RESOUNDING PRAISE FOR

MARY JANE CLARK

LET ME WHISPER IN YOUR EAR

"Mary Jane Clark keeps the reader on the edge of [his or her] seat in LET ME WHISPER IN YOUR EAR. The combination of mind-dazzling suspense and nostalgia for the glory days of Palisades Park is a heady one. Lovers of great romantic mysteries will surely want to read the other novels of Ms. Clark."
— *Romantic Times*

DO YOU PROMISE NOT TO TELL?

"Clark, who in real life is a writer and producer for CBS News, understands how to hang on to her audience. Her characters are the sorts with whom many readers identify. Her first book, *Do You Want To Know A Secret?*, had pluses. It was well told; its characters and plot were compelling. But *Promise* is stronger still . . . it is a fun read with some nifty twists."

— Katy Kelly, *USA Today*

TURN THE PAGE FOR MORE ACCLAIM . . .

ST. MARTIN'S PAPERBACKS TITLES BY MARY JANE CLARK

Do You Want to Know a Secret?
Do You Promise Not to Tell?
Let Me Whisper in Your Ear
Close to You
Nobody Knows
Nowhere to Run

Let Me Whisper In Your Ear

MARY JANE CLARK

St. Martin's Paperbacks

This is a work of fiction. All the characters and events portrayed in this book are either products of the author's imagination or are used fictitiously.

LET ME WHISPER IN YOUR EAR

Copyright © 2000 by Mary Jane Clark.
Excerpt from *Dancing in the Dark* copyright © 2005 by Mary Jane Clark.
Excerpt from *Hide Yourself Away* copyright © 2004 by Mary Jane Clark.

Library of Congress Catalog Card Number: 00-031725

ISBN: 0-312-93809-8
EAN: 80312-93809-3

Printed in the United States of America

St. Martin's Press hardcover edition / September 2000
St. Martin's Paperbacks edition / July 2001

St. Martin's Paperbacks are published by St. Martin's Press, 175 Fifth Avenue, New York, NY 10010.

10 9 8 7 6 5

For my parents,
Doris Boland Behrends, who encouraged me
to follow my dream of working in television news . . .
and
Fred "The Fed" Behrends, who, I hope,
passed on some of his crime-solving genes.

Thank you for taking me to Palisades Park.

Acknowledgments

THE VERY FIRST story I was ever assigned to do at CBS News was an obituary on Rose Kennedy, assigned more than fifteen years before she actually died. I was so proud to be putting my first "piece" together that I didn't pay much attention to the friends and family who thought it gruesome that a story about someone's death was all assembled well before the subject heaved a final breath.

As the years passed, I updated Mrs. Kennedy's obit several times and worked on many others as well, playing the odds that old age or severe illness meant that someone would most likely die soon and we had better have a video life story ready to air. But a few times, I had someone's obit ready when no one really expected the person to die. I had done the stories on hunches . . . feelings that paid off.

Out of those experiences comes this book.

To get from the idea to the book you now hold in your hands required the help of several knowledgeable people whom I would like to thank.

Accomplished musician Russ DeFilippis grew up down the block from the old Palisades Amusement Park. Russ regaled me with the colorful stories of his childhood and put me in touch with others from "the neighborhood."

Acknowledgments

Sister Anne Donnelly generously shared her knowledge of Parkinson's disease, providing the details of how the condition manifests itself and what medication is used to treat it. Sister Anne, happily, was also my sixth-grade teacher and self-esteem builder. But let's blame any errors in sentence structure on her.

Katharine and Joe Hayden helped me when it came time to figure out the legal repercussions of the actions of one of my characters. It's not the first time Katharine and Joe have come to my rescue and, I suspect, it won't be the last.

Sgt. Ed Welch, newly retired New York City Police officer, helped with precinct information and descriptions of the crime scenes. With twenty-five years of NYPD experience under his belt, Ed can paint a vivid picture. I'd love to read his book, should he decide to write it.

Vince Gargiolo's book, *Palisades Park: A Century of Fond Memories*, along with the clippings file at the Cliffside Park Public Library, provided valuable research information on my favorite amusement park.

A new, and I hope continuing, source of inspiration came from Elizabeth Clark, my fifteen-year-old daughter. I was stumped over something and, over lunch one day, asked Elizabeth what she thought. She came up with a terrific solution to the problem I was having. Thank you, Monkey.

Gratitude to Jennifer Weis, my editor at St. Martin's Press, for the attention she gave this book. Jennifer has a keen sense of what makes a story work and her input helped make this one better. Copyeditor Dave Cole did his job carefully and well, finding, though I hate to admit it, a mistake or two along the way. Thank you so much, Dave. Sally Richardson, Matthew Shear, John Murphy, Matthew Baldacci, and Walter

Halee are pulling for me as well. I'm aware of it and greatly appreciate it.

Once again, Laura Dail, my wonderful agent and valued friend, has encouraged me and done her job well. I wish for every writer an agent as devoted, smart, and hardworking as Laura. The bonus for me is that she has a great sense of fun as well. Francheska Farinacci, Laura's able and dear assistant, generously lent her distinctively spelled name for a character.

Finally, I would like to thank Father Paul Holmes. A constant source of encouragement, Paul has been there since the beginning of my dream. Over the years, when things looked pretty bleak, Paul's reassuring voice of reason pulled me up. His editorial skills are extraordinary and I am the extremely fortunate beneficiary of them. Grazie, Paolo.

Prologue

♪ Palisades Amusement Park . . .
Swings all day and after dark . . . ♪

THE TWO YOUNGSTERS sneaked through the hole in the fence as so many others had done before them. That their parents didn't know where they were only increased their guilty pleasure.

Twelve years old and sneaking into Palisades at night. *How cool!* They had done it often enough during the day, when the amusement park was open for business. Just behind the Free Act Stage, there was a hole in the fence that circled the park. Lots of local kids knew about the opening and slipped through it so as to avoid paying the admission fee. Little did they know that the park's good-hearted owner was well aware of the hole but had instructed security guards to turn a blind eye to the young trespassers. He didn't want any child turned away from Palisades Park. And, after all, once inside, the interlopers would have to spend their money just like anyone else.

Sneaking in during the day was one thing. Sneaking in at night, after the park was closed, was another. But with school starting in a few days and the park closing for the winter, they could not wait any longer. If they were going to collect their payment from Emmett, this was the night to do it.

With only the light of the early-September moon to guide them, the children hurried down the darkened midway, eager to collect their reward. Past the boarded-up Balloon Game and Cat Game, past the closed birch beer and roast beef stands. Past the bingo parlor, where just hours before, men and women in their short-sleeved cotton shirts and summer frocks sat eagerly sliding red plastic discs across cardboard game sheets.

And then, there it was. The granddaddy of them all, the Cyclone. The world's largest, fastest, scariest roller coaster loomed before them, darkly sinister against the moonlit sky: their payoff for a season of running errands for Emmett.

The tip of a burning cigarette glowed in the dark, signaling that Emmett was waiting for them. As they drew closer, they saw that Emmett was not alone. That curvy brunette in her tight Wrangler shorts who had been hanging around him all summer was wrapped around him again tonight.

"Hey, squirts. You all set?"

They looked at one another and nodded apprehensively. What had seemed like such a great idea during the day, now, at night, took on a different cast. Their enthusiasm turned to excited fright. What would it feel like to ride the Cyclone, in the dark, all by themselves? Would they really be able to carry out their plan and follow through on the dare they had made to each other?

Neither one wanted to be the first to chicken out, so they climbed into the first white wooden car of the roller coaster. They took their seats side by side, and their hands gripped the metal guard bar. Their hearts pounded against their chest walls as the car slowly pulled out from its starting place; the metallic clanking of the pulling chain echoed eerily in the late-summer night.

Excruciatingly slowly, they made their ascent, high above the Palisades. The New York City skyline glimmered beneath them as they crept inexorably to the Cyclone's summit.

What exactly happened after that would take decades to discover. But when the ride came to an end, the car pulled into the station carrying only one child.

The Holiday Season

1

"WHEN I THINK of you, I think of death."

Laura Walsh, carefully balancing a stack of videotapes in her arms, turned to her boss and grinned.

"Gee, thanks, Mike. I really appreciate that."

She'd done it again. Sometimes it bothered her how much satisfaction she took from it. Professional satisfaction. She'd been prepared and had done her work well.

A human death. Usually, a sad event, leaving complicated repercussions for those left behind. But for Laura Walsh, death was a rush, at least in certain circumstances.

Today, it was an old movie star, long rumored to be failing. Laura had been ready to roll. Within minutes of the death announcement made by the actress's press agent, a two-minute video package recapping the screen legend's life was running on the KEY Television Network for millions of viewers to see.

If they thought of it at all, the TV audience probably marveled at how quickly the television newspeople got everything assembled and on the air. So much research must go into deciding what to include and what to leave out when boiling a lifetime down to two minutes. Let alone coming up with a

7

script. Didn't that take some time to write? Just getting the old movie clips had to be a project. How did they do it all at almost a moment's notice?

The fact was, they didn't. Laura Walsh had written and produced the movie star's obituary months before she actually died.

"Ghoulish," "creepy," "gross," "morbid" were just some of the comments Laura got from people when she told them what she did for a living. But Laura loved her job. When working on her selected project—or "victim," as Mike Schultz called it—Laura did not think of herself as the "Angel of Death" her co-workers teasingly dubbed her. Rather, she saw herself in a position of responsibility. She wanted to do her subject justice, knowing that the images she chose would be seen across the United States and, eventually—through the various and complicated syndication deals that KEY News had with foreign broadcasters—her work would be seen around the world.

The obits were wrap-ups of a noteworthy person's life and career. A mini-biography. She knew others at KEY News might think her corny, but Laura felt honored to produce the video-taped obituaries.

She also knew that she was quite young to be in a position of such responsibility. At twenty-eight, she'd only graduated from college six years ago. Thanks to a lucky internship break, Laura had worked the summer before graduation as a clerical assistant in the offices of Hourglass, the network's top-rated news magazine show. To Laura's continuing good fortune, the always glamorous and sometimes acerbic Gwyneth Gilpatric, the broadcast's star correspondent, took Laura under her very impressive wing.

"Don't let any of these head cases around here scare you,"

Gwyneth had reassured Laura. "Most of these people are really pretty decent. It's the ego and the pressure that make them seem so driven. Just realize that if they scream, or yell, or act like you don't exist, it's because they're so involved in what they're doing and because they're terrified that they aren't going to make deadline or might make a mistake. It's no fun getting it wrong when millions of people are watching."

Laura tried to remember Gwyneth's advice whenever one of the *Hourglass* producers or editors snapped at her that summer. They worried constantly about keeping their jobs. Joel Malcolm, the executive producer of *Hourglass,* had let it be known in no uncertain terms that he intended to knock *60 Minutes* off its first-place perch over at CBS. Anyone who did not do his or her part to further that goal had no place on the *Hourglass* staff.

That had been the general feeling throughout Laura's six years at *KEY News* as she worked her way up from her extremely low-paying first job after graduation as a desk assistant, then broadcast assistant, followed by assistant producer and, now, associate producer. They were taking names at *KEY News*. If you fouled up, you were out. There was no place for excuses or second-bests.

So far, Laura had been more than okay, a golden girl. Her bosses liked her, gradually giving her more and more responsibilities as they grew to trust the judgment and skills they thought remarkable in someone so young. They did not know that she often came to work in the morning with a knot in her stomach, worried about what the day would bring. Or that there were nights she'd wake up at three o'clock, anxiously tossing and turning until dawn, insecure thoughts about how she might mess up running through her head. They did not know about the "feelings" she sometimes got, but everybody seemed happy about the results of those feelings ... unquestioning when Laura had her obits ready even when her subject was not expected to die.

2

"I'M TELLING YOU, Gwyneth, it will be a fantastic segment—'Death at the Amusement Park,'" Joel Malcolm raved, pacing his spacious office. "Your pet Laura Walsh came up with the idea. She's trying to get a job on the broadcast, you know."

"No, I didn't know," said Gwyneth icily.

Joel pressed on. "And if we don't do it soon, it will be too late. All the old-timers will be dead and there will be no one left to interview who was around at the time." Joel lit a cigarette, ignoring the *KEY News* no-smoking dictum.

Gwyneth Gilpatric, dressed in a cornflower-colored cashmere blazer designed to make her keen blue eyes bluer still, sat stone-faced on the sofa. She stared out the picture window, one of the few at *KEY News*, and studied the snow-covered banks of the New Jersey cliffs on the other side of the Hudson River.

"Palisades Amusement Park isn't there anymore, Joel." Gwyneth sighed, her hand going gracefully to her throat, stroking her neck absentmindedly. "They tore it down to build a high-rise condominium complex, remember?"

Undaunted by the lack of enthusiasm from his star, Malcolm pressed on persistently.

"Yeah, but we have great old newsreel stuff. We can paint a picture of the legendary old Palisades Park with its simple Funhouse, Tunnel of Love, and the ancient wooden roller coaster, and tie it in with the death of a boy—a death that's taken thirty years to come to the surface."

Gwyneth carefully picked an expensively tinted ash-blond hair off her jacket shoulder.

Joel continued his pitch. "People were thrilled with simple things then," he reminisced. "Hell, I can remember as a kid, my parents would take me to Palisades every summer. I looked forward to it all year."

"Slumming, Joel?" Gwyneth knew that Malcolm lived in the Fifth Avenue duplex he had grown up in and inherited from his parents. The last time he had the apartment appraised, it was valued at twelve million dollars.

"Tell me you never went to Palisades, Gwyneth. You, who grew up in one of those big houses next door in Fort Lee. You never went to the park?"

"Of course I did, Joel." Gwyneth sighed with exasperation.

"Wasn't it the best?"

"It was okay." Gwyneth was conceding nothing.

"Fine. Sneer if you must. But it's the truth: I loved that old place. Loved riding the Cyclone, loved not getting sick on the Round Up when everyone else did, loved gawking at the two-headed calf in the freak show, and the cow with six legs."

"You would."

Joel looked momentarily hurt, but he shrugged it off. "I suppose I was a showman even then. There is nothing I like better than a good show, and I'm telling you, Gwyneth, this will be a great show for *Hourglass*. We can get it done in time for the February 'book.' "

The "book" was the bible of commercial television. The ratings of the programs broadcast during each of the four sweeps periods determined what advertisers would pay for commercial time in the months to follow. The networks aired what they thought would be their most sensational programming for sweeps in February, May, July and November.

"So there's nothing you like better than a good show, huh?" Gwyneth decided to try distracting him, uncrossing her legs and leaning back slightly against the buttery smooth leather cushions.

His eyes lit up and he stomped out his cigarette. Joel crossed the room and took a seat close to Gwyneth on the sofa.

"We'll make a decision about it in the new year. How's that, kiddo?" he whispered as he began to kiss Gwyneth's long, graceful neck.

No, we won't, thought Gwyneth. *The decision is made. You just don't know it yet.*

3

FELIPE CRUZ'S HAND trembled as he hung up the white receiver onto the telephone mounted on the kitchen wall. Without seeing, he stared at the red tomatoes and orange carrots printed on the wallpaper they'd hung in an effort to cheer up the old kitchen.

How was he going to tell Marta?

The test results were back. The DNA testing, which he'd only first heard of during the O. J. Simpson trial, now solved, at least partially, the agonizing mystery that had plagued their lives for the past thirty years. Three decades spent in despair and depression, worrying and wondering. Half of their lifetimes. Lives that they marked as "before" and "after" Tommy disappeared.

The DNA tests were done on samples taken from a pile of bones found by construction workers in early December as they dug the foundation out of the cold ground for yet another high-rise apartment complex scheduled to perch atop the prime real estate of the Palisades. The Cliffside Park police called the Cruzes to alert them that the examination had shown that the bones were those of an adolescent. Felipe and Marta had not slept through the night in the two weeks since they'd given their own genetic samples to authorities for comparison.

Now they knew. After thirty years of living in a state of heartbroken anticipation, clinging to what became an increasingly desperate and faint hope, they finally knew. DNA, a human being's genetic road map, ultimately marked the location of their only child. The bones were Tommy's.

God, forgive me. It's a relief.

Now, at least this Christmas, they knew that Tommy was not still out there somewhere. The years had just crept along. Tommy's birthdays rolled by. The first without him had been the worst. Then his fourteenth, his fifteenth . . . his fortieth, forty-first, forty-second. Somehow, they had survived, always praying and wondering if their son would turn up one day. And, if he did come back into their lives, what horrors would he have lived through? Many nights, year after year, Felipe had rocked a sobbing Marta in his arms in the dark as they speculated on what could have happened to their son. And then they stopped speculating. Out loud, at least. They could not talk about it anymore. Not if they wanted to go on living.

The pain was so great that at times they discussed how they might kill themselves. They agreed that they would—if not for their religion. Devout Roman Catholics, they believed that they must live out their lives, no matter how painful, according to God's will.

Felipe felt a tug in his chest. *How could God have wanted this?* he wondered.

Marta would be home from the market soon. Felipe paced the kitchen floor, mentally rehearsing what he was going to say. But then he realized that the moment Marta saw his face, she would know. He would not have to come up with the words to tell the mother of his son that their boy was dead and had been rotting less than a mile from their house for the last thirty years.

But Felipe was going to have to come up with a way to tell his wife that the examination of what was left of Tommy's bones showed that almost every one of them had been broken and that the police held out little hope of tracking down the owner of the silver chain and marcasite cross that they had found lying among Tommy's remains.

4

Wednesday, December 22

COLD, GRAY DECEMBER always brought the dreaded Year-enders.

Three days before Christmas, Laura sat at her desk, yellow highlighter in hand, poring over a computer listing of all the people whose deaths had warranted an obituary in the *New York Times* over the past year. The printout was as thick as *Gone with the Wind*.

Next year, I'm not doing this, she promised herself. *While most people are making out their Christmas lists, I'm making my list and checking it twice, all right. A list of the dead.*

Laura swept her blond bangs back from her forehead, instinctively rubbing the thin scar above her browline, and sighed. This was the last thing she wanted to be doing. Not because it was a ghoulish task in the otherwise cheery holiday season. In fact, she found it rather interesting, reading up on who had died over the previous twelve months. Even though she followed the news very closely, there were always some people she'd forgotten or missed—the ones who were not household names, who did not get a full television obit when they died, but who were noteworthy enough to get a write-up in the national newspaper of record.

No, it wasn't the work that bothered her. It was the timing. There was just so much to do at this time of the year. The socializing, the shopping, the rushing, the wrapping. It was stressful enough to get all that done. Who needed to be worried about choosing the top-sixty croakers?

Come on, Laura, she chided herself. *Don't be cynical. You know you want it to be good. Every KEY television station will use it.*

The Yearender piece would run on New Year's Eve. Two minutes and thirty seconds of flashes of the faces of those who had gone on to their rewards, set against some appropriate music. This year, Laura had selected the signature song of a legendary singer who had died a few months earlier.

She knew it would come out well. It always did. She'd done several of these Yearenders now and, each time, when they played out to the network, her newsroom co-workers watched, fascinated. They were a tough crowd, most of them not given to compliments. But even some of the most jaded could be moved by the combination of visual images, wonderful music and thoughts of people who had all made impressive marks on this world, passing on to whatever comes next.

Laura always felt satisfied after the Yearender was done. But mostly she felt relieved. Relieved that she'd made another deadline and that she could then pay a little attention to her personal life, such as it was.

Being a producer assigned to the *KEY News* Bulletin Center meant that Laura's life was not her own. When she accepted the position, she knew it meant that she would be constantly on call. Weekends, holidays and vacations were only fully her own as long as no major news story broke. If something big happened, the beeper, her constant companion, would sound and she was expected to call in to *KEY News* headquarters immediately and, most often, report in person quickly thereafter. In the year she'd worked in the Bulletin Center, she'd left dozens of dinners uneaten, and days off interrupted.

Whenever she felt a bit sorry for herself, when the rest of the world seemed to work a normal schedule, without fear of having a random act of violence or a whim of Mother Nature cut one's plans short, Laura reminded herself that there were lots of people who lived this way. Police and firefighters staffed their departments around the clock. Hospital doctors and nurses had to make sure their institutions were covered twenty-four hours a day, 365 days a year.

In fact, when reflecting on it, Laura thought that *KEY News* was a lot like a hospital. The fine surgery was performed on *KEY Evening Headlines* and on the magazine shows like *Hourglass*, where untold hours of excruciating exactitude were spent perfecting every aspect of each broadcast. The Bulletin Center was more like the hospital emergency room. The correspondents, producers and editors assigned to Bulletin duty dealt with whatever the news gods blew their way, and they dealt with it immediately. Seconds counted in being first on the air with the news and beating the competition.

Laura was so engrossed in going over her obituary list, she jumped when she felt a hand on her shoulder.

"Hey, Laura, how's it going?" Mike Schultz loomed over her desk.

"Getting there," Laura answered, capping her highlighter. "I've whittled down the list to the most important dead people—now we just have to keep our fingers crossed that no one else dies in the next nine days."

"You can bet somebody big will buy the farm before the year's out," Mike replied.

Laura nodded, knowing her boss was right.

5

MIKE SCHULTZ HAILED a cab and told the driver to take him to Penn Station. He really was not looking forward to the commute home, but he *was* looking forward to a double Johnny Walker Black.

Mike was a burly bear of a guy. At six-foot-two, he carried his extra weight well, but his large frame sported fifty pounds of unexercised baggage put on since his college football days. That was only two pounds a year, he rationalized to himself.

His doctor viewed it differently. "You're looking at an early heart attack. Cut the crap out of your diet, get some exercise, quit smoking and stop stressing out over that damn job!"

"Okay, Doc." Mike sighed resignedly. *That's easy for you to say,* he thought.

He tried. He really did. Instead of grabbing a bagel with a double-cream-cheese-and-jelly-"schmear" at the deli across the street from the commuter train platform, he'd take the time to slice a banana and cover it with raisin bran and low-fat milk, scarfing it down before he rushed out the door to catch the train from Park Ridge, New Jersey, to Manhattan. At lunchtime, he'd choose carefully from the cafeteria salad bar, instead of loading up on his usual cheeseburgers, french fries and onion rings. He'd even try to get out of the office at some point during the day to grab a twenty-minute walk.

It was harder, though, when he got home. He ached for a scotch or two, or three, after a day in the Bulletin Center. He wondered what effect always being on alert had on a human being. He was sure it wasn't good. Knowing that anything could happen at any time, and it would ultimately be his responsibility to get the news on the KEY Television Network, was part of the senior producer's job description. True, he had correspondents, producers and editors under his command to fight the war to get the news immediately on television and, in doing so, beat the other networks. But when things went wrong, when human error or logistical nightmares caused the excuses to fly fast and furious, the buck stopped with Mike Schultz.

He wanted out. It was getting to him. At first, it had been a relief just to be working in his field again. He'd been determined to do the job well and show the executives on the front row that he had what it took to be a leader and a valued team player in the *KEY News* hierarchy. Hadn't he always been a good soldier, willing to do what KEY wanted and needed him to do? Someone had to take the hit for the Gwyneth Gilpatric scandal. He still remembered with a shudder the day Yelena Gregory had summoned him to her president's office and explained that, for the good of *KEY News* and the reputation of its star correspondents, Mike would have to take the fall.

He had been dismissed from the staff of *Hourglass,* the second most highly rated news show on television. He went from traveling in the network news fast lane to being persona non grata in the industry. None of the other networks would touch him. For a year, he was out of a job . . . without a job, but with a wife, three kids and a mortgage.

They'd made it, scraping along on Nancy's substitute teaching, Mike's working nights at a local liquor store and dipping into the children's college fund. After months of that nonsense, he had called Yelena Gregory and threatened to expose what had really happened when he worked at *Hourglass* with Gwyneth Gilpatric.

Suddenly, Yelena reassured him that of course they wanted him back. He was a valued part of the team. They had just wanted to give the brouhaha time to settle down.

More time passed, the money oozing from the Schultz bank account, the confidence leaking from Mike's psyche. He didn't want to cause a problem, didn't want to go public. He didn't have the energy, the pocketbook or the heart to fight *KEY News.* He just wanted to work in television news again.

Just as he was steeling himself to call the media critic for the *New York Times,* Yelena Gregory phoned. They had a position for him. They wanted him to be the senior producer at the Bulletin Center, a department far less prestigious to *KEY*

News insiders than the famous *Hourglass* magazine broadcast. Mike would be stuck with the tough, essentially grinding work of honchoing the center.

Mike had been so grateful to be working again, he almost forgot that *KEY News* had screwed him. *KEY News* and Gwyneth Gilpatric.

6

"MISS LAURA WALSH is here," the gray-coated doorman announced.

Laura stood in the warm lobby of the august prewar building on Central Park West, happy to be out of the frosty night air.

"You can go right up, Miss Walsh."

The mahogany-paneled elevator rose smoothly to the top level. Laura watched the polished brass floor indicator as she made her ascent. Penthouse. The doors opened silently and Laura found herself entering directly into the long marble-floored foyer of Gwyneth Gilpatric's apartment. A magnificent Christmas tree dominated the space, its branches densely covered with whimsical and theatrical ornaments. Laura scanned the tree but did not notice what she was looking for.

"Laura, darling!" Gwyneth approached with open arms. "I'm so glad you're here. I don't see nearly enough of you these days. But from what I hear, you may be working at *Hourglass* again." Wearing gray slacks and a tunic with gunmetal icicle beading, Gwyneth gathered the younger woman in an enthusiastic hug. "Come in. Come in."

Gwyneth escorted her guest into the enormous living room. The wall ahead was glass, offering a spectacular view of Central Park and the glittering Manhattan skyline to the south. Laura caught her breath at the beauty of it. On the coffee table sat an hourglass, full of pale pink sand, surrounded by a small army of Emmy Award statuettes.

"Sit in front of the fire, Laura. Will you have a drink? A glass of wine? I have a bottle of merlot open and breathing. I know that you like merlot."

As always, Laura was flattered that Gwyneth remembered anything about her. "Some merlot would be nice," she answered as she sank into the largest and most luxurious white sofa she had ever seen.

"Ma'am, the prime minister is on the phone again."

"Please, Delia. Call me 'Ms. Gilpatric.' 'Ma'am' sounds so old-ladyish. Laura, dear, will you excuse me? I have an interview set up in London next month, and Tony and I keep playing phone tag. This should only take a minute."

Gwyneth disappeared somewhere to take the call, and Laura settled in to enjoy the beautiful surroundings. What it must be like to live in a place like this! As many times as she'd been here, she'd never gotten used to it. It was like stepping into a dream.

Laura reached over to lift the heavy hourglass and turned it upside down. The fine pink sand sifted slowly through the small opening at the middle of the vessel. She read the inscription on the small brass plaque that was mounted on the teak

base: TO GWYNETH, YOU MAKE EVERY HOUR PRIME TIME.
JOEL.

Joel Malcolm, the executive producer of *Hourglass,* was almost the television news legend that Gwyneth was. He had created the award-winning magazine show and Gwyneth Gilpatric had ridden it to stardom.

Laura considered her boss, that first summer at *KEY News.* Malcolm initially had been brusque and uninterested in Laura when she interned that July and August at *Hourglass.* That had changed dramatically when he learned that Gwyneth seemed to consider the young college student a pet project. Malcolm went from indifference to congeniality. When the internship was over, Malcolm had ordered a large cake and champagne to thank Laura and wish her well as she returned to college for her senior year.

"To Laura," he had toasted, raising his glass of Piper-Heidseck, and, turning his handsome head to look at the staffers gathered, he added, "She's been a terrific addition to our team, and she'll be missed around here. But," he continued, smiling over at Gwyneth, who was perched on a desk in the corner of the newsroom, "something tells me we'll be seeing Laura Walsh again here at *KEY News.* And something else tells me that that will be our gain."

Laura remembered how embarrassed she had been at the time. She knew others on the staff had been talking, resentful of what they rightly perceived to be the favoritism lavished on Laura. She was relieved to finish the internship and get back to school. But as the next academic year passed and graduation time neared, Laura was more and more certain that she wanted to work in broadcast journalism. And what better place to work than *KEY News?*

Pulled by the twinkling city lights that magically illuminated the dark, shadowy Manhattan skyscrapers, Laura rose from the sofa and walked out to the terrace. She caught her breath as she was hit by the dry, icy December night air. Wrapping her arms around herself for warmth, Laura stepped over to the telescope that stood at the side of the terrace. She peered through the instrument, squinting and focusing on the roof garden of the Metropolitan Museum of Art across Central Park.

No warm-weather cocktail parties among the sculptures on the deserted roof tonight.

Gwyneth paused for a moment at the entrance to her living room and looked toward the glass window, out to the terrace where Laura, unaware of the eyes upon her, gazed through the telescope. What a lovely young woman she was! Her straight, naturally blond hair was blunt-cut and fell smoothly over her shoulders. Her features were fine, with alert blue eyes, straight nose and a generous mouth that broke easily into a smile revealing dazzling white teeth.

She could probably be on air if she wanted to, Gwyneth thought. *Maybe I should encourage her to try.*

Or maybe not. Being on air wasn't all it was cracked up to be. Gwyneth could attest to that. Funny, once she had thought being on television was so important. God, the things she had done, the people she had stepped on to get where she was, where she thought it had been so damned important to be.

Come on, now, old girl. You love it. What else could you have done that would have brought you as much excitement and satisfaction, not to mention adulation? And don't forget the money. You started with no connections, sweetheart, and now look. A penthouse on Central Park, a beach place in the Hamptons and a flat in London. Though "flat" didn't seem the right word to describe the luxurious setup she had in Kensington.

All that and young enough to enjoy it. Just forty-seven years old. *Just.* Only a short time ago, that would have sounded ancient, but not anymore. Gwyneth was in her prime professionally and that was all that really ever mattered. Or so she always told herself, as she scrutinized the crepelike skin at her neck in the mirror each morning.

There had been no family along the way. Though there had been many affairs, many relationships, there had never been anyone she really wanted to marry. And that had been fine with Gwyneth. Her career was her passion and she did not want to dilute her energies.

Gwyneth knew herself. She knew that she would not be good at the give-and-take, the compromising and the patience that marriage took. She didn't really regret not having married. But she did regret not having a child.

You could have, you know. Adoption, one of the lovers along the way, even the sperm bank. But admit it: you just didn't want to take the time. Didn't want to put in the effort. Didn't want to be distracted. Face it: you wouldn't have been a good mother.

Gwyneth watched as Laura's tall, angular body turned from the telescope to come back inside. The younger woman smiled when she realized Gwyneth was looking at her.

What was it about Laura, Gwyneth asked herself as she stepped into the living room and took a seat on the plush sofa, what was it that had struck such a chord in her? Gwyneth Gilpatric, usually so matter-of-fact, very often hard, always calculating, had an intense interest in Laura Walsh.

Gwyneth knew the answer to her own question. But she did not want to think about that, as she raised her right hand to massage the back of her neck.

Delia was hovering again.

"Yes, Delia? What is it?" Gwyneth was obviously annoyed.

"Dr. Costello is on the phone, Ms. Gilpatric," the maid announced nervously.

Another interruption. Gwyneth winced. She did not want to talk to her plastic surgeon. She knew she had taken the easy way out, canceling her surgery with a phone call to Costello's nurse, Camille Bruno. But it was easier telling Camille than facing Leonard. She didn't want to have to explain why.

Over the years, as she had gone for one relatively simple procedure after another to reverse the toll of aging, Leonard had become her friend. Gwyneth had done her research well. Leonard Costello's name was high on everyone's list of the best plastic surgeons in New York.

When no amount of careful lip lining kept her lipstick from bleeding, she started with collagen injections to fill in the fine lines that had developed around her mouth. The next year, at Leonard's suggestion, she had a blepharoplasty, removing the fatty tissue from her upper and lower eyelids. Then came the neck lift, which ensured that her television profile was well defined and youthful.

She had been putting off the full face-lift as long as she could. But now the stopgap procedures were not enough. Gwyneth's appearance was an essential part of her livelihood. While she supposed even the men on television worried about aging, they could get away with being mature and distinguished-looking. Women agonized about looking old. Though the network brass paid lip service to a non–age discrimination policy, how many older women did you actually see in television news?

She had talked it over with Joel, and she was somewhat hurt but not really surprised when he said he thought it was a good idea. All Joel seemed to care about was that Gwyneth be ready to appear before the *KEY News* cameras again in February for sweeps. When she assured him that, with carefully applied makeup, she would, Joel was all for the surgery. In fact, he'd had the audacity to suggest that they do a segment on her plastic surgery and recovery. Gwyneth had quickly quashed that idea.

Gwyneth went ahead and scheduled a full facial lift with CO_2 and erbium lasers for the first week of January, comforted in knowing that she would be in Leonard Costello's talented hands.

But her confidence had turned to terror when she found out. Leonard Costello had Parkinson's disease.

She thanked her lucky stars that she had befriended Camille Bruno. Gwyneth had liked the friendly nurse immediately upon meeting her and had many conversations with her over the years as she went for her quarterly collagen injections. Each Christmas, Gwyneth remembered the nurse with a gift. She had arranged tours of the Broadcast Center for Camille's family and out-of-town guests, gotten her tickets for the heated and catered *KEY News* Columbus Circle reviewing stand for the Thanksgiving Day Parade and written college letters of recommendation for each of Camille's three daughters. They had all been admitted to the universities of their choice. While Gwyneth had her doubts that the letters had made any difference, Camille was convinced that they had.

When Gwyneth called in mid-December to confirm the details for her upcoming surgery, she sensed the distress in Camille's voice.

"What's wrong, Camille?"

"I think I should tell you something."

"What?"

"Not now," she had whispered. "Can you call me at home? Tonight?"

Gwyneth made the nocturnal call.

"I feel so disloyal to Dr. Costello by telling you this, but you've been so good to me and my girls. Dr. Costello would fire me in a second if he knew that I told anyone." Camille's voice quavered.

"Told anyone *what*?" Gwyneth urged.

"You can't tell him that you know. You can't tell him that I told you."

"I won't. I promise. Now, what is it?"

Camille explained that the Parkinson's was in the early stages, controllable with medication. Dr. Costello was careful to take his medication before any sort of surgery, making sure it had time to kick in before he lifted his scalpel.

"He told you he has Parkinson's?" Gwyneth asked.

"No. He doesn't know that I know. I've noticed his hand tremoring from time to time, but never in surgery. But a few weeks ago, he put off a scheduled surgery though we were all ready to go. I saw him take a pill. He just waited in his office for forty-five minutes before he started the procedure. That's so unlike him, you know. He's such a stickler for keeping to his schedule."

"That doesn't mean he has Parkinson's disease, Camille."

There was silence on the other end of the phone.

"Camille?"

"I am so ashamed." The nurse exhaled deeply.

"Go on. Please, Camille."

"I went into his drawer later and checked the prescription bottle," she had admitted. "It was for Sinemet, the drug to treat Parkinson's."

Now, Leonard was on the phone, wanting an explanation for the canceled surgery. She owed him that. And she might as well get it over with.

"Excuse me, Laura, dear." Gwyneth frowned at her guest and hoped Laura didn't recognize the name of the well-known plastic surgeon. She didn't want Laura, or anyone else, knowing that she had face-work done. "I really must take this call, though I wish I didn't have to. I'll be right back. I promise this will be our last interruption."

She walked quickly down the hallway to her office and closed the door behind her. She took a deep breath as she lifted the receiver from its cradle.

"Leonard! How are you? I'm so looking forward to seeing you and Anne on New Year's Eve," she faked jovially.

"I'm just fine, Gwyneth, but I'm troubled. Camille tells me you canceled your procedure."

"Yes."

"May I ask why?"

"I'm a coward," Gwyneth lied. "I've chickened out, Leonard. I'm afraid to go ahead with it. I'm worried I won't look like myself anymore."

"We've gone over all that, Gwyneth. Many times." She could tell he was trying very hard to sound patient.

"I know we have, Leonard. I'm sorry. But I'm just not ready."

"All right, Gwyneth. Why don't we reschedule in the spring, then?" She could hear him flipping the pages of his calendar.

"No, Leonard. I don't think so." Gwyneth was firm. "I'll let you know when I'm ready."

7

ACROSS CENTRAL PARK, Kitzi Malcolm dressed for the fourth dinner party of the week as she waited for her husband to come home from *KEY News*. Her hands trembled as she struggled to fasten the clasp of her pearl necklace, an anniversary gift from Joel. Her beloved husband.

She clumped the perfectly matched pearls in a ball and slammed them on the dressing table. She reached up behind her shoulder blades, trying to find the zipper of the blond sleeveless cashmere tank, but she could not reach it. *Damn that Joel*. If he didn't make it home in time, the matching cardigan with dyed Norwegian fox trim would hide the open zipper until someone in the ladies' room could zip it up for her.

She was sick to death of being Mrs. Joel Malcolm—and she had no one but herself to blame! She had chosen it.

She should have divorced Joel years ago—she knew that—but there was one problem: she still loved him.

He was dashing and passionate and funny. He could be

warm and loving and understanding. And he was repeatedly unfaithful.

Not that any of them really mattered to him, Kitzi told herself as she expertly applied the thin line of pencil to her lower eyelid. No, they were just diversions.

All except one.

Kitzi made sure Joel didn't know that she watched him. So many, many times. Watched as he stood on their terrace high above Fifth Avenue, his eyes glued to the eyepiece of his telescope, pointed west, trained on Gwyneth's apartment.

8

SOPHISTICATED GWYNETH GILPATRIC tore open the bright green Christmas wrapping paper from the Saks Fifth Avenue box like an excited child and let out a squeal.

"Oh, Laura, I love it!"

"You don't have it?" Laura asked uncertainly.

"Oh, darling, no. No, I don't have this one. He's charming."

In her red-nailed hands, Gwyneth held up a Christmas ornament, three inches high. A little blond boy, with shiny green pants, blew a golden trumpet. In his other hand he held a hand-painted clock that read five minutes to midnight.

"It's called 'Ringing in the New Year,'" volunteered Laura.

"I know you like the Christopher Radkos. I was praying you didn't have this one."

Gwyneth went over to Laura and gave her a hug. "You're right. I adore the Radkos, ever since I saw the White House tree decorated with his ornaments a few years ago. Do you know his story?"

Laura shook her head.

"It's such a wonderful success story, really—we did a piece on him for *Hourglass* some time ago," Gwyneth began, turning the ornament gently in her hand and inspecting the delicate workmanship. "Christopher Radko was working in the mailroom somewhere, not having any real success in moving up the corporate ladder, when over the holidays he accidentally knocked over the family Christmas tree. All the family ornaments, handmade in Europe and collected over years and years, crashed and broke. Radko's grandmother told him he had ruined Christmas forever."

"How horrible," Laura said, imagining how she would feel if she destroyed family heirlooms. Not that she had any.

"Don't be sad, dear. Obviously it has a happy ending."

Gwyneth stopped to elegantly light a cigarette. She closed her eyes as she exhaled.

"Radko went to Poland on his Easter vacation and found an old glassblower who made ornaments in his garage. Radko sketched out some icicles, comets and stars and, when he returned to the U.S. two weeks later, he carried with him over two dozen baubles. When he showed a few of the ornaments to his co-workers, they asked if they could buy some, too.

"So he set up a tiny business in his garage and started importing a few cartons of ornaments, and then more and more. Each ornament takes seven days to make. The glass is heated and blown into a mold, then the new ornament is painted on the inside with sterling silver. The hand painting and lacquering and detailing is done over the final days. As you can see, the Radko concept has caught on. Bottom line is, the last I heard, he had sixteen factories in Europe and employs more than two thousand people in New York alone. He has a Christmas line, a Hanukkah line and ornaments for Halloween, Easter and the Fourth of July."

"What a great story!" Laura smiled approvingly. "I didn't know Radko's history, but I did love looking at all his ornaments at Saks. I found the perfect one for my father . . . a beautiful silver roller coaster."

The smile faded from Gwyneth's face.

"What I love about this story—and I've seen it in my own life—" said Gwyneth as she handed Laura a gleaming gold package, "many times, a seeming tragedy can end up leading to something more wonderful than you would have ever imagined."

9

NANCY SCHULTZ HURRIEDLY poured a box of macaroni into the pot of boiling water. As the pasta cooked, she threw three place mats on the kitchen table and slapped down plates, silverware and paper napkins. Then she poured three tall glasses of milk.

She hated feeding the children this way, she thought, as she drained the pasta elbows and stirred in the milk, butter and orange powder that would magically transform into macaroni and cheese. She forced herself to look at the nutrition information on the side of the blue box that packaged her children's dinner. High fat, high sodium, high calories. Wonderful.

What am I doing? she asked herself as she spooned the mounds onto the kids' plates. *Probably what many mothers in America are doing tonight,* she thought, answering her own question. Mothers who had been working all day in underpaid jobs in offices or restaurants or hospitals or supermarkets. Mothers who had been out battling the crowds and traffic, trying to get holiday shopping done—of course, not getting paid for that. Mothers all, who had too much to do and not enough time to do it in; and, like Nancy, tonight were just too damned tired to stop at the A&P on the way home for easily the sixtieth or seventieth time this year. Couldn't face figuring out another dinner. Couldn't deal with cooking it. Over three hundred dinners cooked this year—well over. Enough was enough.

"Aaron. Brian. Lauren. Dinner's ready."

She heard the hurried stampede of feet as her children ran up from the playroom. She watched their facial expressions to see if they resented what was being presented as "dinner."

"Oh, great! Macaroni and cheese!" eight-year-old Aaron exclaimed. His six-year-old brother Brian just dug right in. Lauren, at four, took her cue from her older brothers.

Relieved, Nancy announced, "Okay, kids, I'm running in to take a shower."

They looked up at her, their expressions puzzled.

"Aren't you eating with us?"

"No. Remember? I'm working tonight. Julie D'Amico is coming over to babysit until Daddy gets home."

"Good," said Aaron as he turned his attention back to the orange food on his plate. "Julie always has gum."

Nancy sighed, not having the energy tonight to attempt the requisite lecture on gum not being good for your teeth.

As she stepped gratefully into the steaming shower, Nancy wished she could stand there forever. She did not look forward to four hours on her feet tonight at Macy's, running the register in the ladies' lingerie department and straightening up the stock. But they needed the extra money, and not just for the holidays. They were trying desperately to get out of debt and eventually put back the money they'd taken from the kids' college fund.

It was amazing what a year out of work for the main breadwinner did to a family's financial position. Sometimes it seemed to Nancy that they'd never get ahead again.

And wait until she told Mike that an invitation to Gwyneth's famous New Year's Eve party had arrived in the mail today.

10

Thursday, December 23

LAURA HUNG HER double-breasted navy wool coat and striped chenille scarf in the crowded Bulletin Center's double closet and went straight to her desk. Booting up her computer, she first checked her e-mail.

Three new messages since she left last night: the DAILY PLANNER, listing the stories that *KEY News* was planning to cover for the day; yesterday's OPPOSITION LOG, listing the stories that ABC, CBS and NBC had aired on their evening news broadcasts last night; and a JOBS AVAILABLE posting.

At this point, Laura was most interested in the jobs bulletin. She wanted to move on from the Bulletin Center and she knew where she wanted to go. She clicked open the e-mail.

There was a job as a producer in the London bureau. Tempting, but she really did not want to leave New York, or Pop, right now. There was also a producer spot unfilled in Washington. That did not appeal to Laura, either.

Both jobs would be a definite promotion for her. She'd be working on "breaking news," working out in the field and doing original reporting. But Laura had her heart set on *Hourglass,* even though there was no posted opening there. She knew full well that the job postings were often mere formalities. Executive producers usually decided who would staff their broadcasts before the mandatory job lists were posted.

By pitching the Palisades Park story to Joel Malcolm, she hoped she'd have won him over to considering her for the next *Hourglass* producer spot. It helped to have Gwyneth on her side, but, as Laura thought about it, Gwyneth had not pursued the idea of Laura joining the *Hourglass* staff as they exchanged Christmas gifts the night before.

11

THINKING ABOUT LAURA'S visit after a fitful night's sleep, Gwyneth took a seat at her desk. Clad in an ice-blue silk dressing robe, she checked her e-mail from her apartment laptop computer. With two days until Christmas and much to do, she wanted to avoid going into the Broadcast Center if she could.

As she read the electronic message from Laura, Gwyneth felt the warmth of blood rising to her cheeks.

TO: Allpersonnel@key.com
FROM: Laurawalsh@key.com
RE: Research

I am working on a piece about the old Palisades Amusement Park. It's been said that Palisades Park, which operated for nearly 75, years, reflected the popular culture of a changing nation.

If you know anyone with a good Palisades Park story to tell, please contact me.

How dare Joel give Laura the go-ahead to do the story! He'd promised the decision would wait until the new year.

Gwyneth logged off the computer and poured herself another cup of herbal tea from the silver pot that Delia had left on the library's refectory table. As she sipped, she tried to organize the thoughts running through her head. Her rage at Joel only grew as she pondered his betrayal—although she knew, when confronted, Joel would deny that he'd broken his word to her. From Joel's point of view, giving Laura the okay to work on the story was in the best interests of *Hourglass* and therefore in the best interests of Gwyneth. That was always the rationalization he used with her as he maneuvered to inevitably get his own way.

But no more, Joel, Gwyneth thought, a triumphant look in her blue eyes as she stared out at snow-covered Central Park. *You won't be getting your way with me anymore.*

She'd been feeling guilty and full of trepidation, not wanting to tell Joel her news. However, in the face of Joel's latest outrage, Gwyneth now thought she'd take some real satisfaction in seeing the look on his handsome face when she told him she was leaving.

Leaving *KEY News,* leaving *Hourglass,* leaving him.

She felt momentarily satisfied. Joel had hurt her, and soon she would hurt him. But her satisfaction quickly gave way to dread. As she remembered that *KEY News* would soon be putting its considerable resources into an investigation of the final days of Palisades Amusement Park, beneath her silk robe Gwyneth felt a bead of cold perspiration trickle down her side.

Decisively, she reached for the telephone and dialed Joel's direct line.

"Just a few days before Christmas, and this is the gift you give me, you son-of-a-bitch!"

Joel winced at the venom in Gwyneth's hiss as he clutched the telephone receiver. "Gwyneth, sweetheart, I can explain."

"Don't 'sweetheart' me, you pathetic liar. You promised that we'd decide together, *after* the holidays, about that Palisades Park story, and you just went ahead and did what you pleased. That's the story of your life, doing what Joel wants. The big executive producer always gets his way."

"That *is* how the system works, baby."

"Well, I'm sick of it. What about keeping the talent happy? Now, *there's* a concept you haven't thought about lately."

Joel paused for an instant, considering which tack to take. Should he show her who the boss was, or should he try to appease her?

"Come on, Gwyneth. What's the big deal?" he implored, choosing appeasement over confrontation. "I just told Laura to continue her research."

"With you so high on the story, that's tantamount to giving her a green light, and we both know it," Gwyneth answered angrily.

"Does this mean that Kitzi and I are off the guest list for your New Year's Eve party?"

"Do whatever you damn well please," Gwyneth answered curtly. She slammed down the phone, knowing very well that Joel would show up for the party. He'd probably come bearing some sort of peace offering, confident that he could make things right.

But not this time. In fact, she had a little surprise ready for him, too. After this, she would take satisfaction in telling him her news. His beloved *Hourglass,* his creation and life's work, would soon be without its star.

12

RETIRED SCHOOLTEACHER MAXINE Dzieskanowski Bronner looked forward to Laura's Christmas Eve visit tomorrow as she had each year for the last twenty. She remembered the first time the little eight-year-old Laura had come to the Bronner house on Lafayette Avenue. It had been just a month after her mother had died.

Laura's father was not taking the death of his wife well. He was drinking heavily, not going to work and crying all the time. Maxine knew all this because Laura had told her. Not verbally, but in her journal.

The third graders that Maxine taught at Epiphany School came to class each day, unpacked their book bags and wrote in their journals the first thing every morning. Mrs. Bronner would give a prompt each day. What will you be when you grow up? What is your favorite spot in the house? Describe your family. What are your plans for the summer? Or the young students had free choice: they could write anything they chose, anything that was on their minds.

It was through the journal that Maxine had witnessed a little girl's loss of her mother.

In September, Laura wrote that her mommy had been sick all summer and had to go to the doctor all the time. In October, her mommy was going to the hospital for treatments, treatments that made her throw up and lose her yellow hair. Mommy said the treatments would make her better. By November, Mommy told Laura that the medicine wasn't working after all.

Maxine's students were aware of what was going on. Part of the journal experience was reading to the class what they had written. No one was forced to, but when the teacher asked the class, "Who would like to share?" Laura's hand would spring up.

The other kids tried to console her.

"Your mother will get better."

"Don't worry, Laura."

"My uncle was sick, too, but he got well."

But as Thanksgiving grew close and the class was learning about the *Mayflower* and Plymouth Rock and the Pilgrims and the Indians, Laura wrote in her journal that she was sleeping with her mommy each night so she could be close to her. After her father fell asleep beside his wife, Laura would sneak into their double bed to snuggle next to her mother, to feel the warmth of her thin body, to listen to the sound of her breathing.

Mommy didn't sleep that well, but she never minded that Laura wasn't acting like a big girl and sleeping in her own bed. She would gather her daughter in her arms and stroke her golden hair and whisper that everything was going to be all right. And in those moments in the dark, safe and warm next to her mother, Laura felt that everything would.

But the last night, Laura wrote, Mommy didn't wake up when Laura came in to curl beside her. Mommy's breathing sounded funny as her chest moved up and down. She tried to wake Daddy, but he didn't budge. She knew that he had been drinking a lot of beer after dinner, and when he did that, it was useless to try to wake him.

So she had lain there, her arms wrapped around her mother, clinging to the person who made her feel safe, the person she loved most in all the world. And Laura prayed that God would make her mother well.

She heard the cuckoo clock chirp in the downstairs hallway and she lay there in the dark, praying. And then she heard the bird sing again. Right after that, Mommy's chest rose one last time.

Maxine's heart had ached as she followed Laura's story and she had tried to do what she could to help the little girl. She had put her arm around the child and told her, "We're always here." Laura had cried in her teacher's arms.

In that first Christmas season after Mrs. Walsh's death, with all the hurt so fresh, it had taken all Maxine had not to cry herself in front of the child. The school Christmas concert went on, the kids sang Christmas carols, Santa Claus came to the classroom and gave out candy canes to each child and Laura had participated as best she could. A brave little soldier in front of the other children.

When the school bell rang out signaling the end of another day, Laura would linger in the classroom. She did not want to go home to the house she had lived in all her life, the house on Grant Avenue, the house without Mommy. Daddy was home, but that was little comfort. She was afraid of how she would find him.

So she stayed after school, and Maxine would find jobs for Laura to do. Erase the blackboard, help decorate the bulletin board, tack class projects on the wall. As the last days before the holiday vacation approached, Maxine got up the courage to ask Laura what she and her dad were doing for Christmas.

Laura hung her head. "Daddy says we aren't having Christmas this year."

"Because of Mommy?"

Laura nodded.

"Do you think Mommy would want you to have Christmas, even though she isn't with you?" asked Maxine gently.

Laura thought about it for a minute. "I don't know," she answered uncertainly.

"Well, Laura, this is a very difficult time for your father. I can understand that he doesn't want to celebrate now. But how would you like it if I asked him if you and he could come over to my house on Christmas Eve? We have a special celebration and we do many things that my family have done for years and years. It would be a different kind of Christmas for you."

The little girl brightened.

That night, Maxine called Emmett Walsh. She could tell by his slurred speech that he had been drinking, but when she extended the Christmas Eve invitation, she was encouraged, in a way, by his response.

"I know Laura should have a Christmas, but I just can't make one for her. I don't deserve one. But she does."

"Of course you deserve one. You aren't responsible for your wife's death."

"She didn't die peacefully. That was because of me." Over the phone line, Maxine could hear him slurp another swig of beer.

She did not know what he meant, but she did not feel it was her place to ask more.

"Mr. Walsh, perhaps you should talk to Father Ryan. Maybe he could help you come to terms with everything that has happened."

"I'm not too big on religion right now, Mrs. Bronner. In fact, I'm quite pissed off at God."

"Well, that, of course, is up to you, Mr. Walsh. But Laura is an innocent child and I know you want what is best for her. Won't you please come for Christmas Eve?"

That was how it started. The first few years, Emmett Walsh came with his daughter to the Bronners' house the night before Christmas. After that, Laura came on her own.

An only child, Laura loved the big family celebration. Alan Bronner was a warm, generous man who clearly loved his "Max" and their two children, Danielle and Justin. Aunts, uncles and cousins filled the house, gathering to celebrate the *Wigilia,* the biggest Polish family feast day of the year.

As dusk gathered, Mrs. Bronner placed a candle in the front window. She explained to Laura that this was once believed to help the spirits of family ancestors find their way "home" for the *Wigilia.*

"Do you think my mommy will find me here?" Laura asked quietly that first year.

Maxine pulled the child close. "Laura, I truly believe your mother is here in spirit, loving you very much. She did everything she could to stay with you and I know she did not want to leave you. But it was her time to pass on, to go to live in heaven with God. I know she wants you to be happy and enjoy your life and all the wonderful things that are in store for you."

"Like tonight?"

The poor child is asking permission to enjoy herself, Maxine thought.

"Yes, especially tonight."

Maxine took Laura's hand and led her into the dining room. Pulling back the corner of the heavily starched white linen tablecloth, Maxine showed the child the straw that had been laid beneath it.

"Hay and straw are the symbols of the birth of Jesus in the stable, Laura. When the first star appears in the sky, we can begin our celebration."

Laura thought about that. "What if there is no star? What if it's too cloudy?"

Maxine laughed. "Then we begin at six o'clock."

But that night, there was a star. The family and guests stood around the table to break and share the *optalek,* the sacred bread that, Mrs. Bronner explained to Laura, was similar to the liturgical water used as the sacred Host at Mass. Instead of the Host's round shape, the *optalek* was a rectangle and was embossed on one side with a Christmas motif. For Poles, it symbolized the strengthening of bonds between peoples.

Laura solemnly ate her piece of the wafer and then took her seat next to her father at the table. She was relieved that Daddy had not been drinking that day. In fact, she noticed that when Mrs. Bronner asked what he would like to drink, Daddy had asked for a ginger ale.

Maybe things were going to get better.

13

IN THE DAYS before her mother died, eight-year-old Laura had been put to bed early, but she had not slept. The familiar bedroom with its multicolored candy-striped wallpaper and single twin-canopy bed, the "princess" bed, Mommy called it, the happy, cozy place where so many nighttime stories had been lovingly told, became a darkened, frightening chamber. During the daytime, there had been school and her teacher, Mrs. Bronner, and Brownies and play dates. At night, however, when all the day's activities were over, Laura would lie in her small bed alone, to think and worry.

She had known something was wrong, though everyone tried to act as if everything were all right when she was around.

Daddy hadn't known that she'd seen him crying in his big red chair late at night. He'd thought she was in bed asleep. But she wasn't. She was up and creeping around. That was how she found out everything.

Laura, ever the little trouper, had acted as though nothing

were amiss. She would chatter through supper, telling Emmett everything that had happened in Mrs. Bronner's classroom each day, careful not to look at the empty chair at the table. Mommy's place. She had acted as if it were not at all strange that Mommy was upstairs in bed at dinnertime, instead of at the kitchen table eating meat loaf with her husband and daughter. Laura drank all her milk and ate all her peas and hoped that being a good girl would make everything all right.

Laura had also pretended not to notice that Daddy was drinking even more than usual.

For as long as she could remember, Daddy drank from the red-and-white cans. Mommy usually didn't say anything, but Laura could tell that her mother was keeping track of the "red-and-whites" piled up in the trash can each day. "Emmett, that's enough, honey," she'd say. Usually, Daddy would stop.

With Mommy unable to keep watch now, Daddy didn't stop. He drank more and more. He slurred his words. He smelled like beer. Sometimes he'd stumble and fall when he got up from his chair.

One night, Laura said, "Daddy, that's enough, now." And her father hit her. After that, Laura pretended not to notice as she heard one beer can after another pop open.

Somehow, even in her little girl's mind, Laura had known that her father had not meant to hit her. He loved her. She knew it. She excused him because she knew that Daddy was worried about Mommy.

She knew because she had heard him. When her parents thought she was safely sound asleep in her room, blond, wispy-haired Laura stood in the hallway outside her parents' door and listened to their hushed voices.

"Oh, Sarah, what will I do without you?" Daddy cried.

"Shh, sweetheart, shh. I'm so sorry, so sorry. But you have to be strong, you have to go on, for our little girl, for Laura."

"I can't."

"Yes, you can. You must. But, Emmett, you've got to stop drinking. Promise me you'll get help."

Laura heard her father whimper and it scared her. If Mommy was leaving her, all she'd have was Daddy, and he was falling apart. Daddy, who she'd always thought was so big and strong. Daddy, whom she'd have to depend on to make everything all right. Daddy, who was sobbing.

"Promise me, Emmett. You have to tell someone. Unburden yourself. You'll never be able to stop drinking with what happened nagging at your conscience. You have to stop feeling guilty and own up to it. Admit to what happened. It was an accident. Go to the police. Confess."

Laura knew what "confess" meant. She had made her First Holy Communion that year—and along with it, her first confession, the other sacrament, Penance. She had had trouble coming up with things to tell the priest, things that would be considered sins.

She stood in her flannel pajamas and bare feet, and wondered, *What did Daddy do that Mommy is so worried about?*

Twenty years later, a childhood and adolescence of secrets and physical abuse behind her, Laura still did not know what her mother had been whispering about. But her forehead carried a constant reminder of her father's sickness and inability to control himself.

14

DR. LEONARD COSTELLO finished his rounds at Mt. Olympia Hospital with a heavy heart. But it was not his last patient, a teenage girl who had been knifed in the face by some lunatic in Central Park, that left him feeling bereft. When he was done with her, several operations and many thousands of dollars later, she might even look better than she had before.

Costello walked slowly down the hospital hallway, the antiseptic scent of recently cleaned linoleum filling the air. Nurses hurried down the hall, their crepe-soled shoes squeaking. Doctors' names crackled over the PA system. But Costello was only faintly aware of the activity around him. He was thinking of his conversation with Gwyneth Gilpatric and it was deeply troubling him.

Did she know? How could she know about the Parkinson's? He hadn't told anyone, not Francheska, not even his own wife.

He had taken such care. When he suspected that something was wrong, he had not consulted with any doctor at Mt. Olympia—he had not spoken to any doctor in New York, for that matter. Instead, he had called his best friend from medical school and flown down to Miami for an examination. His med school pal, now a neurologist, checked him out but wasn't sure at first what was wrong. It could be anything, Parkinson's, multiple sclerosis, or something unknown. But his friend suggested he try some medication. Costello would know within twenty-four hours if it worked. If the Sinemet stopped the trembling, Costello surely had Parkinson's disease.

As he took the yellow tablet for the first time, Costello was ambivalent. He wanted to know what was wrong, but he prayed it wasn't Parkinson's. However, the alternative of multiple sclerosis or a brain malfunction wasn't any better. How he had taken his good health for granted!

By the end of that day, Costello knew. The Sinemet worked. Costello had joined the ranks of actor Michael J. Fox, Attorney General Janet Reno and boxing great Muhammad Ali.

Once the diagnosis was made, his friend swore to tell no one. Costello was sure his buddy would keep his promise. After all, Costello knew things about him, too. Doctors had to take care of one another.

One whiff of suspicion and a crowded waiting room could become an empty tomb. Reputation meant everything in maintaining a thriving practice.

He had worked too long and too hard to build his dream practice. He was an artist. Everyone said so. His bank account proved it. His lifestyle reflected it.

The Jaguar, the Range Rover, the boat moored in the Hudson. The mansion in Scarsdale, the beach house perched on a cliff in St. Martin. The kids in the best private schools. The hot girlfriend ensconced in the Upper East Side apartment.

He was not about to give it all up.

If Gwyneth knew, it would be just a matter of time before she told someone else. The gossip would spread like wildfire. Leonard Costello, the renowned plastic surgeon with the shakes. His well-heeled patients would flee in fright. He shuddered at the thought.

True, eventually he would have to quit. But not yet. He could wait until he could not control the shaking with medication any longer. With luck, that could be years away. Years when he could continue to rake in the cash and force himself to pay more attention to his investing. Time to build the cushion he needed.

He had to find out if Gwyneth knew. If she did, perhaps he could reassure her that he never intended to operate during one of the Parkinson's episodes. Maybe he could appeal to her sympathies and explain what his plans were. She would understand that he just needed some time before he retired. He resolved to get her aside and fish around at the New Year's Eve party. If he saw her face-to-face, he would be able to tell if she knew.

"Hey, Len." Costello's thoughts were interrupted by Greg Koizim, another of the city's top plastic surgeons. Good-looking and ten years younger than Costello, Koizim fell in step beside his colleague.

"Hi, Greg. How's it going?" Costello asked dully.

"Guess who came in to see me the other day?"

"I give up."

"Gwyneth Gilpatric. Isn't she a patient of yours?"

You know damn well she is, you son-of-a-bitch, thought Costello, and he cursed himself for all the name-dropping and bragging he had done over the years. But the fact that he was losing a famous patient did not matter to him now. As long as he kept all the others.

"Oh, yeah? What's she having done?" Costello asked, trying to sound only mildly interested.

"Full face-lift. I fit her in for the first week of January."

Dr. Costello felt his cheeks grow hot. All Gwyneth's crap about being scared, about not being ready. She had been lying.

Gwyneth knew. She definitely knew.

15

LAURA WORKED ON her Yearender all morning and a good part of the afternoon. She screened three cartons of videotapes looking for just the right two seconds of pictures to capture the essence of her dead subjects. By four o'clock, she was eager to go down to the *Evening Headlines* studio for her taping session with Eliza Blake.

As many news staffers as possible tried to take Christmas week off. Laura, with the exception of Christmas Day, would work through the week, finishing her Yearender. Eliza Blake was taking some vacation, but before she left, *KEY News* wanted to be prepared for contingencies.

When Laura arrived in the studio, Eliza was already at the anchor desk going over her copy. She smiled at Laura as the younger woman approached.

"I feel creepy doing this the day before Christmas Eve," Eliza remarked.

Laura nodded. "Me, too. But you know how it works. If

we're prepared, then he won't die. It's only if we're not ready—that's when he'll be sure to go."

"I guess that's one way of looking at it." Eliza shrugged. "I wonder if they know we do this."

"From what I hear, he's in no condition to know much of what's going on," Laura answered.

"Okay. I'm ready when you are."

Laura crossed the studio to the director's booth, leaving Eliza to give an audio level. "Mike check, one, two, three."

"Sounds good," confirmed director J. P. Crawford, as Laura took a seat in the control booth behind him. Crawford counted down, "Eliza Blake, 'Special Report Kevin Kane,' in three, two, one. Cue Eliza."

Laura watched on the television monitor as Eliza looked directly into the camera and read the words on the TelePrompter. "This is a *KEY News* Special Report. Former President Kevin Robert Kane died today at his ranch outside of Tucson, Arizona. He was seventy-three years old. The former president had been fighting a battle against cancer for the last year.

"President Kane's body will lie in state at the Capitol Rotunda and he will be buried on the grounds of the Kevin R. Kane Presidential Library in Tucson.

"We will have more details on the death of President Kane on tonight's *Evening Headlines*. Repeating, former President Kevin Kane is dead at age seventy-three."

"Let's stop and check," directed Crawford.

Laura and the control room staff watched as the tape of Eliza played back on a half-dozen screens across the control room wall.

"You happy?" Crawford asked.

"Fine," replied Laura.

Now, if the former president did die over the next ten days, as he very well could, his demise would be reported on the KEY Television Network, as it should be, by the *Evening Headlines* anchor—even if she was two hundred miles away from the Broadcast Center, vacationing with her daughter in Rhode Island.

Eliza Blake unclipped her microphone.

"Doesn't doing these obits all the time get to you?" she asked.

Laura shrugged. "Not really. In fact, I kind of enjoy them. The fact that the person warrants a network obituary means that he or she has led an extraordinary life. I enjoy doing the research. I always learn things I didn't know."

Eliza nodded. "Any common thread?"

Laura stopped to consider the question.

"Yes," she answered. "Without exception, each subject I've done has had very difficult periods in his or her life. Each has dealt with tough times and gotten through, persevered and, most often, prevailed."

Eliza smiled brightly. "I like that. And on that upbeat note— I wish you happy holidays and I'm off with Janie to visit my parents for Christmas. What are your plans, Laura? You aren't working, I hope."

"No, thank God. I have Christmas off this year. I'm going out to New Jersey to spend the day with my father."

16

Christmas Eve

THE ATMOSPHERE AT *KEY News* on Christmas Eve was festive. Someone had draped strings of colored lights around the ceiling of the Bulletin Center and the largest desk in the room had been cleared to make way for a spread of cakes, cookies and Mike Schultz's wife's baklava. The news world was quiet on the day before the anniversary of Christ's birth and Laura and her co-workers spent a good deal of time joking around, asking each other what their plans were for the holiday, and commiserating with the goats who had to work.

Laura tried to get some work done on the Yearender. She felt she was in pretty good shape for getting the project completed on time, so she decided to duck out of work a little early. She was eager to get to the Bronners'.

Not wanting to be tied down to bus schedules, she had decided to splurge and rent a car for two days. Her presents for the Bronners were already in the trunk. So she left the KEY Broadcast Center and headed directly for the Lincoln Tunnel and New Jersey. As she emerged from the tunnel, the winter sky was already darkening. Her foot itched on the accelerator. She wanted to get there before the first star appeared.

This is my favorite part of Christmas, she thought. *The part that I most look forward to.* For a moment she felt guilty, wishing she most wanted to spend time with her father. That was how it should be. But it wasn't.

The relationship with Emmett was a complicated one. She loved him, to be sure. But the years spent worrying about her father and living in constant anxiety over what he might do next had taken their toll. She never went to see her father without some dread. Would he be sober? Angry? Depressed?

The Bronners, on the other hand, always welcomed her as family. She knew, because she was not related by blood, she did not have to deal with emotional baggage and issues that would be involved if she actually had been part of the family. She could go to their home and just enjoy the charming, tradition-filled Christmas Eve celebration.

Laura found a parking spot on the corner of Lafayette and Palisades Avenues. As she unloaded the packages from the trunk, she realized that she was just across the street from what had once been the site of Palisades Amusement Park and blocks away from where the remains of Tommy Cruz had been discovered. She walked up Lafayette toward the Bronners' house and, as a blast of winter wind bit at her face, she reminded herself to ask Maxine and Alan if they remembered anything from the time the Cruz child disappeared. Climbing the steps to the Bronners' wreath-bedecked front door, she looked up to the sky and saw a star.

"You made it! Just in time!" Maxine greeted Laura with open arms. "Come in, come in."

The familiar smells of the Bronner Christmas wafted from the kitchen. No meat would be served at dinner. There would be pickled herring, and trout stuffed with apples, mushrooms, onions and celery. A meatless hunter's stew with sauerkraut and yellow peas simmered on the stove, minutes away from being served with noodles and poppy seeds. And, of course, there would be Laura's favorite *pierogi,* those Polish dumplings stuffed with potatoes and cheese.

As the Bronners called out their welcomes, Laura placed her presents under the Christmas tree, its boughs laden with angels, stars, candy and glittering tinsel. She took off her coat and revealed a new red form-fitting dress she had just bought as a Christmas present to herself.

"Laura, you look wonderful!" Maxine exclaimed.

"So do you, Mrs. Bronner. You never change."

Maxine laughed. "Laura, how many times have I told you to call me Maxine? And I wish that were so, dear heart. But time is marching on."

"Looking at you, you'd never know it," said Laura. "You look the same as you did when I walked into your third-grade class. And I guess that's why I will always think of you as Mrs. Bronner. But I'll try to remember to call you Maxine."

"Lady Clairol helps a lot, I guess." Maxine shrugged, pulling a strand of dark brown hair behind her ear.

Alan Bronner put his arm around his wife. "You're absolutely right, Laura. Max is as pretty as the day I met her, or should I say, the day I dialed that wrong number. That was the luckiest day of my life."

They all knew the story of how Maxine and Alan had first "connected." Alan had actually been calling another girl and had mistakenly dialed a different number. Maxine Dzieskanowski answered. The two had clicked. At first the relationship was conducted entirely on the telephone. When Alan finally asked her for a date, Maxine met a ponytailed young man with a patch on the crotch of his jeans at her front door. The young man went on to start a basement computer company—a company that grew to employ thirty-five people at offices in Mahwah. The Bronners could easily have moved from Cliffside Park to a bigger house in a more affluent New Jersey suburb. But they chose to stay where they were, their ties to the community very strong.

"Come on, everybody. It's time for the *Wigilia*," called Maxine. The *optalek* was broken, the meal savored amid warm conversation and laughter. When Maxine brought out dessert—warm, heart-shaped honey spice cake, a compote of dried fruit, nut pudding and a poppyseed coffee cake—Laura groaned.

"I can't eat one more thing."

But she filled her plate anyway.

After dinner, Maxine sat down at the piano in the living room. Playing since she was five years old, she was an accomplished pianist. Laura joined in with the others and sang Christmas songs enthusiastically. Then they opened presents.

Laura sat next to Maxine on the upholstered love seat in the corner of the room, watching and enjoying the oohs and aahs as the gifts were opened.

"So how are things at *KEY News*, Laura?"

"Actually, things are going pretty well."

"Still doing the obituaries?"

"Yes. But I'm trying to get a new job, at *Hourglass*."

Maxine's eyes widened. "Oh, Laura, that would be wonderful for you! We watch that show every week. It's terrific."

Laura nodded. "I've come up with an idea for a segment that the executive producer really likes."

Maxine waited.

"Palisades Amusement Park and the death of Tommy Cruz."

Maxine's face darkened.

"What's wrong?"

Maxine shook her head. "That was a terrible, tragic time. I remember the search for that little boy. It seemed to go on forever. Day after day, week after week, they found nothing. I remember Tommy's best friend Ricky Potenza had a nervous breakdown, poor child. He was never the same. The family eventually moved away, but I still get a Christmas card from his mother."

Maxine looked away for a moment, seeming to collect herself.

"Gradually, the hubbub died down," she continued. "But for the Cruzes, the nightmare went on and on, all these years. To this day, when I see Felipe in church or bump into Marta at the supermarket, I don't know what to say to them. I hope now, at least, there is some closure for them."

"Yes and no," said Laura. "The police are opening up the investigation again."

"I'd think the trail would be dead after all these years."

17

Christmas Day

NOT WANTING TO spend the night at her father's house after dinner with the Bronners, Laura drove back into Manhattan and slept at her own apartment.

On Christmas morning, she was putting her gaily wrapped gifts for her father into a red Bloomingdale's shopping bag to carry with her back out to New Jersey when her apartment telephone rang.

"Merry Christmas," whispered the voice.

"Francheska?"

"Uh-hum."

"Why are you whispering?"

"I'm not alone."

"Oh, God," Laura groaned. "Is Len there?"

"He's lying right beside me. Fast asleep."

"I'm going to throw up. Christmas morning, and he's in bed with you? When his wife and kids are home in Westchester? Slimeball. When are you going to get rid of that animal?"

"Oh, come on, Laura," Francheska pleaded. "Don't nag me. Not today. It's Christmas."

"All right." Laura sighed, resigned for the moment to her

friend and former roommate's situation. "But just tell me one thing. How does he manage it? I mean, what reason did he give his wife for not being home this morning to open the presents from Santa?"

"He's a doctor, remember?"

"Oh, yeah, I forgot," Laura replied sarcastically. "Another 'emergency' at the hospital. Big hotshot plastic surgeon. It's pathetic. And I don't care what you say, Fran, Mrs. Costello has *got* to suspect something. Either that or she's the dumbest woman in Scarsdale."

"Going out to see Emmett?" Francheska whispered, changing the subject.

"Yes. And I wish you'd come with me. Emmett would be happy to see you. He loves you, you know, and he's making your favorite, prime rib. Come on. It's Christmas, Francheska. I don't want you to be in the city all alone after Dr. Wonderful leaves."

"Thanks, honey. The thought of spending some time down in your dad's basement playing with the park is really tempting. If I change my mind, I know where to find you."

"Hey, I've got to go," she whispered hurriedly. "He's starting to wake up."

As she heard the phone go dead, Laura wished she'd had time to tell her friend that her cheating lover had called Gwyneth Gilpatric the other night.

18

THE AROMA OF roasting beef greeted Laura as she let herself into her father's half of the two-family house on Grant Avenue. There was no one there to greet her in either the small living/dining-room combination or the tiny kitchen. She struggled with the large, heavy box she carried, along with the shopping bag filled with gifts. She laid everything on the floor.

"Pop?" she called. "I'm home."

"Down here, Munk."

Of course, that's where he would be, she thought. The basement was his favorite place in the house.

Stuffing her gloves into the pocket of her coat, she hung it in the closet next to the front door. Laura carried the box and the Bloomingdale's bag over toward the tabletop Christmas tree Emmett had set up on top of the television console. Her father had threaded a strand of colored lights through the branches of the miniature fir and he had hung the ornaments he treasured most: Laura's artwork done over her school years. A butterfly with a clothespin body and tissue-paper wings, a caterpillar fashioned from a cardboard egg carton and some green pipe-cleaner antennae, a tiny wreath of strung macaroni sprayed gold.

Laura smiled at Emmett's sentimentality. He'd had his parental failings over the years, but in his own way, she supposed, he had tried to be both mother and father.

She arranged her presents on the floor in front of the television and was glad that she'd ignored their rule of keeping down the holiday spending. She'd brought a half dozen boxes wrapped in red-and-green plaid and tied with shiny silver bows, containing things that Emmett would never buy for himself. There was one small box and Laura carried it with her as she walked though the kitchen to the basement door.

"Pop?"

As she descended the old wooden steps, she heard the sound she'd heard over and over again since her childhood. The Palisades Park theme song tinkled from the basement below.

Some grown men had train sets, some played with miniature battlefield scenes and moved their battalions of soldiers through the various stages of combat. Laura's father had painstakingly fashioned a diminutive Palisades Amusement Park, the place where he had worked for the summers that, he said, were among the most memorable of his life.

It was all there, amazingly constructed to scale. The carousel with the tiniest hand-carved horses; the saltwater pool that Emmett filled with an eyedropper; the Sky Ride's teeny cars that dangled from a thin wire thread; the tiny angry black gorilla that stood menacingly guarding the Jungleland ride; the really miniature, miniature golf course. Every attraction and amusement of the legendary park was represented in Emmett's basement world.

After her mother died, Laura and her dad spent hours together working on the park. Laura loved to listen to Emmett's stories about the rides, contests and music that brought people from all walks of life streaming through the gates. Her father had seen Jackie Kennedy with Caroline and John-John eating ice-cream cones, and Walter Cronkite and his daughter driving the Antique Cars. A movie star named Debbie Reynolds announced her engagement to a singer named Eddie Fisher at the park, though the marriage didn't last, Emmett always remarked, shaking his head. Elizabeth Taylor stole Eddie away from Debbie. It was very sad.

Pop was there the day the crown prince of Saudi Arabia came with his entire entourage to see the two-headed cow at the animal freak show. Once, the king and queen of Nepal came—and wouldn't leave. The park had to stay open late while the royal pair rode every ride and played every game.

Top entertainers came to perform for record summer crowds. Pop had heard Tony Bennett, Diana Ross, Frankie Avalon, Chubby Checker and the Jackson Five sing their hearts out on the open-air stage.

To young Laura, growing up after the park had been torn down to make way for high-rise condominiums, it was magical to hear that Cliffside Park had once drawn people from all over the world.

"Laura, honey. I'm glad you're home. Merry Christmas, Munk. Did you bring Francheska?"

Father and daughter hugged each other. Laura instinctively sniffed and was relieved to smell Old Spice instead of the Budweiser that had led to so many fits of violence. She blinked, remembering the stinging smacks across the face she had received over the years. He didn't mean it. He couldn't help it. It was the alcohol that made him do it. The alcohol and the anger at his situation. Laura understood it better now, but the emotional scars ran deep.

"Merry Christmas, Pop. No, Francheska couldn't come." Laura handed her package to Emmett. "Go ahead, open it right away."

Emmett hesitated. "Well, wait just a minute. I have your presents upstairs. Let me go get them." He started for the basement stairs, but Laura pulled him back.

"We can open the other presents later, but I want you to open this one now, down here."

"Okay, Monkey. If that's what you want."

Emmett took his customary seat in a chair he kept next to the miniature Cyclone. Carefully, he pulled at the tape that fastened the bow.

"Just rip it open," Laura urged. If her father knew how much she had paid for the glass roller-coaster ornament, he would choke.

Emmett's face broke into a wide smile as he held up the shiny ornament. "This is terrific, sweetie. Thank you. I'm going to put it right on the tree."

Laura followed her father up the stairs.

"Hey, Munk, did I tell you that they asked me to bring my park to the fund-raiser that they are having next month to raise money for a real Palisades Park museum?" he called over his shoulder.

"Yes, Pop, you mentioned it. That's wonderful." He had already told her at least half a dozen times.

Afterward they went upstairs to open the other presents. Emmett was much more excited about his new VCR than he was over the Christopher Radko ornament.

"Honey, you shouldn't have spent so much money on me."
Laura smiled with pleasure.

"That old VCR of yours is always breaking down, Pop, or
eating tapes. I wanted you to have a new one."

"That's just too much money to spend, Laura," her father
insisted, but Laura could tell he was enthusiastic about his gift.
Emmett was forever taping shows and watching them at his
leisure.

"Is dinner almost ready?" asked Laura, changing the subject.
"It smells wonderful." She rose from the worn sofa and went
to the kitchen, Emmett following her. Together they put the
finishing touches on their Christmas feast.

$\approx$

"So, Munk, are you still working on those funeral stories?"
Emmett asked as he cut into his rare prime rib.

Laura nodded as she tried the whipped potatoes. "They're
called obituaries, Pop."

"The whole thing gives me the willies. If you ask me, it's
just plain creepy to do stories on somebody's death before they
are actually dead." Emmett shook his head as he spread butter
on a flaky popover.

"Well, Pop, you'll be glad to know that I'm trying to branch
out. I've proposed a story for *Hourglass* and the executive producer is interested in it. I'm hoping that I can do a good job
on it and earn a position on his staff."

"Good for you, honey. I'm so proud of you. Who'd have
ever thought that a daughter of mine would become a big
television producer!"

Laura laughed. "Hold on a minute, Pop. I don't have the
job yet."

"But you will, Munk, you will," said Emmett, looking pleased. "You've always done everything you've set your mind to. What's the story?"

Knowing his obsession and fascination with her subject, Laura was eager to tell her father. "Palisades Park and the disappearance of Tommy Cruz."

The pleased look fell from Emmett's face.

"What's wrong, Pop?"

"Munk, why do you want to dredge all that up? Think about how the poor Cruzes will feel having all that on television."

"I would think they'd take some satisfaction that Tommy's death is finally getting the attention it deserves. Maybe we'll be able to find out what really happened. I'm sure the Cruzes would want to know that."

"I doubt it, Munk. I sincerely doubt it. Let them rest in peace." Emmett rose and retrieved a can of beer from the refrigerator.

Laura groaned inwardly. Not wanting to distress Emmett further, especially at Christmas dinner, Laura decided to change the subject.

"Hey, Pop, guess where I'm going New Year's Eve."

19

WORKING ON CASPER'S Ghostland on Christmas night was truly sick, but so were all obsessions.

The computer screen glowed in the darkened room. Against the bright white background, the names of America's media elite were listed in bold block letters.

The editors and publishers of *Time, Newsweek,* the *New York Times,* the *Wall Street Journal,* the heads of the television networks, the executive producers of the major news broadcasts, as well as the familiar personalities that anchored them made the list. One hundred names in all.

Fortunately, John Kennedy, Jr., even as the head of his magazine *George,* had never made the list, so the pot had been growing for a long time. No one expected someone so young to die. None of the newshounds had been prepared for that.

Casper's Ghostland was a secret pool, and anonymity was guaranteed. For one thousand dollars a month, high-rolling members of the pool placed a bet. A bet on who would die next.

Casper's Ghostland was also a lottery. The names were assigned to the bettors. No one could choose who they were placing their money on. Except, of course, the organizer of the game.

One name to a customer—and only for thirty days, please. You paid your thousand bucks, got a name, and waited. If the month went by without a winner, everyone was assigned a different name in the pool. Casper, of course, kept the same name: that was the plan. The pool grew and grew, one hundred thousand dollars amassing each month. Now over two million dollars sat in the account.

For twenty months it had been hard to sit and wait. But now the payoff was near.

Just another week.

Casper offered up a "Friendly Ghost's" prayer. *Please, God, don't call any of the other names home to their heavenly rewards.*

20

Sunday, December 26

THE EAST HARLEM Tutorial Project was housed in an old four-story brownstone painted neon blue on a horrible inner-city block, Second Avenue between 105th and 106th Streets. No sessions were being held Christmas week, but Laura hurried to meet her student anyway, the sound of boom boxes and police sirens blaring in her ears.

East Harlem was the city's original Puerto Rican enclave. Traditionally an entry-level immigrant neighborhood, arriving waves of Germans, Irish and Italians had settled there. But in the fifties, when Puerto Ricans began coming to New York in significant numbers, East Harlem became home for those who had left the sunny island.

East Harlem, Spanish Harlem, El Barrio were interchangeable names for the area roughly defined by 96th Street to the south and 140th Street to the north, from Fifth Avenue to the East River. El Barrio was widely acknowledged as the birthplace of salsa music, and in the busy streets, pulsing rhythms filled the air.

The neighborhood was poor. Junky stores lined the trashstrewn sidewalk. The abandoned lot next to the tutorial building was strewn with cans, broken bottles, cigarette butts, used condoms and, more often than not, Laura noticed, hypodermic needles. A wonderful atmosphere for learning.

The tutorial program was not remedial. The kids enrolled were bright enough. But they needed to be given opportunity and exposure to life beyond their limiting city blocks and economic situations. Once a week, for two hours, Laura had signed on to help a child develop the life of the mind.

Ten-year-old Jade Figueroa was Laura's student. They had been meeting on Saturday mornings since school started in September and Laura was happy with the relationship that was developing between them. The little girl with black bangs and pigtails lived with her mother and grandmother in a small apartment near the tutorial building. Jade's dad was not on the scene. Jade didn't talk about him.

As Laura approached the building, she spotted Jade and her mother, Myra, waiting outside the entrance. They'd arranged to meet here. Laura knew that it would save time. The Figueroas' apartment building had just two elevator banks for hundreds of apartments. Laura had dropped Jade home once, and they had had to wait almost a full half hour to catch the smelly elevator.

Jade stood on the sidewalk now, looking excited. Her dark brown eyes shone, her white uneven teeth beamed from her scrubbed round face. Myra had carefully braided her daughter's shining hair and adorned it with little plastic butterflies. As she held tightly to her mother's hand, she bounced up and down. Laura knew that this would be Jade's first trip just forty blocks south, but a world away, to FAO Schwarz.

When Laura had told her that the toy store let every kid play with any toy in the place, Jade had listened wide-eyed.

"Really?"

"Um-hmm. You can try out anything you want and see if you want to buy it."

Jade's face fell.

"What's wrong?" Laura asked.

"You need money to buy the toys. I don't have any."

"Well, I'll tell you what," Laura had proposed a few weeks ago. "You ask your mother if it's okay with her, and I'll take you to FAO Schwarz for Christmas and you can try the toys out. If you find one you really like, I'll buy it for you."

Today, the day after Christmas, was the day they had agreed upon for their excursion.

Myra eyed Laura a bit warily as she handed over her daughter.

"Jade's been lookin' forward to this for weeks. She didn't sleep last night, she was so excited that Christmas would last one more day."

"Well, I'm excited about this, too." Laura smiled. "Thank you for letting me take her."

"When you be home?" Myra's thick Hispanic accent sometimes made it difficult for Laura to understand her.

"Four o'clock okay?"

Myra nodded. "I'll be here waiting at four o'clock."

Jade pulled her hand from her mother's. Myra zipped up the child's blue ski jacket tight around her neck and adjusted her red wool scarf.

"You be a good girl, Jade."

"Yes, Mama. I'll be good. I promise."

The subway ride downtown seemed quick to Laura, but Jade asked when they were going to get there a dozen times.

Laura watched Jade's awed expression as a real-life toy soldier greeted them at the entrance to the Fifth Avenue store. The child was hypnotized by the endless spinning, bobbing, bouncing and flashing of the Clock Tower. The rolling blue eyes and the chattering red lips of the animated, singing timepiece mesmerized her. They stood for ten minutes watching its tiers of chugging trains and floating blimps.

Together, they toured the aisles of wonderful distractions in the world's most fabulous toy store. Radio-controlled race cars zipped past their feet. Barbie dolls smiled in their glittering designer ball gowns, GI Joes in their camouflage posted sentry. Star Wars figures loomed. There were towers of board games, and video games flashed from shiny monitors. Electronic and science toys filled one buzzing section. Another area was stocked floor to ceiling with stuffed animals of all whimsical shapes and sizes.

Laura steered Jade to the Lollipop Forest in the candy area. The Gummy Bear totem pole and a twelve-foot chocolate soldier greeted them. Jade looked longingly at the world's largest M&M selection.

"Want some?" Laura asked.

Jade hesitated.

"It doesn't count as your present," Laura reassured her.

As Jade carefully ate her candies, one at a time, Laura asked her if she had made a decision.

"I saw a dog I liked. Mama says we can't have a real dog in our apartment. Maybe I could get that dog?" she asked uncertainly.

"The dog it is. Let's go."

From the array of dozens of soft, creamy-colored stuffed dogs, all named Patrick the Pup, the FAO Schwarz mascot, Jade chose the one whose ears weren't quite so perky as the others.

"He looks like he needs a good home," she said satisfied. "I want him."

Afterward, they walked along Central Park South together, the winter wind blowing into their happy faces. But Jade's beam faded as she looked up at her older companion.

"What's that?" she asked solemnly, pointing to Laura's bare forehead, the bangs now blown back by the cold breeze.

Caught off guard, Laura reached up and touched the space over her brow.

"Oh, this? It's just a scar I got when I fell and hit the corner of a table. I was just a little older than you when it happened."

Jade nodded, satisfied with what she did not know was only a partial explanation.

Laura was careful to leave out the part about her father's drunken anger and frustration that had led to his striking his young daughter, sending her careening into the table's edge.

21

Tuesday, December 28

FRANCHESKA SKIMMED THROUGH the glossy pages of the *Lifestyles of the Rich and Famous Cookbook,* settling on Ivana Trump's recipe for beef goulash. She had prepared it before and Leonard loved it.

She slid the emerald ring off her index finger, and the pearl-and-diamond one off her right ring finger, and placed both of Leonard's lavish gifts on the ledge above the sink so that she could prepare dinner unencumbered.

After expertly cutting the cubes of beef and dusting them with flour and paprika, Francheska sautéed them in butter and oil, adding minced onions and crushed garlic. She added the water and marjoram the recipe called for and slid the casserole dish into the oven to bake. A bottle of red wine sat already opened, breathing on the kitchen counter.

Carefully, she set the table for two. A creamy linen tablecloth and napkins. The Villeroy & Boch dinner plates and the Christofle crystal wineglasses she had purchased at Bloomingdale's. The two Tiffany sterling place settings that she had charged to the American Express Card that Leonard had given her. At five hundred dollars a pop, Francheska had known that Leonard wasn't too happy with that, but that had been early on in the relationship, when he accepted anything she bought, so eager was he to keep her happy.

Before he had started taking her for granted.

Francheska loved beautiful things. She scanned the apartment living room and was satisfied with the way it looked. She had pored over issues of *Architectural Digest* and *Town and Country* long and hard, educating herself in the ways the wealthy decorated.

She had instructed the painters to cover the walls in egg-yolk-yellow paint with a dramatic lacquer finish. She had ordered rich coral draperies to match the damask-covered camelback sofa. The armchairs that flanked the fireplace were upholstered in a Scalamandré paisley fabric that picked up the colors in the sofa and rug. Elegantly framed English prints graced the walls. A large Chinese-Chippendale-style gilded mirror hung over the fireplace, reflecting the light from a dozen candles perched in sterling holders that were grouped on the mantelpiece.

Yes, she had made a beautiful place for their trysts. And, for a while, that had been enough.

But where was she going? Though she denied it to Laura in their myriad conversations about her affair with Leonard, Francheska was not content with being the "other woman." It was not how she had been raised. If her parents knew that she was being kept by a married man, it would kill them, and God knew they had already had a tough enough time of it.

She loved her parents and their good and decent ways. And yet, she had wanted to escape them. She didn't want to repeat their lives of hard work that got them nowhere. Francheska had realized early on that her looks were her ticket out of a world where one lived from paycheck to paycheck.

She had still been living with her aunt since her parents had moved to Puerto Rico, working on a painfully sporadic modeling career, when she met Laura at the World Gym near Lincoln Center. As they got to know one another, panting through aerobics classes, Francheska learned that Laura had just moved into a small Manhattan apartment at a good address, but was having to budget carefully to come up with the ridiculous New York City rent each month. Francheska seized the opportunity to get away from home and asked Laura if she would consider a roommate.

They had had a lot of fun together in that apartment, but Francheska's modeling assignments were not dependable enough. Some months, Laura had to advance Francheska's portion of the rent. When Leonard Costello came along, Francheska was ready to be taken care of.

Glancing at her watch, Francheska realized that Leonard should be arriving in about a half hour. She went in to take a shower and dress.

She dropped her clothes on the bathroom floor and, twisting up her long dark hair and clipping it to the top of her head, she stepped into the tub. The sliding glass shower door was covered with steam as Francheska let the hot spray douse her sleek body.

She had to talk to Leonard. Maybe he did care enough about her to leave his wife—though, in her heart, she was afraid she knew already what his answer would be. But she felt compelled to bring things to a head. If she had no real future with Leonard, painful though it may be, it was time to move on.

She was practicing in her mind what she would say when the shower door slid open. Leonard stood naked before her. And, God help her, she was excited by the sight of him.

Afterward, as Francheska dried his well-exercised body with a thick towel, she told him that she had his favorite dinner waiting.

Leonard looked uncomfortable.

"Don't tell me." Francheska pulled away from him.

"I'm sorry, Francie, but I can't stay. Anne has something planned with the kids tonight. I thought I could get out of it, but I can't."

Biting the corner of her lip, she answered him with silence. Pulling a robe from the hook on the back of the bathroom door and covering herself, she stormed into the bedroom. Leonard followed behind her and began to dress quickly.

"Do you have any idea how this makes me feel, Leonard? Do you even care how this makes me feel?" Francheska exploded. She could dissolve into tears if she let herself, but she wouldn't. Not now. There would be the whole lonely night in front of her to do that.

"Come on, Francheska. I've had a long day and I don't need to get into this crap now." He was strapping on his Rolex.

"Great. That's just great." She stalked out of the bedroom, pulling the tie of her bathrobe tight around her waist. She was taking the goulash from the oven when Leonard, now fully dressed, came up behind her and began to nuzzle her neck.

"I'm sorry, Francie. I'll make it up to you, I promise."

"Um-hmm." She wouldn't look at him.

Leonard tried to change the subject. "Hey, you'll never guess who is lying at Mt. Olympia on life support."

22

"WHY DON'T YOU get in a cab and come over here right now?" Laura urged her distraught friend. "Sleep over. It will be just like the old days."

They had been on the telephone for the better part of an hour now, going over and over the same old thing. Francheska's humiliation tonight was just the latest episode in the ongoing saga. She had to get rid of that guy. She knew it. But she could never bring herself to do it.

Laura hated to hear her friend's alternating sobbing and angered anguish. And, though she hated to admit it to herself, Laura was losing patience with Francheska. No matter how much she tried to encourage Francheska and reassure her that she would be better off out of this relationship no matter what she had to give up, Francheska didn't budge. While Laura hoped that Leonard's actions tonight might be the final nail in the coffin of the affair, she sensed that Francheska still held out hope. Big mistake.

Laura tried to put herself in her friend's shoes. How would Francheska support herself once she lost the Dr. Costello meal ticket? She had given up modeling in the years she had been with Leonard. But she had purchased a computer and taken a few business courses at Fordham during her empty afternoons.

Maybe she could get some sort of job and finish her degree at night. Francheska was bright enough. Other people did it; so could she. But she had to want it. No amount of encouraging pep talks from Laura, helpful though they were, could make Francheska do it. Francheska had to want it herself.

Francheska sniffled on the other end of the phone line. "Thanks, Laura. But I'm just too tired to come over. I'm just going to wash my face and go to bed."

"You're sure?"

"Mm-hmm."

"All right, then. I'll call you tomorrow." Laura was about to hang up.

"Hey, so that the night won't be a total waste, I did get something out of Leonard's visit," Francheska remembered.

"And that would be what?" Laura asked.

"That tennis player? The one who won Wimbledon and the U.S. Open last year . . . ?" Francheska's voice trailed off as she tried to pull the name from her tired brain.

Laura prompted her with the name.

"Yeah, that's the one. Well, Leonard told me he's on life-support machines at Mt. Olympia. Drug overdose. His parents are flying in tonight to pull the plug."

23

Wednesday, December 29

THE FIRST THING Laura did when she arrived at her desk the next morning was call the tape library and order some video of last summer's U.S. Open. With two days before the Year-ender was to air, she knew right where she could use the pictures of the strapping, healthy tennis player in her video montage. So confident was she of Francheska's information that Laura went ahead and edited the video into her piece well before the Associated Press wire service issued a bulletin on the athlete's death.

As she exited the editing room, Mike Schultz was waiting for her.

"Laura, I've got an obit for you to do."

"I've got the tapes right here," Laura responded.

Mike looked surprised as he looked at the videotapes labeled with the tennis star's name that Laura held in her hands.

"How did you know that?" he asked in wonder, shaking his head.

"I have my sources," Laura said with a shrug as she headed toward her desk to write her obituary script.

24

WHEN GWYNETH HUNG up the phone after her conversation with her agent, her heart was pounding. She sank gratefully into the tufted slipper chair that sat in front of her dressing table and smiled slyly at her reflection in the mirror.

It was done! The *I*s were dotted and the *T*s were crossed in the contract, and CBS had given her everything she had wanted, and then some, to lure her over to their team.

Now came the even better part. She got to tell Joel.

Gwyneth wanted to do it herself, and right away, before he had a chance to hear it through the immediate and superactive broadcasting grapevine. She didn't want him to have time to think or couch his response to her news. The fun would be in getting his raw reaction, catching him completely off guard. She wished she could tell him in person and see Joel's face as he heard the news, but she didn't dare wait even the time it would take to catch a cab over to the Broadcast Center. Someone from CBS could call him to gloat before she got there.

She glanced at the crystal timepiece on the bedside table. Six o'clock. He'd still be there, waiting to watch the *Evening Headlines*. Gwyneth's manicured fingers plucked nervously at the chair's velvet piping as she waited for Joel to pick up his private line.

"Yes?" Joel's voice was clipped and she could hear him exhaling a drag of his cigarette.

"It's me, Joel."

"Gwyneth, baby!" His voice changed to his best purr as he instantly recognized her voice. "How are you, kiddo? All set for your party?"

"Sure. Everything should be wonderful, Joel, but I'm not so sure you'll want to come after you hear what I have to tell you."

"Tell me what?" he asked cautiously.

"I'm leaving *Hourglass,* Joel. Leaving KEY and going over to CBS. The contract is all set."

She listened quietly, smirking at her reflection in the beveled glass of the mirror as Joel let loose with the expletives she had anticipated. It felt good to anger him, to hurt him, to pay him back for the hurt that he had caused her.

A marriage between them probably would have been a disaster. Gwyneth knew that. But as much as she always declared that she was not the marrying kind, she had been deeply wounded that Joel had never, in all the time that they had carried on their affair, suggested that he would leave Kitzi and make an honest woman of his star. If he had, Gwyneth wasn't even sure what she would have answered. But it didn't matter. He should have asked. And, over the years, Joel's omission had festered within her.

Now, as she listened to him yelling into the telephone and pictured the rage in his reddened face, Gwyneth felt smug satisfaction in rejecting him.

"Goddamn it, Gwyneth, you owe me more than this!" Joel demanded.

"I don't owe you anything, Joel," Gwyneth answered determinedly. "You owe *me*. I'm the reason for your success, and the success of *Hourglass*. We both know that."

"No! We don't both know that!" Joel sputtered. "I've made you the star that you've become, and don't you ever forget it! If it weren't for me, you'd be nowhere. You and your kind are a dime a dozen, baby. Don't kid yourself, Gwyneth, you'll be easily replaced. And, I might add, by a younger, fresher, prettier version."

Gwyneth rose to Joel's bait. She screamed into the phone, calling him every foul name she could think of. "You can go to hell!" she hissed as she went to slam down the receiver.

"I'll see you there," answered the executive producer. "I'll see you there."

25

New Year's Eve

LAURA WAS EAGER to get to the Broadcast Center on New Year's Eve morning. All the hard work was done. Now she would have the pleasure of watching her Yearender air on the KEY Television Network.

She tucked a starched white cotton shirt into her favorite pair of jeans and pulled a loose-fitting dark green sweater over her head. No need to dress up today. Only a skeleton staff would be working. Almost all the executives were on holiday vacation, available on beeper if any big news story broke. Those who reported to the Broadcast Center today were the worker bees.

She hoped this would be the last time that she would be responsible for the Yearender. If things went the way she planned, this time next year, she'd be producing for *Hourglass*.

Laura lifted the Murphy bed up into the wall and wished for the thousandth time that she had more space. It seemed amazing to her, now, that Francheska and she had once shared this apartment.

If she got the new job, the first thing she was going to do was look for a bigger apartment. Hopefully, something would open up in the same building. She loved the Oliver Cromwell on West 72nd Street. Just a half block from Central Park and a pleasant walk to the Broadcast Center. The neighborhood was wonderful. Lots of good restaurants, interesting shops, multiple movie theaters and, of course, Lincoln Center. She'd made a New Year's resolution to take better advantage of the cultural opportunities that were just blocks from her front door.

Raising the shade at the picture window, Laura glanced at her "view," the apartment across the alley. No one was stirring at the Pilsners'. She laughed to herself.

She really had no idea what the people who lived in that apartment were really named. But every night she watched the family gather for dinner, the father always drinking beer from a Pilsner glass. And so Laura had christened them.

She did not think that the Pilsners noticed that she watched them. In the beginning, she kept track of how many beers the father drank. Usually he stopped at two, and Laura was relieved for the little boy who sat at the table with his parents.

Fleetingly, Laura wondered if she would miss the Pilsners when she moved. No. The next view she had was going to be a more interesting one. Perhaps the expansive Manhattan skyline to the south, or at least the broad boulevard scene of 72nd Street to the north.

As she waited for the kettle to boil on the old stove in the closet-sized kitchen, Laura carefully lifted the hanging bag that was hooked to the top of the bathroom door frame. Pulling back the plastic, she inspected the midnight-blue velvet cocktail dress she would wear tonight to Gwyneth's party. It fit like skin and she was glad that she had been keeping up with her jogging even as the weather had gotten cold.

She had spent almost a week's salary on the dress. But it was worth it. She knew she would feel confident wearing it to the party, whose guests probably never worried about price tags.

Of course, with a dress like this, she needed shoes to do it justice, and she had spent almost an equal amount on the Manolo Blahnik silk crepe de chine high-heeled mules that she and Francheska found at a Madison Avenue boutique. She rationalized that the purchases were investments, though she doubted she'd have many occasions to wear them again. But one could hope.

The kettle whistled as Laura pulled the plastic down over the velvet dress. She walked over to the stove and poured the steaming water over a tea bag and considered the possibilities of the evening ahead. Joel Malcolm would be at the party and that would provide another opportunity to talk with him. Another chance to remind him that she wanted to work for him.

Naturally, she would not even bring up the fact that she wanted the job. They both knew it. But it would be beneficial for Joel to see that Gwyneth thought enough of Laura to invite her.

And you never know. Maybe she would meet someone tonight. Someone exciting. Francheska was always nagging Laura about her love life, or rather the lack of it. But things could change in an instant, couldn't they?

26

"GREAT JOB." "I didn't know she was dead."

"I thought he had died a long time ago!"

"Nice work, Laura."

The Yearender aired and Laura basked in the reactions from her co-workers in the Bulletin Center. Praise was not dispensed freely at *KEY News,* although you were always quick to find out when you fouled up.

"You get better every year," said Mike Schultz. "That was a first-rate piece of work, Laura. You got fifty people in there beautifully."

"Thanks, Mike. Thanks a lot. From you, I consider that quite a compliment."

"Come in to see me when you have a minute."

"Sure. Just let me check that the script information is in the computer. I want to make sure that the stations know they have to pay music rights when they air this thing."

Ten minutes later, Laura approached the open door of Mike Schultz's office. She overheard the tail end of his telephone conversation.

"Listen, honey, I don't want to go, either, but we have to. That's all there is to it. I'll meet you there at nine."

Laura heard the phone receiver returned firmly to its cradle. She waited a moment and knocked tentatively on the side of the open door.

"Come on in and sit down, Laura." Mike sighed. "if you can find a place. And close the door."

Laura smiled as she glanced around the small office. Mike's desk was crowded with piles of papers and stacks of videotapes. The extra chair was covered with a bundle of newspapers. Laura lifted it and put it on the floor.

"I'm dying for a cigarette," Mike grumbled as he rummaged through his desk. "Do you mind?"

"Not at all." Laura laughed. "But aren't you worried about the smoking police?"

"Screw 'em." Mike lit the end of a Marlboro Light.

Laura waited expectantly.

"I got a call from Joel Malcolm yesterday."

"And?"

"He was asking a lot of questions about you and your work." Mike took another drag on his cigarette. "I, of course, told him the truth. Your work is terrific. And so is your attitude. A rare combination to come by around this place."

"Thanks, Mike, I appreciate that." Laura, feeling uncomfortable, shifted position in her chair. "I've been meaning to tell you, but it's been so busy around here, there hasn't been the right time. But, as you've probably figured out, I'm trying to get a job on *Hourglass*."

Mike nodded. "That makes a lot of sense. It's a good career move for you, Laura. But I'm sure as hell going to miss you."

"Well, I don't have the job yet."

"I think it looks good," Mike assured her. "Malcolm was very enthused about you, especially when I told him that you seemed to have an uncanny ability to predict whose obits to have ready. He got a big charge out of that."

Laura smiled. "We both know, Mike, that comes from common sense, some research and a little bit of luck."

"Some well-placed contacts don't hurt, either."

"That, too," Laura admitted.

Mike dropped his cigarette butt into an empty Coke can. "Well, when things get firmed up, let's talk again. I spent some time at *Hourglass* myself. I'll fill you in on how they get things done there."

Laura detected a trace of bitterness in his voice.

27

TO MAKE THE guest list for Gwyneth Gilpatric's renowned New Year's Eve parties, the famous television news personality had to find you interesting. Having wealth and power helped, but those alone wouldn't open the door. Gwyneth had to think you were fascinating in some particular way. This meant that, at times, there was an unlikely mix at the penthouse on Central Park West.

Waiters in black pants, white shirts, red cummerbunds, and matching bow ties moved unobtrusively through the guests who milled around Gwyneth's expansive living room. Gleaming silver trays bore hors d'oeuvres of smoked salmon pillows, miniature crab cakes and grilled herbed-chicken satays. The champagne flowed freely and the wet bar in the library did a steady business.

Dressed in a floor-length, very full black velvet skirt and a ruby wrap top that sashed around her trim waist, Gwyneth greeted her guests at the door. Delia stood at her side, taking coats. When Laura arrived, Gwyneth gave her a big hug.

"I'm so glad you could come, Laura, darling. And who is this beauty you've brought with you?" Gwyneth inquired, extending her hand.

"This is my best friend, Francheska. Francheska Lamb."

"Welcome, Francheska Lamb. Any friend of Laura's is welcome here. You girls go ahead in and mingle. There are lots of stimulating people here."

Throughout the evening, Gwyneth would play the gracious hostess, making introductions and hoping that her guests would click and enjoy one another. If they didn't, that was regrettable, but not tragic. Gwyneth supplied the atmosphere for a fabulous party. She felt it was up to her guests to put their energy into having a good time.

When Gwyneth was confident that most of her guests had arrived, she swept across the foyer and into the living room to talk to Dr. Leonard Costello and his wife, Anne.

"Leonard, Leonard. It's so good to see you. And Anne, what a beautiful dress! You look terrific!" Gwyneth kissed the air beside the couple's cheeks.

"You're looking fabulous as always, Gwyneth," replied Dr. Costello coolly, as his eyes scanned her face. She sensed that Costello, one of New York's leading plastic surgeons, was checking for any telltale signs of failure in his artistry. He would have a busy night if he kept that up, since he had worked on the faces of more than half of the women and men in the room.

As the Costellos left to take in the view of the Manhattan skyline, Gwyneth had a few moments to stand back and observe the party. Laura and Francheska were engrossed in conversation with Mike Schultz and his wife. It occurred to Gwyneth that when she had told Laura to bring a friend, she had hoped Laura would be on the arm of a handsome young man. Oh, well, the dark-haired beauty added to the glamour of the party.

Gwyneth made a mental note to get over there soon and break up that little group. Laura could talk to Mike anytime. There were other people Gwyneth wanted her to be exposed to tonight.

Joel didn't look any too happy. What gall he had in even coming tonight, after their bitter fight yesterday.

She wouldn't put it past him to think that he could charm her into changing her mind and staying at *Hourglass*! And she'd also bet that he had probably had one of his notorious fights with Kitzi before he arrived. Joel had often told her that whenever he and Kitzi were required to show up as a couple at anything that had to do with Gwyneth,

Kitzi would fly into a rage. That's probably why Kitzi hadn't come with him tonight—not the "headache" Joel claimed she had.

Gwyneth chuckled inwardly.

28

KITZI MALCOLM FUMED. What a hell of a way to spend New Year's Eve. Feigning a headache and alone.

Of course, she reassured herself that the old saying was true: it was better to be miserable in mink. And that she was.

Three minks hung in the foyer closet, and a sable and two beavers. She hardly ever wore them, though, always afraid that some animal activist would spray red paint on them as she came out of Saks Fifth Avenue. What was the use of having them anyway?

What was the use of having any of this stuff? The designer dresses, the Italian shoes, the Cartier watches and the Harry Winston jewelry. They really didn't make a tinker's damn bit of difference in the long run. Not when your personal life was in shreds.

She had sold out a long time ago, accepting Joel's peace offerings. Allowing him to mollify her with expensive gifts which they both knew did nothing to heal the emotional rift between them. Never really addressing the problems that they had.

The situation seemed to suit Joel just fine. He had his trophy wife safe at home in the duplex overlooking Central Park while he did just as he pleased. Kitzi presided over their social life, arranging dinner parties and chairing charity events that Joel hosted and got publicity for. He loved having his name out there as one of the players in the competitive New York City social scene. It helped *Hourglass,* he explained.

Everything was about the show. The people they socialized with, the vacations they took, the charities they supported. They spent very little time together. Joel was always too busy with *Hourglass.*

Birthdays, anniversaries, any illness Kitzi had over the years were only paid attention to if *Hourglass* didn't need Joel. The broadcast schedule was a demanding one, she knew. Every week another hour of prime-time television had to be produced. And not just any old hour. It had to be strong enough to keep the broadcast at the top of the ratings heap. A heap that grew increasingly more competitive as all the networks continued to add magazine shows to their schedules.

When she complained about it, Joel grew angry. Did she want to be some little housewife somewhere in the boondocks? He insisted that she knew what she had signed on for when she married him.

But she had not counted on his philandering. Not as much philandering, anyway. No, she was not naive. She knew that many men strayed, especially in the circles she and Joel traveled in. Her friends said it went with the territory. Power was a great aphrodisiac.

Women, young and old, were turned on by Joel's power and prestige. Joel was well aware of it and enjoyed it. Kitzi had seen it. At *KEY News* functions, women reporters and producers who wanted to work on *Hourglass* flirted shamelessly with him, acting as though Kitzi weren't even there.

But Joel was past screwing around at the office. A sexual harassment lawsuit had seen to that. There were plenty of women outside of *KEY News* who were eager for flings.

But like all of Joel's rules, this one had an exception.

Gwyneth Gilpatric.

He could not get over his obsession with her, and Kitzi had often thought that Joel would leave her for his anchorwoman. But he hadn't. Not yet anyway.

Kitzi had confronted him about it, more than once. The fight tonight had been especially fierce.

"If you think I am going to spend New Year's Eve watching you fawn over that woman, you have another thing coming."

"Kitzi, Kitzi. I always have to keep Gwyneth happy. It's always been for the good of the show." Joel smirked.

"The show, my ass. I'm telling you, Joel, I've had it. With the show, with Gwyneth, with you."

"And what, my dear, are you going to do about it?" Joel purred sarcastically, defiantly.

Kitzi knew she was cornered. What *was* she going to do about it? Was she finally ready to divorce him? No, not yet. Not until she got all her ducks in a row.

"Well, I'm sure as hell not going to her damn party!"

"Suit yourself." Joel shrugged. He had calmly walked off to take a shower and dress, leaving Kitzi to stew alone.

It was time to make an appointment with a lawyer.

Kitzi pulled the tie closer at the waist of her peach silk lounging robe, walked over to the built-in mahogany bar and poured herself another vodka on ice. Happy New Year.

She hated herself for what she was going to do next. She crossed the expansive living room, over the antique Persian carpet, past the sumptuously upholstered sofas and the Regency chairs, beneath the Baccarat chandelier, heading for the terrace. A gust of biting winter wind smacked against her as she opened the French doors, whipping her thin dressing gown around her legs. Tufts of old, crusted snow dotted the terracotta tile that floored the terrace, her silk-covered mules stepping carelessly through them. Her ringed, manicured hands gripped the nozzle of the frozen telescope.

She did not have to aim it. It was already trained on Gwyneth's apartment across the park.

29

"DID YOU SEE his expression when he spotted you? I've heard the phrase 'the color drained from his face' many times . . . this is the first time I've actually seen it happen. He was ashen."

Laura and Francheska huddled together in the powder room, ignoring the polite knocks on the door as other guests waited outside. Francheska calmly brushed lipstick within the lines of her full lips as Laura continued agitatedly.

"You knew he was going to be here, didn't you, Fran?" Laura asked, talking to her friend's reflection in the mirror.

Francheska nodded, her mane of dark hair shining in the powder room's strong light. She wore a form-fitting bronze strapless gown, the bodice trimmed with natural brown mink. She was dressed to command attention.

"Len did mention he was coming. You, if anyone, know how he is, Laura. He loves dropping names and trying to impress me with whom he knows and what he's doing."

"Why didn't you *tell* me?"

"Because, if I had, you would have freaked out and been worried that there was going to be a scene. You would have been too nervous to bring me as your guest. When you asked me to come to this party, I wrestled with the question of 'should I' or 'shouldn't I' tell you that Len and his wife were on the guest list. But I really wanted to come and I didn't want to run the risk of you taking back the invitation."

"Oh, Fran, don't do anything like this to me again. Okay? I don't like that kind of surprise."

"Relax, Laura. This is going to be fun."

Another knock on the door signaled they really had to go back to the festivities and Laura gave a last tug at her wispy bangs, making sure they covered her scar.

"What are you going to do now?" whispered Laura as the pair walked back toward the living room.

Francheska giggled. "Maybe I should go up to the Costellos and start a conversation. I've never met 'the Mrs.,' though I've heard so much about her."

Laura laughed despite herself. "You wouldn't dare."

"I'm thinking about it."

"Well, if you do that, I'll pull the good doctor aside and thank him for all the inside dope he's unknowingly provided on who was going to die next. Though he doesn't know it, he's really helped my career."

30

RICKY POTENZA DID not feel the cold as he paced up and down the Central Park West block outside Gwyneth Gilpatric's apartment building. He was not sure if he was going to be able to get past the doorman, but he had a plan.

He'd been waiting for this night for a long time—thirty years, really. Actually planning the specifics over the last year since reading in the hospital last January about Gwyneth's annual New Year's Eve party. He remembered it very clearly. Sitting with the other chain-smokers at Rockland Psychiatric Center, flipping the pages of *People* magazine. Reading about the schmaltzy party *KEY News* star Gwyneth Gilpatric threw each year for the rich and famous. Haunted by the smiling image of the woman who stared back at him from the glossy pages. Gwyneth Gilpatric, the woman who had changed his life forever.

Of course, he had been seeing her on television for years. There had been lots of time to watch television at the mental hospitals. And when he was home in between hospitalizations, television was his main pastime. He made it a point to watch *Hourglass* every week.

It galled Ricky to hear his mother rave about Gwyneth. She thought Gwyneth Gilpatric was so wonderful, a Jersey girl made good. "Gwyneth grew up in neighboring Fort Lee, you know," his mother repeatedly told him. If she only knew.

Ricky listened silently to his mother's enthusiastic admiration, listened silently and fumed. It wasn't fair. Gwyneth, a national figure, feted and awarded, while poor Tommy lay rotting in the mud.

But now they had found Tommy. He saw it on TV, though his mother had been quick to snap off the set. She didn't want him to relive all that, she said. Didn't she know that he had been reliving it all again and again, day after day, for the last three decades? Reliving it in his head, but never bringing himself to talk about it.

Everyone had tried to get him to talk. His worried parents, the suspicious police, and, over the years, the concerned doctors. They thought he was traumatized simply by the disappearance of his best friend. If they knew that Ricky had been part of his best friend Tommy's death they would not have treated him so well.

By the time the Cruzes realized that their son was missing the morning after Tommy was killed at Palisades Park, Ricky was home safe in his own bed, pretending to be asleep. He feigned ignorance when his mother broke the news to him that Tommy was missing, swore that he hadn't seen his buddy since they parted company at dinnertime the night before. But as his parents and the police continued to question him over the days that followed, Ricky began to shut down. Silence was his defense.

We all have a breaking point. That's what the doctor told Ricky's parents. Ricky has met his breaking point. You must not push him.

So they had not pushed. They'd followed the doctor's orders, gently trying to get the increasingly brooding, introverted Ricky interested in things again. They encouraged him to go out and play with the other kids, to get involved in sports or clubs at school. They tried to get him to audition for the school plays, hoping to find something that would bring him outside himself. Nothing worked.

Adolescence and the hormonal changes that went with it made things worse. Ricky grew more angry and violent. The acting out grew more angry and violent as well. One day after school, he climbed on the roof of the Potenzas' three-story brick home and hurled the family's cat to the ground below. That night he took his father's razor blades to his wrists.

There followed the first of a lifetime's worth of stays in various mental institutions.

At first the Potenzas had tried the private hospitals, thinking that money could cure their son. Ricky, heavily sedated, would seem better for a while, but the psychiatrists all agreed that medication alone would never cure him. The young man refused to open up in talk-therapy sessions. Until he did, Ricky was not going to get well.

The years passed and the hospital debts grew. The Potenzas sold their house in Cliffside Park and moved to a small bungalow over the state line in Rockland County, New York. There Mr. Potenza died. Three days after the funeral, Ricky was picked up by the police as he tried to jump into Lake Tappan.

The police brought him straightaway to the nearby Rockland Psychiatric Center, a state-run facility. With little money and exhausted, Ricky's mother had no choice but to leave him there. As time went on, she resigned herself to the fact that it made no difference where he was. Her son was not going to get well.

So it went, a pattern developing. Ricky would stay at Rockland for months at a time. Then the staff would say he was well enough to come home. Another crisis sent him back. And on and on.

Now he was on another of his home furloughs.

His mother tried to make a normal life for them, tried to make Ricky appear as if he were normal. She did not want him to look like some sort of seedy, scary-looking crazy person. She made dental appointments, took long walks with him for exercise, made sure he got frequent haircuts. For Christmas, she saved from her modest secretary's salary and bought him a camel hair overcoat, wanting her son to look the part of a handsome, well-dressed forty-two-year-old man.

Now on Central Park West, no one looked askance at Ricky Potenza. He looked like he belonged there.

Ricky watched as a half dozen men and women approached, and prayed that they would turn into the doorway of Gwyneth's building. As they did, he fell inconspicuously behind them. One of the men told the uniformed doorman his name, said they were going to the Gilpatric party, and the doorman nodded.

"Go right up, sir."

They all went up in the elevator together.

Gwyneth had gone on and thrived. It wasn't fair.

31

OVER THE PARTY din, Joel Malcolm was explaining the concept of Casper's Ghostland to his amused *Hourglass* producer Matthew Voigt.

"And this is supposed to be a secret death pool?" asked Matthew.

Joel grinned defiantly. "Yeah, it's done anonymously, on the Internet. We all get a monthly bulletin that's sent to our e-mail address, letting us know whose name we're holding for the month. And if nobody in the pool dies over the next thirty days, we all ante up and Casper assigns us a new name. I've had Bryant Gumbel over at CBS three different times during the last two years. He's still going strong, damn it!"

"And it's *how* much a month?"

"A thousand bucks. But think how much you can win! The pot is really growing."

"Too rich for my blood." Matthew laughed. "Besides, they wouldn't let me in anyway—I'm not high enough on the media totem pole."

Joel shrugged and looked over Matthew's shoulder, his keen eyes scanning the party. "There she is. The blonde in the dark blue dress." He elbowed Matthew. "That's Laura Walsh, the one I told you about."

Matthew Voigt caught sight of Laura as she stood across Gwyneth's opulent living room. "Whoa. This is going to be a pleasure."

"Hold on," warned Joel. "This is work, remember?"

"Who says work can't be fun?" answered Matthew as he took off in Laura's direction.

He followed her over to the bar and listened as she ordered a Cosmopolitan. As Laura took a sip of the pale pink cocktail, he introduced himself.

"I'm Matthew Voigt. I hear you're coming to work with us."

Laura looked up quizzically at the dark-haired man, her interest aroused. She had seen him around the Broadcast Center, noticed him in the cafeteria. He was tall, lean and reasonably good-looking. Intense brown eyes sparkled intelligently beneath his dark eyebrows. As she assessed Matthew's sharp nose and angular jaw, Laura was momentarily reminded of a hawk, the bird of prey with the curved beak that loved to hunt.

She was intrigued, but wary. Focusing now on what he was saying, her interest was piqued by the phrase "working with *us*."

"You know," he insisted, "at *Hourglass*."

"Well, you must know something that I don't know." Laura laughed.

Matthew looked surprised. "Oh, I thought it was a done deal."

"Maybe in other people's minds, but not in mine. I haven't heard anything from the boss."

"That's odd. Joel was just telling me all about you."

"Well, that certainly puts me at a disadvantage, because I know nothing about you." Laura took another drink from her stemmed glass.

Matthew looked disappointed. "I had hoped my reputation would have preceded me."

"Sorry."

He laughed and shrugged. "That's probably better. At least you haven't heard anything bad about me. I've been a producer at *Hourglass* for a few years now, since Joel brought me over from ABC. One of the many *Hourglass* producers, but we all like to think we are integral to the show's success."

"I'm sure you must be. I'm sorry I didn't know who you were."

"No problem. I'm just a legend in my own mind." He turned to the bartender. "Glenlivet, rocks," he ordered.

Laura wanted to know more. "Do you mind my asking what exactly Joel told you?"

"What's it worth to you?"

She ignored him and waited.

"Okay. I can see being obnoxious is not going to work." *God, she had pretty eyes.* They were an amazing shade of blue. Almost the color of the clear sky on a Midwest summer's day. The color of the July sky atop Lake Michigan, the sky he stared up at as a teenager while he lay on the shoreline and fantasized about what he wanted to do with his life. He was an electrician's son from Waukegan, Illinois, who dreamed of living in New York City and working at one of the television networks. Well his dream had come true, but it wasn't always what he'd thought it would be, and increasingly it wasn't enough.

Laura's words pulled him from his brief reflection.

"You're a smart man, Matthew. I'd expect nothing less from an *Hourglass* producer, seeing as I hope to be one."

Matthew's white teeth flashed as he smiled appreciatively. "Seriously, now, Joel spoke highly of you and mentioned this project you've brought to us. The Palisades Amusement Park story? It sounds like it has all the makings of a great segment."

"I think so. I grew up in Cliffside Park, the town where the old amusement park used to stand. My father ran the Cyclone the year the park closed down."

"And there's some sort of unsolved murder connected to the park?"

"It looks like it. They've just found a boy's body that has been missing for thirty years, buried a stone's throw from the park's perimeter, and they've identified it."

"Cool."

Laura briefly thought how sick they were to be enthused about such a grotesque turn of events, so excited about the details of someone else's agony. But that was the business. A nightmare made a compelling story.

"What are you doing at KEY now?" Matthew changed the subject.

"I work in the Bulletin Center."

"Doing?"

"Hard news pieces. Obits seem to be my specialty."

"Fun. No wonder you want to get out."

"It hasn't been so bad, really," Laura protested. "I've kind of enjoyed doing them."

Matthew considered her comments and nodded in agreement. "Come to think of it, you're right, Laura. I can think of a few people whose obits I'd like to see run."

32

"YOU'VE BEEN AVOIDING me all night, Doctor." Francheska stood behind Leonard Costello and whispered in his ear.

Leonard turned and smiled warmly, but hissed his answer. "What the hell do you think you are doing?" He cast a furtive glance around the party to see where his wife was.

"Don't worry, lover. Mrs. Costello is on line for the powder room. You're safe." Francheska smiled.

"Stop it, Francheska. This isn't funny."

"I think it is. I think the whole situation is very amusing. And exciting, too. Want to slip away for a quickie?"

For a split instant, Francheska recognized that Leonard was actually considering her proposition. Then his survival instincts kicked in. His wife and many of his patients were at this party.

"Cut it out, Francie. How did you get in here, anyway?"

"I have friends in high places, too, Len. Laura brought me." Francheska plucked a champagne cocktail as a waiter passed with a silver tray. "I thought it would be fun to surprise you."

"Well, you did. Now let's say good night. I'll call you tomorrow."

"I don't like being dismissed, Leonard."

"That's part of the deal, Francheska, and you know it. You get the posh Upper East Side digs and the credit cards and anything your heart desires. I can tell that dress you're wearing must have set me back plenty. And that's fine. But the price is discretion. My wife finds out and it's all over. You've known that from the beginning."

"You could at least make some pretense that you're going to leave her for me."

"I've never said that I would. Please, let's not get into all of this now." Leonard's eyes searched for his wife.

Francheska cast her eyes downward, not wanting him to see the hurt she was sure he would recognize there. She turned and walked away.

33

THOUGH GWYNETH'S NEW YEAR'S Eve party was costly to host, the main attraction of the night didn't cost her a penny.

The magical fireworks display over Central Park at midnight.

As the new year inched closer, the guests, some of them getting their coats first, trailed out to the wraparound terrace. Drinks in hand, they waited on their privileged perch for the fireworks to begin.

When she thought that all of the partygoers had made their way out to the terrace, Gwyneth went down the hall to her quiet bedroom to get her Pashmina shawl to wrap around herself. She heard the first pop of the fireworks explode outside as she pulled the soft wrap from her closet, and she jumped as she felt a tap on her shoulder.

"My God, you scared the hell out of me."

"I'm sorry. But I need to talk to you."

"What is it?"

"It's really very important, but not here. Someone might hear us. Want to go up on the roof and have a cigarette for 'auld lang syne'?"

"But my guests . . ." Gwyneth trailed off.

"They won't miss you. Their attention is on the fireworks. Come on. You'll only be gone a few minutes. It will be worth your time. I promise you."

34

"FIVE, FOUR, THREE, two, one. Happy New Year!"

Alone in his living room, Emmett watched, as he had for dozens of years, the televised New Year's Eve celebration from Times Square. The revelers cheered and danced around, horns tooted and blared and confetti fell as another year began.

Amateur night.

He did not understand those idiots who bothered to go into the city to be crowded and jostled in the freezing cold and wait for the Waterford crystal ball to fall. It was pathetic, really. Didn't they have anything better to do? He suspected this was the one night of the year that they got out. Why else would anyone go there? He took another swig of Budweiser.

He'd rather be alone. Or so he told himself.

But he was glad that Laura had been invited to that swanky uptown party. He wanted her to have a good time, a good life. He knew that it hadn't been easy for her.

Emmett knew that he should have paid more attention to Laura. He should have stopped drinking, should have straightened himself out. But he couldn't. Instead he'd gone from one lousy job to another, barely making ends meet. Each job loss led to another bender. If those checks hadn't come regularly, he didn't know what they would have done.

But Laura, in spite of everything, had succeeded. She was her mother's daughter. Smart, conscientious, determined. Laura was in the big leagues now. A producer at *KEY News*. New Year's Eve at Gwyneth Gilpatric's.

Emmett rose from his armchair and switched off the television set. He walked into the kitchen, stopping at the refrigerator to take out another beer. Then he opened the door to the basement, stumbling at the top step. He grabbed the handrail, righted himself and continued down the wooden steps.

The amusement park was lit for the holidays. He took his seat next to the Cyclone and gently pushed the tiny rollercoaster car up the tracks to the zenith. He held it there for a while before he let it go, watching it as it swooshed downward.

Such a long time ago. But that one night had changed his life forever.

It had started so innocently.

It was just an accident.

He hadn't had the courage to own up to what had happened. If he had, things would have been so different.

But would he have gone to jail? Would Sarah have married him? Would there have been a Laura? They said that God worked in mysterious ways. Maybe that had been his plan, that Emmett not tell, so that his life went on as it did. God surely wanted a world with Laura in it.

Did God forgive him?

But he knew from his old religious training that God would only forgive him if he confessed, admitted what he had done.

It was too late for that now.

He finished off the can of beer and switched off the amusement park lights. As he headed upstairs, he wondered if Gigi knew that Laura was working on a story about the park and Tommy Cruz. If Gwyneth Gilpatric did, she surely wouldn't like it. He chuckled in spite of himself.

35

ONCE BEFORE, SHE'D felt this way.

The car accident on Route 95 as she had driven up to college. Gwyneth had grasped the steering wheel tight, years ago, her body stiffening as the car hydroplaned across the rain-covered highway. She knew she'd been driving too fast. She always did.

She had waited for another car to smash into hers as she

glided across the sheet of water that coated first one lane and then another, on her way to the heavy steel guardrail. Coming from the other direction, a huge tractor-trailer approached. She knew that if the guardrail didn't do its job, if her car flipped over to the other side of the superhighway, she would certainly collide with the giant gray eighteen-wheeler. The truck driver must have known that, too. She heard his warning horn blast angrily.

The windshield wipers continued their rhythmic slapping and she'd wondered how many cars would ultimately be involved in the accident as, one by one, they'd be unable to stop, skidding on the slippery macadam into the car in front of them. How many other people were going to have their lives altered or ended?

She'd listened as an old Beatles song blared from the radio and thought of the things she wouldn't want her parents, or whoever went through her things, to find.

She'd wondered if she was going to die.

She'd thought of all those things, observed all those details in five seconds. Five seconds from beginning to end: the car skidding, hitting the guardrail and then fishtailing around the back and smashing into the rail again, leaving the automobile looking like a giant accordion. Totaled.

No other cars had hit hers. And she had walked away that time, without a scratch. Miraculous, the state trooper later described it. A charmed life.

Five seconds. Yet, after the accident, she recalled with great clarity that everything had seemed as though it had been moving in slow motion, like videotape played frame by painstaking frame.

That's what it felt like now. Slow motion.

But there would be no miracle this time. This time, she didn't wonder if she was going to die. She knew it.

The cold winter air whipped her long black velvet evening skirt. She wondered if, when they found her, the skirt would be up around her waist. Pantyhose but no underwear, a smoother line. Interesting detail. Someone would be sure to report that.

She heard the firecracker pops of gunpowder and saw the fireworks flashing, sparkling white, green and red against the charcoal night. Diamonds, emeralds and rubies. Her own jewels, a rope of Akoya pearls, blew up from her neck across her face in a strangely comforting caress.

The inevitable was coming. Closer, closer. But what they said was wrong. Your life didn't pass before your eyes. She thought now of only one thing. One regret. One person.

The moment before she hit the icy sidewalk, she thought her last thought.

This is how Tommy Cruz must have felt.

The New Year

36

New Year's Day

THEY DIDN'T WAIT for the elevator. Laura and Mike Schultz raced down the flights of stairs—her legs moving like rapid-fire, graceful pistons; his, clomping and heavy—both as fast as they could. As they flew through the elegant lobby and out toward the frosty street, Mike barked over his shoulder to the doorman.

"Call 911."

The sidewalk was eerily deserted except for the lifeless velvet form collapsed on the cold concrete. It flashed through Laura's mind that in this exclusive, protected neighborhood, one of the world's wealthiest, people were snug and protected inside, busy doing what they were doing to celebrate the New Year. As they sipped their Dom Perignon or Veuve Clicquot, they were completely unaware that one of their own, illustrious and renowned, lay bloodied and broken below them.

"Jesus," whispered Mike as they crouched down beside Gwyneth. She was lying face up, her eyes wide open, staring unseeingly into the clear night sky. A halo of dark blood pooled about her shattered head. A trickle of red oozed from the corner of her carefully painted mouth. Mike reached to feel the side of her neck, already certain that he would not find a pulse.

Laura tugged at the hem of Gwyneth's velvet skirt, trying to pull it down to give the woman some semblance of dignity as she lay exposed. She noticed that pearls lay scattered like luminescent drops of hail around Gwyneth's body as she heard a wailing police siren grow increasingly stronger.

Mike pulled his cell phone from his rear pocket.

"Who are you calling now?"

"The office."

"Oh, God, Mike. No. You're not calling for a crew."

He did not answer her, but listening to the one-sided conversation told her everything she needed to know. The cameras were coming.

She actually hesitated for only a moment and then she told him.

"Gwyneth's obit is ready to air, Mike. It's in my desk drawer."

37

ROWS OF WATERFORD champagne flutes and platters of uneaten petits fours were spread across the marble countertops in Gwyneth's gleaming kitchen. Delia stood in the corner, eyes downcast, her arms wrapped around herself to steady her shaking.

Blue-uniformed police officers and overcoated detectives were systematically making their way through the apartment, questioning both partygoers and staff alike. Delia knew that her turn was coming.

She ached for a cigarette, but she didn't dare.

Delia looked up to see a middle-aged man in a dark gray coat coming in her direction.

"Detective Alberto Ortiz, Twentieth Precinct," he identified himself routinely. "And you are?"

"Delia. Delia Beehan."

"And you were just working here for the evening?" he asked expressionlessly, as he eyed her starched white apron.

"No, sir. I am Ms. Gilpatric's personal maid. I work for Madam full-time."

The passive look on Ortiz's face changed to intense interest and he stared at Delia keenly. The maid's lower lip was quivering.

"Any ideas on what happened here tonight?"

"No, sir."

"Had Miss Gilpatric been upset about anything?"

"I don't know, sir."

"Was she depressed?" the detective tried to draw her out.

"Not that I knew of, sir."

"Can you think of any reason why she might want to kill herself?"

At that, Delia began to cry uncontrollably.

38

A SHAKEN NANCY Schultz drove home alone.

Carefully, she followed the string of red taillights up the West Side Highway. It was almost two A.M., but the highway traffic was steady. The New Year's Eve revelers were on their way back to suburbia.

Thank God, the night was clear. No snow or icy rain. She'd been on her third martini when the party ended so abruptly. Nancy had wanted to numb herself. She hadn't realized she'd be doing the driving home.

She should have. KEY News and Gwyneth Gilpatric always had a way of invading their lives.

Nancy steered her six-year-old Taurus station wagon across the upper span of the George Washington Bridge and glanced out the driver's window, down the Hudson River to the illuminated Manhattan skyline. The Empire State Building glowed prominently.

The angry blare of another driver's horn forced her to swerve back into her lane and concentrate on her driving. The last thing they needed was a car accident. They couldn't afford it. As it was, she dreaded coughing up the fifty dollars she'd have to pay Julie for babysitting tonight.

She switched on the car radio and scanned the stations, stopping when she found what she was listening for.

"The forty-seven-year-old *KEY News* anchorwoman was pronounced dead on the scene. Police are investigating. Again, *KEY News* correspondent Gwyneth Gilpatric died tonight after falling from the roof of her Central Park West apartment."

Nancy opened up the glove box and rifled around until her fingers felt the cigarette pack Mike kept there. She waited for the lighter to pop out from the dashboard, lit up and inhaled deeply.

What goes around, comes around.

39

AMERICA LEARNED OF the life and death of Gwyneth Gilpatric as the obit that Laura Walsh had produced ran on the KEY Television Network. The video package opened with tape from the very first *Hourglass* broadcast.

"Good Evening. I'm Gwyneth Gilpatric. And this is *Hourglass.*"

Then Eliza Blake's narration began, while viewers watched scenes of Gwyneth as she reported from around the world over the past fifteen years for *Key News*, ten of those years on *Hourglass.*

"Gwyneth Gilpatric has been a regular visitor in American homes each Tuesday evening as the host of the *KEY News* magazine broadcast *Hourglass.* Through her eyes, we've watched the stories of our times."

Video played of Gwyneth interviewing kings and presidents, walking with movie stars, standing atop the Berlin Wall as Germans swung at the concrete beneath her feet to tear down the ultimate symbol of Communism.

"Not only did she cover the obvious stories. If anything, Gwyneth Gilpatric's passion was finding and reporting the stories that no one else did. The stories that hadn't been told. She was the winner of scores of awards for her investigative reporting."

Gwyneth appeared on the screen in a white cotton coat, walking among cow carcasses hanging in a contaminated meatpacking plant. She crouched beside a little girl in a wheelchair, a child who would never walk or talk because of medical malpractice at the hospital where she was born. Gwyneth patted the hand of an elderly woman who had been swindled out of her life savings by a wily con artist.

"America trusted Gwyneth Gilpatric and turned to her in times of national mourning."

A clip of Gwyneth at one of the memorial services for the massacred Columbine High School students followed. Gwyneth spoke into her microphone.

"When I was a senior in high school, my biggest concern was getting into college and having a date for the senior prom. For today's students, the worries are far more basic. Will they survive the school day?"

Up came a black-and-white picture of Gwyneth from her own high school yearbook. She looked like so many other girls of her time. Long dark shoulder-length hair, parted in the middle. The traditional black drape pulled out toward her shoulders. A cross on a chain hanging from her young neck.

"She grew up in Fort Lee, New Jersey, the only child in a middle-class family. While attending Boston College, she decided what she wanted: a career in broadcast journalism. And to the benefit of us all, Gwyneth Gilpatric never looked back.

"Eliza Blake, *KEY News,* New York."

40

IT WAS DAYLIGHT when Joel came home from *KEY News*. After they had taken Gwyneth's body away, there had been police questions to answer. Then he went to the Broadcast Center to make some decisions about how he and *KEY News* were going handle the next *Hourglass* broadcast. The network went right on—with Gwyneth or without her. But Joel didn't know what he was going to do.

He was surprised to see Kitzi up and sitting on the sofa in the living room. She still wore the peach robe he had left her in the night before.

Just last night.

"Happy New Year, darling," Kitzi whispered.

She was drunk.

"I guess you heard," he said, ignoring her inebriation, though normally he would be disgusted by it. He didn't care about her anymore. Didn't care about anything at this moment. "You must be very happy."

"And you, dear Joel, must be very sad. Your poor Gwyneth gone. Whatever will you do without her?"

"Cut the crap, Kitzi."

But Kitzi was enjoying her moment. Enjoying seeing him hurt. Hadn't he hurt her again and again and again?

"What will you do now, Joel? No Gwyneth to star in *Hour glass* and bring it to those rating heights. No Gwyneth to work so hard with late at night. No Gwyneth to spy on so pathetically with your trusty telescope.

"You disgust me." Joel turned to walk away.

"Hey, Joel, don't you want to know how I found out the sad news?" Kitzi called after him tauntingly.

"I know you're going to tell me. On television, on the radio?" he asked dully.

Kitzi shook her mane of auburn hair and laughed defiantly.

"Better than that, dear Joel. Much, much better than that. You'll appreciate this. I saw it *live*!

Joel stopped and turned toward her. "What do you mean?" he snapped.

Kitzi stalled. "You know I've always hated that damn telescope of yours. Hated what you did with it. Hated that you gave one to Gwyneth so the two of you could play your coy little games across the park. Hated that you'd rather study Gwyneth than me. You always found her so damned fascinating. What about me, Joel, what about me?"

Joel ignored her question but pressed for an answer to his own. "What do you mean? What did you see?"

Kitzi tried to read Joel's eyes but was uncertain what she saw there. Was it fear? Panic?

"I watched your darling Gwyneth fall to her death, Joel. Watched it on your own precious telescope."

41

"I STILL DON'T understand why in the world you had Gwyneth's obit ready. I know you had a relationship with her, Laura. Had she told you she was sick?"

Mike Schultz and Laura, still dressed in their party clothes, stood in the Bulletin Center. The piece Laura had produced had been fed out three times now on the network line to the KEY affiliates. Viewers around the United States had gotten their instant thumbnail video sketch of the anchorwoman's life.

"No. Gwyneth hadn't told me she was sick. I actually did the piece a long time ago. It was kind of a practice thing."

Mike looked at her skeptically.

"Really, Mike," Laura insisted. "I worked on it a few years ago, when I was just starting to do the obits, and I've updated the video a few times since. Gwyneth was always jetting all over the place, doing stories on wars and insurrections and natural disasters. I remember thinking she could be risking her life. I knew we had lots of great material on Gwyneth in the archives and I thought it would be interesting to do a profile on her. I even thought I might show it to her and see what she thought. I never actually did, though. I thought better of it. I didn't want her to take any sort of offense."

Mike nodded. "Yeah, I don't think many of us like to think

that our obituaries are already done." Mike thought for a moment. "But Eliza Blake narrated it. Didn't she ask any questions? Didn't she think it was weird?"

Laura tried to recall. "Eliza was anchoring *KEY to America* at the time. I slipped it into a pile of narrations she recorded after the broadcast one morning. I don't remember her asking anything about it. Maybe she thought it was something we were doing for the RTNDA."

The Radio and Television News Directors Association met yearly in different cities. The network news divisions lavishly wined and dined the affiliate news directors, spending lots of money and effort to keep them satisfied and loyal. Splashy video presentations touting the networks' news accomplishments and stars were produced to be shown at the convention. With *Hourglass* a major component of *KEY News'* success, it could make sense that a piece would be done on Gwyneth.

Mike seemed convinced. "Well, lucky for us, once again, you saved our collective ass, Laura. Thanks a lot."

42

THE BUSES RAN a reduced holiday schedule on New Year's morning and it took forever to get back to Pearl River. Ricky was relieved that his mother was not there when he arrived home. She was probably at church. She was always running off to Mass.

When his mother did get home, she would ask him where he had been all night. He would answer her as he always did, with silence.

Ricky hung his new camel hair overcoat in the jammed front closet and snapped on the television. He clicked the button on the remote control until he found what he was looking for. Gwyneth Gilpatric's face.

The news announcer was telling the story of the sensational death. The fall to death as the fireworks exploded over Central Park. There was speculation as to suicide, but the police were questioning everyone on the guest list.

Ricky smiled as he went to his tiny bedroom. He peeled off his clothes and changed into blue jeans and an Islanders sweatshirt. Everything was going to be all right now. It didn't really matter how it had happened. Gwyneth was dead. Fair was fair.

Ricky had stood at the back of the car, behind the other partygoers, when the elevator doors had opened. As Gwyneth greeted her guests, Ricky had been able to slip to the side, avoiding her view. He followed the maid, with her arms full of coats, and handed over his own. Then he hid in one of the bedrooms.

The police would not be looking for Ricky to ask him any questions. He had sneaked out of the party before the police came and his name did not appear on Gwyneth's fancy guest list.

The new year was starting off right.

43

IT WAS ALMOST noon when Laura returned to her apartment. Gratefully, she kicked off the new expensive shoes that were pinching her toes. She had been up for the last thirty hours, but she knew she was not going to be able to sleep. Her mind was racing.

The red button on her answering machine blinked insistently. Automatically, she played back the messages.

"Laura, it's me, Francheska. Are you okay? That was some party. Call me."

"Laura, it's Pop. I heard what happened. Are you all right, honey? Please call me."

"Laura, this is Maxine. Mrs. Bronner. I remember your saying you were going to Gwyneth Gilpatric's New Year's Eve

Party. I'm so sorry. Please call me when you can. I'm worried about you."

"Laura, this is Joel Malcolm. I'm sorry to bother you at home, but with everything that's happening I want to get all my ducks in a row. The job is yours. I just spoke with Mike Schultz and explained that I want you to start with us right away, and grudgingly he agreed to let you go next week. I want to get this Palisades Park story together in time for February sweeps. Everyone is going to be watching to see how *Hourglass* does without Gwyneth. I'm determined to show them that *Hourglass* is bigger than any one personality."

It was the news she had been waiting for.

44

Sunday, January 2

FINALLY, THE PAYOFF. All the plotting, all the patience, all the waiting had been worth it. It hadn't been easy. The nights spent tossing and turning, twisted with anxiety. Worrying that someone else would die before Gwyneth did. Praying that the ninety-nine other media elite who populated Casper's Ghost-land would stay healthy.

Casper, the friendly ghost. But not a friend to Gwyneth Gilpatric.

Now winning the overflowing pot meant complete financial independence.

A new year, a new leaf.

45

WITH NO OFFICE hours on New Year's weekend, Leonard Costello stood in his enormous Scarsdale kitchen, carefully measured out a quarter teaspoon of creme of tartar and stirred it into the pot of sugar and water on top of the stove. A half hour had passed since he had taken his medication and his hands were steady.

He threw in a dash of salt and cooked and stirred until the sugar dissolved and the mixture bubbled. He separated some egg whites into a mixing bowl and added a little vanilla. Bit by bit, he poured the warm sugar mixture from the pot into the bowl, whipping it with an electric mixer. In seven minutes, the stiff peaks would form, and he could begin.

He knew many of the best plastic surgeons had hobbies that they took quite seriously. Some painted, using oils or watercolors to express themselves. A few sculpted with clay or carved their fantasies from stone. Leonard loved to decorate cakes.

Staring intently into the bowl as the fluffy white frosting gradually appeared, Leonard felt the tension slowly leaving his body. He had been so worried about Gwyneth. She could have ruined everything.

Having worked so hard over the years to keep Gwyneth Gilpatric beautiful, how ironic that it was he who pronounced the woman dead as she lay on the unforgiving concrete sidewalk.

Leonard clicked off the electric mixer, picked up a shiny spatula and began to rhythmically smooth the fresh icing over a yellow tube cake.

Another prosperous year lay before him. He was grateful.

46

Monday, January 3

JOEL MALCOLM WAS not in when Laura reported to the *Hourglass* offices the next morning, but his pretty secretary, Claire Dowd, was expecting her.

"Joel is at Lincoln Center," Claire told Laura. "He wanted to attend to some of the details of Gwyneth's memorial service himself."

"That's quick," Laura said with some surprise.

"That's Joel," the secretary said matter-of-factly. "If something is important to him, he takes care of it right away."

Laura nodded. "So should I come back later?"

"No. Joel said you should see Matthew Voigt. Down the hall, the last office on the left. And there's a staff meeting at three o'clock in the conference room."

Laura walked slowly down the *Hourglass* hallway, a hallway so much quieter than the others in the Broadcast Center. This was an insulated world, the world created by Joel Malcolm, a world protected by the tremendous amount of money it made for *KEY News*.

Laura took a deep breath as she reached Matthew Voigt's office.

Matthew was on the telephone and scribbling notes on a yellow pad. His dark head looked up as he sensed Laura standing in the doorway. He smiled, motioned for her to come in and pointed to a gray couch that hugged the wall across from his desk. Laura took a seat on its edge.

As she waited for Matthew to finish his conversation, Laura scanned his small work space. An autographed Bruce Springsteen concert poster hung on the wall behind his cluttered desk. Two Emmy statuettes rested on a crowded bookcase. A gym bag and a pair of worn Nikes were tossed in the corner.

"It's not much, but it's home." Matthew grinned as he hung up the phone. "Welcome to *Hourglass*."

Laura laughed. "Listen, having an office of my own has been a big dream of mine. I've only worked in a communal newsroom where you're lucky to get your own drawer. I think your office is great."

"Well, that's a good thing, Laura, because then you won't

be too disappointed in the closet you've been assigned to work in. Space is at such a goddamned premium around this place. Come on, I'll show you. It's around the corner."

Laura followed Matthew to her new office. He opened the door for her and switched on the light. The room did not seem that much smaller than his office, though only a desk and chair furnished it now. She could not wait to add the touches that would make it her own.

"It's fine. Absolutely fine," Laura declared with pleasure.

"You're easily pleased. I like that. We have a lot of prima donnas around here. They drive me nuts," he said, shaking his head. "Now let's go back to my office so we can talk. Or better yet, want to take a walk with me to the cafeteria? I'm dying for another cup of coffee—I need the strong stuff, and Claire's coffee up here is more like weak tea."

Once they were settled in a booth at Station Break with two cups of high-test steaming before them, Matthew broke the news. He would be working with Laura on the Palisades Park story.

Laura's first reaction was one of disappointment and it showed in her facial expression.

"But it's *my* story," she protested.

"Of course it is. You came up with the idea. But you're in the big leagues here, Laura. I'd think you'd be glad to get all the help you can. Not to mention that usually *Hourglass* segments are worked on for months and months. This one has to be put together in only six weeks. Didn't Joel tell you that he wants to run this during the February sweeps?"

She nodded, staring into her Styrofoam coffee cup.

"Come on," he prodded. "I'm not going to bigfoot you.

You'll get your credit. Just think of me as your mentor. God, that sounds old. I'm too young to be anybody's mentor." He laughed and took another sip of his coffee.

What choice did she have? If Joel wanted Matthew to oversee the Palisades story, that was the way it was going to be. Maybe it wouldn't be such a bad thing. It would take some of the pressure off. It could be worse. Joel could have assigned another producer to the story with her, a producer she wouldn't like as much as she was beginning to like Matthew.

"Okay," she answered determinedly. "Where do you want to start?"

"You tell me, Laura. It's your piece."

So she recounted for him the story as she knew it so far. He listened intently. When she was finished, he asked her questions.

"I'm thinking about who we want to interview for this. Of course, we'll want to talk to the investigators who worked on the case then, if any of them are still around. And we'll try to track down the friend of the boy who disappeared that night. And the dead boy's parents, if they'll talk." Matthew drank the last of the coffee from his cup. "I've been thinking, you mentioned at the party that your father ran the roller coaster at Palisades. He might be a good one to start with. I bet he could give us a lot of colorful stuff on the amusement park, as well as what he remembers from the time of Tommy Cruz's disappearance that last summer."

Laura hesitated. The thought of Matthew Voigt meeting her father wasn't an appealing one.

"Problem?" he asked.

"No. Of course not."

47

THE *HOURGLASS* STAFF gathered in the large conference room, awaiting the arrival of their executive producer. Laura took a seat against the back wall. She wondered if she looked as nervous as she felt.

As she tried to keep the foot at the end of her crossed leg from shaking up and down, she realized that she recognized about half of the people in the room as those who had been there when she had done her internship. But there were many people she did not know. Most were busy talking to their neighbors and Laura listened to snippets of different conversations.

"Joel must be beside himself. What is he going to do without her?"

"I saw him at lunch. He looked just fine to me."

"If I know Joel, he has a plan."

"Watch out. This isn't going to be pretty."

As the executive producer entered the conference room, the conversations ceased. All eyes were on Malcolm, dressed in a gray cashmere sports jacket, black turtleneck and black trousers, and carrying a can of soda as he strode to the front of the room.

"We all know why we are here," he began. "We've lost Gwyneth. I'm sure every one of us is struggling with our own personal feelings about her death. She was a legend in our industry, an extremely talented professional with whom each of us was privileged to work. She was also a true friend, a commodity that is pretty damned scarce these days." He stopped to take a swallow of his Diet Coke.

"But, my friends," he continued, "this, of course, does not mean the end of *Hourglass*. To the contrary. Some may find me crass to say this, but Gwyneth's death will mean higher ratings for *Hourglass*. At least initially. Just out of curiosity, more viewers will tune in than ever before. And we are going to capitalize on this opportunity."

Someone coughed and broke the thick silence that engulfed the room. Laura wondered if the other people sitting there were as creeped out by what Joel was saying as she was. She shot a look in Matthew Voigt's direction. He was staring intently at Joel, but didn't look like any of this was bothering him.

"Every single person in this room is expected to do his or her part toward holding on to this new audience. I want us to move toward February sweeps forcefully. When the ratings are tallied next month, it is my goal not just to beat *60 Minutes*, but to have *Hourglass* command the highest advertising rates on TV.

"To this end and, of course, in Gwyneth's memory, *Hourglass* will be conducting its own investigation of Gwyneth Gilpatric's death. We should be ahead of the police. We *will* be ahead of the police. Viewers will look to us for the latest breaks in the case. And we *will not* disappoint them. Every week, we are going to have something new. Something nobody knows. Something the audience can't get from any other source."

Joel nodded at his secretary. "Claire?" he prompted.

The secretary passed out sheets to those assembled. Laura scanned the written outline of the month's *Hourglass* shows. Joel expounded on what the staff was reading.

"First, our next show is just two days away. The audience is going to watch just because it is the first show without Gwyneth. Eliza Blake, who, of course, will continue anchoring *KEY Evening Headlines,* will, for the foreseeable future, be taking Gwyneth's place as *Hourglass* anchor. At the end of this week's broadcast, we will promise to have exclusive new information on the case in next week's show."

"Shouldn't we be absolutely sure we can deliver on our promise before we make it?" someone asked bravely.

Joel shot the questioner a withering look. "We already have our exclusive, but I'm not going to divulge what it is at this time. In the weeks that follow, however, I'm expecting this staff to come up with new material for our continuing investigation."

Laura's stomach was in knots. What had she gotten herself into by coming here? She wished she could make herself invisible as she felt Joel's eyes bearing down on her.

"Before we break up here, everybody, I'd like to introduce, to those of you who don't know her already, Laura Walsh."

Everyone turned to stare at Laura and she felt her face flush.

"Laura comes to us from the Bulletin Center, where, I might add, she—amazingly—had Gwyneth's obit ready to go. I expect Laura's prescience and industry to be of great benefit to *Hourglass.* Welcome aboard, Laura."

Welcome, indeed.

48

DESPITE THE BITING January wind, Homicide Detective Alberto Ortiz, his hands on his hips, stood with his overcoat wide open outside Gwyneth Gilpatric's apartment building on Central Park West. It was a bright, sunny winter afternoon and he stared up toward the top of the massive building, shuddering as he tried to imagine what the final moments of the famous anchorwoman's life must have been like as she sailed through the dark night to her violent death.

Ortiz was more and more certain that Gwyneth Gilpatric had not taken her own life. While the autopsy showed that she had been drinking, the study of her body showed signs of a struggle. There were marks on her upper arms and there was skin under her fingernails. DNA results were not back yet, but the detective felt sure that it would turn out that the skin was not Gilpatric's. Decades of experience told him that this was a homicide.

Ortiz had volunteered for New Year's Eve duty, covering for a younger detective who usually worked the overnight shift, but desperately wanted the holiday night off. The senior detective had been glad to do it. Divorced and with no one special in his life, he had no plans for that evening. He remembered what it had been like when he was a young cop, what a drag it was when Michael was young, to always work the holidays. It had taken a toll on their family life. Now Ortiz was just past his fiftieth birthday and his son was grown and out on his own, but he had seniority, the best shift, and he could get time off pretty much whenever he needed it. *Screwy system.*

Ortiz's voluntary good deed had led to the biggest case of his career. When the call came in to the squad, Ortiz briefly felt sorry for the young guy who was out somewhere partying, but would find out in the morning that he had missed the opportunity of a lifetime. A case like this one made a career.

Ortiz was just a few years from retirement and he hoped this murder might be his defining legacy. He had a solid reputation, but he'd never had such a high-visibility case. He was determined to find out what had happened to Gwyneth Gilpatric, not only to feed his hungry midlife ego, but because he hoped Michael would be proud of him. Things between the two of them had not been good since the divorce. Ortiz knew that Michael blamed his father and the police work for the dissolution of his parents' marriage.

Patting back the wind-blown wisp of graying hair that remained on the top of his balding head, Detective Ortiz walked the last steps down the sidewalk to the entrance of the apartment building. He entered the lobby, identifying himself to the doorman, who called upstairs to announce his arrival.

"Go right up, sir."

How some people live! Ortiz marveled as the elevator doors opened onto the expansive foyer. *This hallway is bigger than my first apartment.*

The large Christmas tree still stood eerily in the entrance hall. Gilpatric's maid, Delia Beehan, was halfway through taking down the luminescent ornaments. Packing boxes and tissue paper lay on the floor beneath the tree.

Wiping her hands on her apron, Delia greeted him. "Detective."

"Miss Beehan. Thank you for making yourself available." As he shook her cold hand, he thought he felt it trembling.

"We can talk in the living room if you'd like, sir."

The detective followed her and took a seat at the edge of the large white down-stuffed sofa and briefly fantasized about lying down on it with a beer on a Sunday afternoon to watch the Giants game. *Heaven.*

"I know you were very upset when we talked the night of the party, but I have a couple of things I hope you can help me with now, Miss Beehan."

The maid nodded solemnly. "I'll try, sir."

"Did Miss Gilpatric have any enemies that you know of?"

"No, sir. I don't know of any."

"Had she been upset about anything?"

"She really didn't tell me much, sir. I was her maid, not her friend."

"I understand." Ortiz nodded. "But maybe you overheard her talking to someone. A telephone conversation, perhaps," the detective fished.

Delia stared down at the hands clasped in her lap.

"Please, Miss Beehan. Anything you can tell me might be a big help."

"Well," the maid began reluctantly, looking into Ortiz's surprisingly gentle brown eyes, "I know she had words with Mr. Malcolm."

"That would be Joel Malcolm, the executive producer of *Hourglass*?" Ortiz prompted.

"Um-hmm."

"When was this?"

"The day before the party. Well, the night, actually."

Ortiz scribbled in his notebook. "So Mr. Malcolm was here that evening?"

"No. Madam talked to him on the phone in her bedroom."

"What did you hear?"

Delia was clearly uncomfortable as she tried to explain. "I've never heard her use the language she used that night. I'm ashamed to admit it, but I listened outside in the hallway."

Ortiz's face betrayed no judgment. He waited for her to continue.

"I heard her tell Mr. Malcolm that she was leaving *Hourglass*." Delia watched the detective's face for a reaction. She got none.

"And."

"Well, of course, I didn't hear what Mr. Malcolm said, but Madam was very angry. She said that she didn't owe him anything. That he owed *her*. That she was the reason for his success. Then he must have said something that really made her mad because she started calling him all sorts of names and yelling terrible things he should do to himself."

"Okay," said Ortiz approvingly. "That's a big help. Now I want to ask you about just a few other things. As you know, we took some of Miss Gilpatric's things with us the night of the party. One was her appointment book. I see she had some surgery scheduled this week?"

"Yes, sir."

"Do you know what it was for?"

"She didn't tell me, sir."

Again Ortiz sensed her hesitation. "She may not have told you, but do you know anyway?"

The maid reddened slightly. "I think it was plastic surgery."

"Face-lift?"

"Yes."

"Has the doctor's office called about confirming her appointment?"

"No, sir, but why would they? I think everyone knows about Madam's accident. In fact, Dr. Costello was here at the party."

"Dr. Costello was her plastic surgeon?"

The maid nodded.

"But the Day-Timer entry says 'Dr. Koizim.' "

Delia looked puzzled and shrugged.

"Okay, Miss Beehan. One last thing. Miss Gilpatric's checkbook. There are very few entries in it."

"That's because her accountant takes care of most of her business. She has the other checkbook just for spur-of-the-moment things that come up."

Or checks she doesn't want anyone to know about, thought Ortiz.

"That makes sense," he agreed. "But there is a recurrent name here. It seems Miss Gilpatric wrote a check every month to someone named Emmett Walsh. Do you know who that is?"

Delia paused to consider the detective's question. "No, I never met or heard Madam speak of any Emmett Walsh. But she was very fond of a young woman at *KEY News* named *Laura* Walsh. Ms. Walsh was here just before Christmas."

Ortiz flipped back the pages of his notebook until he found the list of people he was looking for.

"Oh, yes. Miss Walsh was at the party, too, wasn't she?"

"Yes, sir, she was."

Detective Ortiz closed his notebook.

49

SHE HAD WAITED what seemed like forever for his decision, but once Joel Malcolm's call had come, Laura had had to move quickly to *Hourglass*. She hadn't even had time to clear out her old desk in the Bulletin Center.

At the end of her first day in her new position, Laura ached to get home, heat up a bowl of soup and soak in a hot, sudsy bathtub. Instead, she had to make a stop at her old office and clean out her drawers for whoever would be taking her place. Then she had promised to have dinner with Francheska, who wanted to take her out to celebrate the new job.

Her makeup having worn off hours before, Laura knew she looked as tired as she felt when she bumped into Mike Schultz as he was leaving the Bulletin Center for the day.

"Whoa. You look beat. What are they doing to you over there?" Mike asked jokingly. "I knew that you'd really appreciate working for me once you had a taste of Joel Malcolm."

Laura shook her head and pulled Mike aside to a spot in

the hallway where fewer people might overhear their conversation.

"Mike, that guy's a ratings-driven madman!"

Mike laughed out loud. "Well put. But he's also a television genius. You are going to learn a lot from him. Tell me what happened today."

Laura briefed him on the high points of the staff meeting and Joel's plan for ratings glory.

"What you're telling me doesn't surprise me, Laura. Malcolm is a fanatic about his baby. It has always galled the hell out of him that *Hourglass* doesn't beat *60 Minutes*. He smells blood now. As he sees it, this is the opportunity of a lifetime for the broadcast and he is not about to blow it."

Laura grimaced. "The whole meeting left a rotten taste in my mouth. Mike, what have I gotten myself into?" she wondered aloud.

Mike put his big paw on her shoulder. "Hang in there, kid. You'll get used to him. This was your dream, wasn't it?"

"Yeah," Laura agreed wryly. "Be careful what you wish for."

50

WITH NEWSPAPER SPREAD over the kitchen table, Emmett was peeling potatoes when the telephone rang. He quickly washed his hands at the sink and got to the wall phone on the fourth ring.

"Mr. Walsh?"

"Yes?"

"Hello, sir. My name is Matthew Voigt. I work with your daughter at KEY News."

"Is Laura all right?" Emmett asked anxiously.

"Oh, yes, sir. She's just fine. In fact, we are working on a story together. Laura may have told you about it, a piece on Palisades Amusement Park?"

Emmett clenched his fist around the telephone receiver.

"Yes. She mentioned something about it."

"Well, Mr. Walsh, Laura tells me you operated the Cyclone for the last few seasons at Palisades. I bet you have some wonderful stories to tell."

"What kind of stories?" Emmett asked suspiciously. He'd be damned if he was going to get into the Tommy Cruz thing, not even for Laura.

"Memories, Mr. Walsh. What the park was like. The people

who came. Any celebrities you buckled into the roller coaster. That sort of thing."

"I'm not much for storytellin'."

Matthew was not to be dissuaded. "You know, Mr. Walsh, this is Laura's first story for *Hourglass*. It's important that it turn out well."

"Why isn't Laura calling me herself?"

"It's better if I do, sir. Of course this is Laura's story, but since you are her father, it would make more sense for me to interview you. We want to avoid any conflict of interest."

Emmett wasn't sure what exactly "conflict of interest" was, but he understood that his daughter needed to do a good job on her story. He guessed he could be careful about what he told this Matthew fellow.

"All right," Emmett agreed reluctantly.

"Wonderful! I'll call you in a few days to set up a time when we can come out there to interview you. Maybe we could do it on the site of where the old roller coaster used to stand."

"I doubt that, mister. There's a big fat condominium complex sitting right on top of it."

"At your home, then?"

Emmett glanced around the kitchen, seeing it through a stranger's eyes. He didn't want this tired old place on national television.

"I have an idea, Mr. Voigt. Did Laura tell you about the miniature Palisades Park I built in the basement? Maybe you'd like to see that and we could do the interview down there."

"Sounds perfect."

Returning to the cut potatoes, Emmett threw them into hot Mazola corn oil and watched them fry. When they were a crispy, golden brown, he scooped the potatoes from the oil and drained them on paper towels. A liberal sprinkling of salt and Heinz malt vinegar followed. He tasted one of them, relishing the flavor.

Just like they used to make them at Palisades Park.

51

LAURA DEPOSITED THE large cardboard box packed with the last of her things from the Bulletin Center in her new office, switched off the lights, locked the door and headed toward the ladies' room to freshen up before meeting Francheska. She looked into Matthew's office as she passed. He was still at his desk.

"You are making me feel guilty." She stopped at his doorway, smiling. "Should I be staying late, too?"

Matthew grinned. "Not tonight, my pretty. But you are going to have plenty of late nights here. Get out now, while you can. Hey, I could knock off now, too. Want to stop and have a drink?"

"Can I have a rain check? I'm meeting a friend for dinner tonight." Laura glanced at her watch. "And I'm going to be late."

"Sure, we'll do it another time. Where are you going for dinner?"

"Picholine."

"Mmmm. May I ask, male friend or female friend?"

"My best friend, Francheska. She's treating me in honor of my new job."

"Generous friend."

"Yup. And she's going to be livid if I don't make our reservation. I'll see you tomorrow." Laura turned to leave.

"Hey, Laura," Matthew called after her, "I just talked to your father."

Laura froze in her tracks and turned back to the doorway.

"You did? How come?"

"I thought I'd get his interview set up."

"What did he say?" Laura asked, trying not to show she was bothered. *Matthew should have asked me if he could call, talked to me about it in advance. This is my story. My father.*

"He seemed a bit reluctant at first, but finally he agreed to talk. That little amusement park of his sounds cool. I think it should make a great visual for the piece."

Laura thought of the dark basement with the steep, chipped wooden stairs that led down to it. She pictured Matthew and the camera crew carrying their gear over the worn carpeting in the living room, through the tight kitchen and down the old stairs to the musty-smelling cellar. What would they think, knowing that this was where she came from? It shouldn't matter what they thought. Though she was disappointed in herself for feeling this way, she did care.

Even more worrisome was what her father might do and say. *If he drinks that day, I'll die,* she thought. If Emmett drank, he would slur his words and rant on and on. Even worse was the possibility of his getting angry and mean.

Please, God, let him have one of his good days.

This story idea of hers, her ticket to *Hourglass*, had seemed like such a good one.

She knew the town, knew the history of the amusement park, and had always been intrigued by the stories she had heard about the little boy who had disappeared that last summer. Why hadn't she foreseen how complicated it could become for her personally? Nothing that involved Emmett was ever easy. *Why don't I ever learn?*

Laura said good night to Matthew, freshened her makeup and left the Broadcast Center, hailing a cab on the cold dark street outside. She got into the yellow car, told the driver her destination and, settling back onto the black plastic seat, heaved a deep sigh.

Definitely not a good first day.

52

THE RAVEN-HAIRED BEAUTY sat at the bar at Picholine on West 64th Street, waiting for her friend and savoring her vodka martini. She was well aware that she was getting the long once-over from almost every man who walked into the restaurant. She didn't bother trying to pull down the hem of her dress, which had risen just a bit too high on her crossed, shear-black-stocking-clad thigh.

You never knew when you were going to meet someone

interesting and it paid to go to good places. That was how she had met Leonard. She knew the guy was a sleazeball when he tried to pick her up at the bar at the Carlyle, while his wife sat unsuspectingly at the hotel restaurant nearby. But she had given him her phone number anyway, swayed by his rugged good looks, his beautiful suit, an intoxicating aftershave and the Rolex watch gleaming from beneath his starched white cuff. What a stupid fool she had been!

She had spent two years of her life on Leonard. Two years too much.

Francheska drained the last of her drink from its stemmed glass and ordered another. She rolled the olive around in her mouth a few times before she bit down, chewed and swallowed it. *Where was Laura?*

Her momentary exasperation changed to admiration tinged with envy when she thought of her best friend. Laura had spent the last years paying her dues and now she was reaping the rewards of her labors. *KEY News Hourglass* producer!

Francheska had watched her friend work long hours, in the beginning, for little money. After she got involved with Leonard, Francheska had all the time in the world to do as she pleased, but Laura had been devoting herself to her broadcast journalism career. Francheska had partied and shopped and vacationed. Laura had spent her hours at *KEY News*.

Not that Laura didn't like to go out and have a good time. On the contrary, Laura could party with the best of them. Yet Laura never let a good time interfere with her first priority, her career. Francheska wished now that she had been more like her former roommate. But it had been easier to let Leonard pay the freight and sit back and enjoy the good life.

Unfortunately, she had fallen in love with Leonard Costello. Fatal mistake.

Francheska took another sip of martini and wished that she had brought along a pack of cigarettes. She was trying, once again, to quit. But she knew that her abstinence wouldn't last. Giving up smoking was biting off too much right now, if she was going to go through with her plan to finally break it off with Leonard.

The New Year's Eve encounter had been the last straw. She never wanted to feel that humiliation and hurt again. Besides, weren't there plenty of other fish in Manhattan's very wealthy sea?

"Oh, Francheska, I'm so, so sorry I'm late." Laura stood beside her, cheeks flushed either from hurrying or from the cold outside.

"No problema, honey." Francheska kissed her friend on the cheek. "I'm used to it. Check your coat and let's get to our table. I haven't eaten all day and I'm starving."

The maître d' escorted them beneath the glistening chandeliers to their linen-covered table in the main dining room. The waiter took their wine order and the women perused the menu.

Laura chose the tournedos of salmon, Francheska the roasted rack of lamb.

"Well, how was the first day?" asked Francheska, as she appraised the wonderful breads in the basket the waiter had placed on the table.

Laura groaned.

"That good, huh?"

"Oh, Francie. I hope I haven't made a big mistake," and Laura proceeded to explain Joel Malcolm's plans for *Hourglass*.

"He sounds like one cold fish to me," said Francheska, finishing the martini she had started at the bar. "I know they say it's a cutthroat business, but didn't I hear somewhere that Malcolm and Gwyneth Gilpatric were having an affair? You'd think the guy would be a little more delicate and a lot more upset about her death than what you've just described to me."

The waiter arrived with their appetizers. Laura cut into the silver-dollar-sized truffles drizzled with wild mushroom puree. Ecstasy.

"I'm probably the one who told you they'd had an affair. It was common knowledge at KEY. I don't know if it was still going on or not. But Joel certainly didn't look heartbroken this afternoon. I had heard stories about Joel's fanaticism about the show, but I swear, Francie, he was almost salivating as he described how he wanted to capitalize on Gwyneth's death."

"Speaking of salivating . . ." Laura's voice trailed off as the entrées were set before them.

Laura's salmon was prepared with a horseradish crust and garnished with cucumbers and salmon caviar. Francheska's succulent lamb was served with potato goat cheese gratin and artichokes Barigoule.

As the women savored their fabulously delicious meals, Laura also told Francheska about Matthew Voigt and her uneasiness with the planned interview of Emmett. After the waiter presented the famed Picholine cheese tray for their selections, Laura apologized to her friend for monopolizing the conversation.

"That's okay, sweetheart," said Francheska. "But I do have one piece of news that I know you'll be thrilled about. I'm breaking it off with the 'Facemaker.' "

"That's great, Francie. I'm absolutely thrilled. I won't add that it's about time."

"Good, don't."

"Why now, though?"

Francheska shrugged. "Well, I figure that now that you aren't doing obits anymore, you don't need Leonard's inside skinny about who's in the hospital ready to kick, which I'd so generously whisper in your ear every now and again."

Laura laughed. "Yeah, I have to admit, Dr. Costello was a terrific, if unwitting, source. I got quite a few obituaries done well ahead of time because of him. He was a big help to my career. Hey, Francie, speaking of careers, what are you going to do without your funding?"

Francheska finished the last of her expresso and sat back in her chair.

"Come on, Laura. Don't nag me tonight about getting a job."

53

Tuesday, January 4

IT WAS ALMOST ten o'clock before the supper was finished, the kitchen cleaned up, the homework completed, the fight to turn off the television won, the baths done, the teeth brushed and the kids safely tucked in bed for the night. Nancy Schultz knew she should get on the treadmill and walk two miles, but she couldn't make herself. Her thighs had gone to hell, but she was too tired to care.

Her life had become a treadmill of its own. When Mike lost his job, she had to let the cleaning woman go and the house had not looked the same since. If the home was a reflection of the self, Nancy had only to look around to know she was in bad shape.

Not that Mike, sweet guy that he was, ever complained. He hadn't married her for her housekeeping abilities, he told her. Nancy asked herself sometimes if Mike wondered now why he had married her. She knew that she was less fun than she used to be and she hated herself for it. Every time she vowed to herself to be more upbeat and positive, her resolution was short-lived. She found herself worrying constantly and always feeling stressed. Mike had suggested she get some therapy, but she could not bring herself to pick up the phone and make an appointment.

She consoled herself that she was just like many women in America today. Oprah wouldn't be doing so many shows on overwhelmed females if there weren't a big audience for the subject.

Mike was in the dining room, piles of bills and paperwork spread out on the table before him.

"How are we doing?" she asked her husband, taking a seat on a chair beside him.

Mike leaned back in his chair and ran his fingers through his hair. "Holding our own, honey. But the Christmas bills haven't come in yet."

"Mike, what are we going to do? You make a good salary,

but we're always living from paycheck to paycheck. We never seem to get ahead. I wish I contributed more. The sub jobs are so infrequent and the piddling amount I make at Macy's is nothing."

Mike leaned over and kissed his wife on the cheek. "Listen, it's enough that you work part-time. You can't be worrying about this all the time. We are going to be fine. We decided when we had the kids that it would be best for you to be home to raise them."

"That was before everything happened."

Mike went back to his checkbook, signaling that he didn't want to talk about that subject. They had gone over it again and again until Mike finally declared that he wasn't going to talk about his *Hourglass* job loss anymore. They had to move on, he said. Bitterness over how he had been treated at *KEY News* was poisoning their lives.

"You're right," said Nancy, putting her arm around her husband. *Besides,* she thought, *Gwyneth Gilpatric is dead now. There is no one left to hate.*

54

THE THEME MUSIC played and the hot-pink sand began to pour from the waist of the large hourglass that dominated the television screen as the first broadcast since Gwyneth Gilpatric's death started to air on the KEY Television Network. The hourglass faded from view and Eliza Blake appeared on the screen.

"Good evening, I'm Eliza Blake, and this is *Hourglass*."

Joel Malcolm watched from the executive producer's seat on the platform behind director J. P. Crawford in the control room. Crawford and his crew of assistant directors and technicians sat at their multi-instrumented control panels, dozens of television screens positioned on the wall in front of them.

This is going to work out just fine, thought Joel. *Eliza looks wonderful. She has beauty, brains and presence. And something, at least for now, that Gwyneth hadn't. Youth.*

"Tonight's broadcast will be a tribute to Gwyneth Gilpatric, the host of *Hourglass* since its inception ten years ago. Gwyneth, a legend in this business, fell to her death from the top of her New York City apartment building on New Year's Eve. Police are investigating. And we here at *KEY News* have resolved that we will use all the resources at our disposal to try to find out what happened to Gwyneth Gilpatric. Each week we will keep you informed on the progress of the investigation, beginning next week with an eyewitness to what happened."

Joel couldn't wait to see the ratings.

55

ANGRILY, ALBERTO ORTIZ snapped off his television.

KEY News was promising an eyewitness to Gwyneth Gilpatric's death. *Damn them!*

Did those pompous bastards think they were above the law? They were withholding information regarding a crime!

56

Wednesday, January 5

THE *HOURGLASS* OFFICE was abuzz about the overnight ratings, the highest ever gotten. Joel was strutting around the halls, shaking hands and backslapping like a proud papa.

Uncomfortable, Laura stayed in her office, making calls on her story. Her first was to Maxine Bronner. She explained that she was trying to find Ricky Potenza.

"I remember you saying that you still exchanged Christmas cards with his mother. Would you mind giving me her address?"

Laura could hear Maxine's hesitation in the momentary silence on the telephone line.

"Maxine?"

"I don't know, Laura. That poor woman has been through so much."

"How about this?" Laura suggested. "Would you like to call her yourself and explain what I'm working on? See if she would be amenable to my contacting her?"

"I guess that would be all right," Maxine answered uncertainly. "I'll call information and see if her number is listed."

57

SHE WAS PAID until the end of the month and Delia was faithfully coming to work each morning at Gwyneth's apartment, though why she did not know. The copy of Gwyneth's will that the big-shot lawyer had sent her made it very clear how little Gwyneth valued her.

The Christopher Radko ornament collection. Big deal. Delia hated those damn things. They were so delicate and so easily breakable. Just something else to dust and take care of. How stupid she had been to ooh and aah over them in front of Madam. Now they were her big inheritance.

The ornaments and nothing more. Delia seethed as she thought about it. In the domestic community, you were always hearing about wealthy people who provided generously in their wills for their faithful servants. But not Gwyneth Gilpatric. Seven years of dependable service meant little to her.

But, by God, Laura Walsh had meant something to her. The apartment and everything in it was now Laura's, along with more money than Delia could get her mind around.

Had Laura put up with Gwyneth's demands and bossiness? Delia doubted it. Not from what she had observed the few times she had seen them together. No, Gwyneth was all sweetness and light as far as Laura Walsh was concerned.

But, as Delia reflected on it, had she really expected Gwyneth to come through for her? There had never been a warm relationship between them. Gwyneth had always made it very clear that she was the mistress of the house and was not looking for a friendship with her maid. Delia had never been comfortable around her boss.

And Gwyneth was sharp. Had she sensed that Delia was envious?

Well, who wouldn't be jealous? Delia asked herself as she walked across the expansive living room and looked out the huge windows down at Central Park. Gwyneth lived like royalty. Who wouldn't want to live like Gwyneth did? It had been fun to pretend, when she was alone in the apartment, that it was her own. Fun to be around all the luxurious things. Fun to try on Gwyneth's clothes. Fun to dream.

Now reality had come crashing in. She had to go looking for another job, unless Laura Walsh wanted her to stay on.

It wasn't fair.

Delia made up her mind. She had been holding back what she knew, not telling that Detective Ortiz all she had seen.

She went to the telephone and dialed information, praying for and yet dreading to get the telephone number.

58

ROSE POTENZA PULLED her gray sweater closer around herself as she watched her son concentrating on the jumbo jigsaw puzzle spread over the living room coffee table. Ricky seemed to be doing better lately. Rose didn't want to rock the boat.

Her first reaction to Maxine Bronner's telephone call was fear. Bringing up the old nightmare could not be good for Rose. But Maxine had encouraged her to at least speak with producer Laura Walsh, assuring Rose that Laura could be trusted and would respect her wishes and right to privacy if she should decide that it was best that Ricky not be contacted.

Over the telephone, Rose liked Laura. She had expected the newswoman to be pushy, aggressive and intrusive. Instead, she found her to be sensitive and concerned about Ricky's well-being.

"Mrs. Potenza, I must tell you that *Hourglass* is going to do this story, whether or not we interview Ricky. So I don't want you to feel any pressure on this. On the other hand, couldn't this possibly be a positive thing for Ricky? A chance to speak out about his friend, about what he remembers of him and that time? A catharsis of sorts?"

"Ricky has never opened up about Tommy's disappearance.

Not even now, now that they found . . . what was left of Tommy."

"So Ricky knows Tommy's remains were found?" Laura asked.

"Yes, he saw it on the news. He watches television all the time. I couldn't keep it from him. Actually, it's ironic that you are working on this story and calling us. Ricky is a big *Hourglass* fan. He's watched almost every episode for years. He won't miss it."

"Maybe he would like to be part of one of our stories?" Laura asked hopefully. "Would it hurt to ask Ricky? You have my word, Mrs. Potenza. I won't push him."

Rose had hung up, promising to think about it. She called Ricky's doctor at Rockland Psychiatric Center. He had no clear-cut answer for her, but suggested that possibly Ricky, so fascinated by television, might open up for the camera. It could be beneficial for him. But then again, it might be traumatic. As usual, the decision on what to do with her forty-two-year-old son was up to her.

"Ricky?"

"Yeah, Mom?" her son answered, not looking up from his puzzle.

"I want to talk to you about something, honey."

Maybe it would help. She prayed it wouldn't hurt.

59

DETECTIVE ORTIZ WAS ushered into the executive producer's office and offered coffee by Claire Dowd. He politely refused.

The light that streamed in from the large plate-glass window forced Ortiz to squint to see the three *KEY News* lawyers lined up on the leather sofa. Joel Malcolm was sitting behind his desk, but rose to shake the detective's hand. He gestured to Ortiz to take the seat across from his desk.

"What can I do for you, Detective?"

"First and foremost, Mr. Malcolm, I am here regarding the claim on your show last night that you have an eyewitness to what happened to Gwyneth Gilpatric."

"That's correct."

"Who would that be?"

One of the suits on the couch piped up. "It is *KEY News* policy not to reveal the identities of sources to whom we have pledged confidentiality. Strict adherence to this policy is essential to maintain the trust of potential news sources."

"We can get a subpoena," Ortiz snapped.

"We'll resist it in court," replied Malcolm smoothly. "Our broadcast will air before all the legal wrangling is through. I suggest you be patient, Detective. Tune in next week and your questions will be answered."

Ortiz knew the cocky producer had him there. The attorneys could easily stall things until next week.

"Withholding the eyewitness for a full week takes away valuable time from the investigation of the case. Would it do any good to appeal to your sense of honor about what is the right thing to do?"

Silence was Malcolm's response.

Son-of-a-bitch.

Ortiz tried not to show his anger. "All right, Mr. Malcolm. I have some other questions to ask you, questions of a personal nature."

"Shoot."

Ortiz glanced over at the lawyers.

"They can stay," said Malcolm.

The detective flipped back a couple of pages of his notebook. "Is it true that Gwyneth Gilpatric was planning to leave *Hourglass*?"

"Yes. Her contract with *KEY News* was up. She wasn't going to renew."

"Do you know why?"

"She told me that she wanted a change. CBS had offered her the moon."

"How did you feel about that, sir?"

Malcolm shrugged. "Of course I was sorry to be losing Gwyneth. We started *Hourglass* together and it has developed into a helluva show. But, as you must know, Detective Ortiz, television is a visual medium. Not to be unkind, but Gwyneth was aging. Her best 'face' years were behind her. I thought it might actually be better for *Hourglass* to get some new blood."

"So when Miss Gilpatric told you she was leaving *Hourglass*, you weren't upset?"

"No. In fact, I was relieved. I was very fond of Gwyneth." Malcolm looked over at the lawyers before continuing. "I'm sure you'll hear in your poking around that Gwyneth and I had been romantically involved. But that was over some time ago. I had agonized over the fact that one day soon I would have to let her go from the broadcast. Her decision saved me from that. When Gwyneth told me she was planning to go to CBS, I wished her well."

Ortiz knew the executive producer was lying and thus he would not be able to trust anything else Malcolm might say. But he went on with the questioning anyway.

"Can you think of anyone who might want to see Miss Gilpatric dead, Mr. Malcolm?"

Joel frowned as he considered his response. "Reporters make enemies, Detective. It goes with the territory."

"Any *specific* enemies come to mind?"

"Go to the *KEY News* archives, Detective Ortiz. And get the transcripts of just about any investigative piece Gwyneth reported. I'm sure you'll find scores of people who would be very happy if Gwyneth Gilpatric never existed," Malcolm suggested, a little too nonchalantly for Ortiz's taste.

"And what about here at *KEY News*?" pushed the detective. "Any enemies in the workplace?"

Malcolm shifted uncomfortably in his high-backed armchair. Ortiz stared piercingly at the producer as he waited for his answer.

"Well, there is one situation that I can think of," Malcolm began, seemingly hesitant to offer the information.

The lawyers leaned forward on the couch. Malcolm was ad-libbing, and they didn't like his improvising on the script that they had worked out.

"Please, go on, Mr. Malcolm"

"We did a story for February sweeps a few years ago, about the mean streets up in East Harlem. We had a confidential source, a young guy who was trying to do some good up there." Malcolm closed his eyes and rubbed his forehead. "I can't remember the kid's name right now, but it will come to me."

"What does this have to do with Gwyneth Gilpatric?" Ortiz pressed.

Malcolm took out a pack of Chesterfields from his pocket, offered one to Ortiz, who shook his head no, and lit up.

"Well," Malcolm continued, exhaling the white smoke through his nostrils, "the kid gave us lots of great stuff on the El Barrio drug pushers and he was willing to go on camera to tell it. We shot him in disguise, of course. You know, shadowing his face and distorting his voice."

Ortiz nodded.

"The trouble was, when the edited package aired, one of the shots we used ID'd the kid. Gwyneth's 'standup' showed her walking through an abandoned lot full of discarded drug paraphernalia. When editing the story, the producer didn't notice that Cordero—now I remember, the kid's name was Cordero— was standing at the corner of the shot." Malcolm inhaled deeply.

"And?"

"The week after the story aired, Cordero was found dead. The body had a couple dozen syringes sticking out of it."

Malcolm stamped out his cigarette.

"So where does the Gilpatric–*KEY News* enemy come in?" asked Ortiz.

"As you can imagine, we took a lot of heat for that screwup. It was in all the papers. Management was so worried about a lawsuit that I had a camera crew and half my staff attend the funeral in hopes of mollifying the family," remembered Malcolm.

Ortiz studied the executive producer's face.

"But Cordero's family didn't sue," Malcolm continued. "They said that they were proud of their son for doing what he did, and they didn't want to profit from his death. Refreshing, huh?

"Still, we had to look like we were doing something. We felt that someone had to take the fall. Gwyneth was adamant about it. She felt her reputation was on the line."

"Who took it?"

"The producer, Mike Schultz. He was fired."

60

DAMN! THE MAID had seen them walking out of Gwyneth's apartment on their way to the roof. And she wanted money to keep her mouth shut.

Even if the payment was made, she would still be out there, knowing what she knew. Blackmail never ended.

Since Delia Beehan's phone call, the mind had been racing, the heart pounding.

This is no time to panic. Breathe deeply. Get a hold of your-

self. Think. You can figure this out. You've come too far to blow it now.

You had the presence of mind to agree to a meeting right away. That was smart. Take care of this immediately, before Delia has second thoughts and goes to the police. The maid was ashamed enough to agree to meet after dark. What a dope.

Those shiny scissors would be as good a way as any to do it.

61

SINCE KITZI WATCHED *Hourglass* alone the night before, she had been dreading her next meeting with Joel. They were going to have a major fight over this. She was sure of it.

Eliza Blake's announcement had caught Kitzi unaware. It had actually taken her a few minutes, through her alcoholic haze, to realize that it was she that *Hourglass* was promising would "tell all" next week.

Kitzi had been stunned as she sat on the sofa, transfixed by what she saw on the television screen. She had long since known that Joel put *Hourglass* above everything, including his wife. But with this, he had gone too far.

Kitzi made sure that she was already in bed in the guest room, feigning sleep, when Joel got home from the Broadcast

Center last night. She would confront her husband when she had her wits about her, not when she was tired and had been drinking.

Now the clock in the hallway chimed seven. Joel would be home soon, since it was early in the *Hourglass* production week. The late nights came a night or two before the actual broadcast.

She ached to pour herself a drink, but she mustered up considerable willpower to refrain. Kitzi checked her hair and makeup in the bathroom mirror and dabbed perfume behind her ears and on her wrist pulse points. She needed to go into this battle armed.

The door in the entry hall clicked shut. *Show time.*

Kitzi walked slowly to the living room. Joel had made a beeline to the bar.

"Want one?" he offered, dropping ice cubes into a double-old-fashioned glass.

"No, thanks."

Joel looked up quizzically. "What's wrong? Aren't you feeling well?" he asked sarcastically.

Kitzi cocked her head to the side, considering his question. "Actually, I'm feeling quite well for a woman whose husband wants to hang her out to dry for the sake of his horrific ego and all-consuming ambition."

"Oh, Kitzi. Don't start with me." He poured the Glenfiddich generously over the crystal cubes. "I'm not in the mood."

"Not in the mood? That's rich. What about *my* mood? You want me to go on national television and tell the world—not to mention some sick killer out there—that I saw Gwyneth

Gilpatric pushed off her roof! Believe me, Joel, that doesn't leave me in a good mood." She could hear her own voice approaching a scream. *Calm down,* she told herself. *You've got to stay in control.*

"Sit down, Kitzi," Joel commanded. "Let's talk about this."

"There's nothing to talk about. I'm not going to do it."

"Oh, *yes,* you are, and I'll tell you why. If you *do,* I will give you your divorce and make sure that you are set for life in the style to which you have so expensively become accustomed. If you *don't,* I will make sure that our divorce proceedings are a living hell. I'll make sure you waste years of your life with lawyers and depositions and courtrooms. You're not getting any younger, Kitzi. Don't waste the good years you've got left with such a financial and emotional drain. Better you spend the time finding some other rich schnook."

"It would be a waste for you, too, Joel."

Joel savored his argument along with his single-malt. "You forget something, my dear. I relish that kind of a fight. *You* don't have the stomach for it."

Why had she thought she could ever win with him? If she wanted to salvage what was left of her dignity, she had to get out of this marriage. But she was not about to start worrying over money at this stage of the game. Joel was a bastard, and he had an appetite for conflict. Kitzi knew she was no match for his viciousness.

"Even if I agreed to do the interview, Joel, I can't imagine what you think I'll be able to say. I've already told you what I saw. Only shadows. I couldn't see faces. I couldn't even tell if it was a man or a woman up there with Gwyneth."

Joel knew he had won.

62

ON THE WAY home from work, Laura stopped at D'Agostino's to pick up a few groceries. She was in the mood for some linguine and white clam sauce. The canned version would do just fine.

As usual, once she was in the market, she realized that she needed other things, so when she reached her apartment lobby, her arms were laden with grocery bags. She would come down and check her mailbox later.

The answering machine was blinking in the darkened apartment as she entered, but she hung up her coat, put away her purchases and started a pot of water to heat on the stove before she pushed the button to see who was trying to reach her.

The voice was a pleasant one, with a slight Hispanic accent. Laura recognized it immediately.

"Miss Walsh. This is Detective Alberto Ortiz. We met the night of Gwyneth Gilpatric's death. I would like to speak with you, Miss Walsh. Would you please call me tomorrow?"

Laura scribbled down the number he left, her chest tightening. *What did he want?*

As she stirred the boiling pasta, she tried to recall what she had said as the police questioned everyone left at the party after Gwyneth's fall. No, she hadn't noticed that Gwyneth wasn't out on the balcony with everyone else. No, she couldn't remember specifically who was or wasn't outside. She had just been enjoying the fireworks.

Laura ate her dinner sitting on the couch, the television on before her, though she paid little attention to it. Tomorrow was going to be a busy day. She would have to call Detective Ortiz first thing in the morning because she and Matthew were going out to New Jersey to shoot for the Palisades story all day. She was nervous about that, too. The interview with Emmett was first on their agenda.

She waited to see if she could get the *Final Jeopardy!* question and then rose and took her plate to the kitchen, rinsing it in the sink. She was about to get undressed for the night when she remembered she had not picked up the mail.

Inside the lobby mailbox, a heavy, legal-sized manila envelope waited. The return address read ALBERT, HAYDEN AND NEWSOME, COUNSELORS AT LAW.

As she rode back up the elevator, Laura began to read the letter.

Dear Ms. Walsh:

This is your notice that you have been named the primary beneficiary under the last will and testament of Gwyneth Gilpatric. A copy of the will is enclosed herewith for your review.

63

THE COLORFUL PALISADES Amusement Park website entertained Matthew Voigt for most of the evening before his interview of Emmett Walsh. The site was a fairly elaborate one with a photo gallery, a jukebox, a history of the park, a place where people could share their memories of the park—and even a souvenir shop. He ordered a pair of black Palisades Park baseball caps for himself and Laura.

A transplanted midwesterner, Matthew had never been to the amusement park. Even if he had grown up in the New York metropolitan area, he was too young to have gone there. But he had heard it referred to often.

He clicked on PARK HISTORY. He scrolled down each page, reading about the park's inception through to its closing.

The Palisades Park era stretched back to 1898 when the densely wooded acreage overlooking the Hudson River had been fitted with picnic groves and playgrounds to lure riders to the end of the trolley line.

As the century turned, the park was used as a location by the infant motion picture industry, which was then centered in Fort Lee. The famous *Perils of Pauline* was thought to have been shot at the park and Mary

Pickford and Buster Keaton made their early two-reelers there.

As the years went by, a bandstand was built, refreshment stands were added and a carousel appeared. In those days the big attraction was balloon ascensions, and flights from Palisades to Times Square earned front-page headlines.

Eventually, the world's largest saltwater pool, 400 feet wide, 600 feet long was built and filled daily with over two million gallons of water pumped up the high bluff from the Hudson River.

In the 1930s, a pair of enterprising show-business brothers named Irving and Jack Rosenthal bought the park and added more rides and replaced the park's green and white color scheme with a wild assortment of colors. The park's publicists claimed that every season three thousand cans of paint in as many as two hundred different hues were used to make the park a riot of color.

Over the years, thousands of people, most of whom lived in the immediate area, were employed at the park during its four-month seasons. For many youngsters, Palisades Park offered their first job. A position was almost guaranteed if you lived in the area and wanted to work. Senior citizens were hired as ticket takers, gate-keepers and concessionaires, giving the park the "Mom and Pop" atmosphere for which it became known. All the old people who collected tickets for the sixteen-week season could collect unemployment when the winter months came.

There was always something going on. Babies were

born in the park and people got married on the sky ride or merry-go-round. Once, a jungle ride was built and the monkeys climbed the light cables to escape. The monkeys were found all over town. Press agents used every possible opportunity to thrust the park's name before the public. Two or three special events were held each week, including contests to pick Miss American Teen-Ager, Little Miss America, Miss Polish, Latin, German and Italian America, Miss American Starlet, World's Best-Looking Grandmother and even Miss Fat America and Miss Hot Pants. The pageants became so popular that at one point a sign that framed an entrance to the park read: THROUGH THESE PORTALS PASS THE MOST BEAUTIFUL GIRLS IN THE WORLD!

Music was always a part of the park's drawing power, but when the rock-and-roll era began, large crowds of teenagers from the very influential New York City media market flocked to Palisades. Near the end of the "Fabulous Fifties," "Cousin" Bruce Morrow, a high-profile New York disc jockey, began to do shows at Palisades. His programs broadcast from the park attracted many of the hottest names in show business. Frankie Avalon, Bobby Rydell, Fabian, Little Anthony, Petula Clark, the Jackson Five, Diana Ross and the Supremes, the Fifth Dimension, the Rascals, the Lovin' Spoonful, the Shangri-Las and the Comets all sang their hearts out at Palisades to the delight of their screaming fans.

Advertising for the park floated over the airwaves. Television commercials ran between the hours of three and six o'clock when the kids had arrived home from school. Children would watch their twenty-seven minutes of Huckleberry Hound or the Three Stooges interrupted by five Palisades Park ads. Throughout the metropolitan area, billboards and posters beckoned patrons to "come on over." Matchbooks featured ads, guaranteeing free admission if presented at the gate. Those who were lucky enough to find the face of Pál, the park's mascot, under the flap would also receive tickets for free rides. Comic books had discount coupons and free admission passes on the back pages.

Irving Rosenthal encouraged the park's association with comic book characters. In a deal he made with Harvey Comics, he changed the old Tunnel of Love into Casper's Ghostland. The popularity of the automobile had lessened the tunnel's attraction to young lovers who wanted to kiss and caress in the darkness. Casper, Wendy the Witch and Spooky the Tough Little Ghost roamed the redesigned attraction. Casper's Ghostland became one of the park's most successful attractions.

Of course, there were less than favorable things that happened at the park, but the publicist learned how to tone down the stories of accidents or violence. He had good relationships with the media, so most negative news was kept out of the newspapers. Palisades Park was fun, fun, fun for generations of families who came from miles around. But as time went on and the crowds grew, local residents began to view the park less favorably. They complained about the bright lights, the noise and the traffic that jammed the streets and blocked their driveways. The high-rise apartments that were beginning to dot the cliffs facing Manhattan offered an opportunity to boost property-tax revenues. When the Palisades Park property was rezoned for high-rise use, the days remaining for the granddaddy of amusement parks were numbered. At the time the park closed, Cliffside Park was collecting $50,000 a year in property taxes from the site. When the first two Winston Tower high-rises were built and occupied on the Palisades Amusement Park acreage, approximately $3 million went into the town coffers.

Feeling melancholy, Matthew left the computer running and went to the refrigerator for a beer. *Why did it always come down to money?* He remembered that, when he was a child, his parents worried about money, as his father's business always seemed to be struggling. His parents fought often about money, very often ending with his mother in tears and his father storming angrily from their small Waukegan house. Young Matthew worried that his parents would divorce, but they never did. To this day, they lived in the house of his childhood, but Matthew didn't like to go back there very much.

He supposed that the situation of his childhood had something to do with why, at thirty-five, he was still single. He had wanted to establish himself, professionally and financially, before he even thought about marriage. That and the fact that no one had ever really lived up to his dream about whom he would want to spend the rest of his life with.

Now there was Laura.

He was extremely attracted to her physically, admired her

brightness, and saw a vulnerability in her that touched him deeply. He wanted to get closer to her and get to know her better, but he sensed a reticence on her part. She seemed to be holding herself back. And he wasn't sure what to do to bring her around.

He went back to his desk and played around at the computer screen some more, downloading the Chuck Barris song about Palisades Park from the JUKE BOX. Matthew found himself humming the tune and thinking of Laura as he clicked onto FOND MEMORIES. Listed there were reminiscences of people who had loved the park.

- "I remember each summer, it was a big treat to go to Palisades Park. My sister and I would look forward to it all winter long."
- "The ride operators would play matchmaker, pairing together single men and women. I met my first wife on the Himalaya."
- "My brothers and I would gorge ourselves on those mouthwatering roast beef sandwiches. The Palisades Park french fries were the best."
- "I've spent my life in a wheelchair. One of my happiest childhood memories is being bused to the park by off-duty police officers and being given free tickets for rides and food."
- "It was such a big thrill when I won by throwing that Ping-Pong ball into the narrow opening of that fishbowl filled with colored water and a single goldfish. But my parents made me dump the fish into the water at Jungleland. I still I have the fishbowl."

Matthew made special note of the next entry.

- "I lived next door to the park, in Fort Lee, so I got to spend a lot of time there. The last summer that it was open, I used to think it was so cool that the guy who operated the Cyclone would give me free rides after the park closed for the night, if I'd just run and get him Cokes or cigarettes during the day when he couldn't leave his post. Of course that was when little kids had no problem buying cigarettes. Anyway, I used to feel so special. Then I found out that the Cyclone guy had lots of kids working for him."

Something to ask Laura's father about tomorrow.

64

Thursday, January 6

LAURA STOPPED AT Dunkin' Donuts, picked up a cup of coffee and a low-fat blueberry muffin, and walked the last few blocks to the Broadcast Center, dreading the call she would make when she got to her office. Did Detective Ortiz know about Gwyneth's will? Was that why he wanted to talk to her?

She was still in absolute shock over the lawyer's letter. What had she done to deserve Gwyneth's bequest? Laura hardly knew Gwyneth Gilpatric, really, and although she had been flattered by the anchorwoman's attention, she had never quite understood why Gwyneth had singled her out. Laura liked to think that she held few illusions about herself. She knew she was bright and hardworking and had some talent, but she didn't consider herself all that outstanding, considering the highly gifted people she worked with every day. Most of them had keen minds and some of them were driven to work even harder than she did, totally sacrificing their personal lives for the sake of their professional careers.

Why had Gwyneth focused on her? Why had she left her a fortune? It was unbelievable, really, like winning the lottery!

Of course, it will be great to have all that money, she thought, as her gloved hand reached beneath her wispy bangs and rubbed the scar on her forehead. The first thing she would do was schedule the expensive elective plastic surgery to wipe away the painful reminder of Emmett's anger.

Worrying about the rent and bills would be, incredibly, a thing of the past. She wouldn't have to budget, wouldn't have to carefully calculate how much of her credit card bills to pay off each month. She could afford to live anywhere she wanted, even if she chose not to live in Gwyneth's opulent penthouse. She could sell it and find a place of her own choosing, a smaller apartment that fit her better. Or maybe she would move into Gwyneth's for a while, and see what it was like to live as only a very small number of people were privileged to live.

Laura could do anything she wanted and the realization of the infinite possibilities of that fact was only slowly seeping into her mind.

The biting January wind whipped off the Hudson River, blowing across Laura's exposed face and temporarily distracting her from the thoughts of what Gwyneth's bequest would mean for her. She was chilled to the bone and cursed herself for not bothering to wear a hat.

Gratefully, she reached the heavy revolving door to the warm Broadcast Center lobby. She greeted the receptionist and the uniformed guards, slipped her identification card across the security scanner and hurried to the elevator. Matthew Voigt, his own Styrofoam cup of coffee in hand, greeted her as the elevator doors slid open.

"I just saw the crew downstairs in the cafeteria. We can leave in about twenty minutes."

"Fine," Laura answered. "I have a phone call I have to make and then I'll be ready to go."

She didn't take off her coat when she got to her office. Slipping off the lid of the steaming cup of coffee, Laura took several sips to fortify herself. Then she dialed the number.

"Twentieth Precinct."

"Detective Ortiz, please."

Laura waited.

"Ortiz here."

"Detective Ortiz? This is Laura Walsh returning your call."

"Oh, yes, Miss Walsh. Thank you for getting back to me so promptly. I hope you can help me with something."

"Surely, if I can."

"In going through some of Miss Gilpatric's papers, I've come across the name Emmett Walsh. Before I ran a national computer search, I thought I'd try you and see if that name means anything to you."

Laura's heart pounded and she forgot completely about being cold.

"Miss Walsh?"

"My father's name is Emmett Walsh."

"Then he knew Gwyneth Gilpatric also?"

"Not as far as I know," Laura answered, puzzled. "Of course, he knew *of* her from *Hourglass* and I spoke of her sometimes to him, but they didn't have any personal contact."

"He never met her?"

"No. Not that I know of."

Ortiz tried another tack. "Prior to the party, when did you last see Miss Gilpatric?"

"A few days before Christmas. We exchanged gifts at her apartment."

"How would you describe her when you saw her? Her demeanor, I mean."

"She was fine."

"Could you tell if anything was bothering her?"

"No. She seemed to be in a good mood when I got there. She was very cheerful." Then Laura remembered the phone call. "But, as a matter of fact, she did get a phone call while I was there that she didn't seem too happy about taking."

"Do you know who it was from?"

"A doctor. Dr. Leonard Costello."

"You have a good memory, Miss Walsh."

Laura didn't share the reason why the name of the caller was familiar enough for her to remember. Wait until she told Francheska about this conversation! A conversation Laura wished would end, but Detective Ortiz pushed on.

"Could you tell me more about your relationship with Miss Gilpatric? I know on the night of the party you told me that she was a mentor to you?"

"Yes. Gwyneth was very good to me. I first met her when I did my college internship here at *KEY News*. She took an interest in me then and she encouraged me to come back and work at KEY after graduation."

"So you've been working at *Hourglass* for several years now?"

"No. Actually, less than a week. I found out I had gotten the new job on New Year's Day."

"That is strange, is it not? Finding out about a new job on a holiday?" Ortiz's voice trailed off.

"In other businesses, maybe. But not in this one. Joel Malcolm called me at home and left a message on my machine."

"You weren't home, then, on New Year's Day?"

"I was in the office in the morning. I guess you can imagine, work was very busy."

"You mean with the reporting of Miss Gilpatric's murder?"

"Yes. Everyone was stunned, but we had to get the news on the air."

"I'm interested in television news, Miss Walsh. What part did you play in the reporting of Miss Gilpatric's death?"

"I did her obit."

"Her obituary?"

"Ah-huh."

"That must have been hard for you, under the circumstances," the detective suggested. His accent was hardly noticeable.

"Actually, I had done the obit already." Why not tell him? He could find out if he asked around.

"Really? Why would you have done that?"

"We do it all the time, Detective. When someone is important enough to warrant a full television obituary, we often prepare them in advance."

"So KEY News has obits done on everyone big? All the celebrities and heads of state and people famous in their fields?"

"No. Not everyone. But when we hear a rumor that someone noteworthy might die, we get working on the obit right away."

"Then you thought Miss Gilpatric was going to die, Miss Walsh?"

Laura stuttered as she tried to explain to the detective why she had Gwyneth's obit ready. Whether or not Alberto Ortiz believed her explanation, she could not tell. But she realized that the detective might be looking at her as a suspect in Gwyneth's death.

You have nothing to worry about, she told herself. *Stay calm. Don't protest.*

Matthew appeared at her office doorway, pointing to his watch and mouthing, *Let's go!*

"Detective Ortiz, I'm afraid I have to go now. I have a camera crew waiting for me to go out on a shoot. Can we continue this conversation some other time?"

"Of course, Miss Walsh. I'll be in touch."

Before she said goodbye, she blurted out, "Detective, you should probably know, I received a letter from Gwyneth's lawyers yesterday. She had named me as a beneficiary in her will. I am inheriting a large portion of her estate."

He would find out anyhow, she thought. *Better to volunteer the information.*

65

EMMETT WENT THROUGH three different plaid flannel shirts as he waited for his daughter and the *KEY News* crew to arrive. The first he changed because he spilled coffee over himself. The second because he was perspiring so heavily.

He had done what Laura had asked him to do. Vacuuming and dusting upstairs, sweeping out the basement below. He had sprayed the cellar with so much air freshener that now it smelled like a flower shop, or rather a funeral parlor, he thought grimly. Most importantly, he kept his promise to his daughter and had not had a drink yet today.

Of course, it was only eleven A.M.

He had two six-packs chilling in the fridge, waiting for him to break open the minute Laura and company left. It couldn't come fast enough.

The doorbell rang and Emmett coughed and swallowed hard as he went to answer it. Laura hugged her father, introduced her colleagues and pointed them to the stairs.

"Matthew, why don't you go take the crew downstairs so they can set up? I'll stay up here with my dad and make some coffee."

"There's a pot on the stove," Emmett volunteered.

"I'll make us a fresh pot, okay, Pop?" She wanted to speak with Emmett alone before the interview. She had debated the whole ride out to New Jersey about whether to talk to Emmett about her phone conversation with Detective Ortiz. She did not want to upset her father, but she had to know what, if anything, went on between him and Gwyneth. The sooner the better.

She heard the camera gear bumping against the wall as the crew made its way down the narrow steps. When conversation started to drift up from the cellar below, Laura silently shut the basement door. She turned to Emmett.

"Pop, I know you're nervous enough about this interview and I don't want to upset you, but I got a very disturbing phone call today."

Emmett glanced furtively at the refrigerator. "Yeah?"

"A detective investigating Gwyneth's death called. He asked me if I knew an Emmett Walsh."

"What did you tell him?"

"What do you think I told him?" Laura asked in consternation. "I told him my father's name is Emmett Walsh."

"So?"

"He said that he found your name in paperwork of Gwyneth's."

"That's odd." Emmett shrugged. "I guess she must have known some other Emmett Walsh."

"Then I was right in telling him that you didn't know Gwyneth?"

"Absolutely right. It must be some kind of coincidence," Emmett assured his daughter.

The basement door opened and Matthew poked his head into the kitchen. "We're ready when you are, Mr. Walsh."

As Laura followed her father downstairs, she asked herself what were the odds that Gwyneth had known another Emmett Walsh. Pretty infinitesimal. She knew that her father was good at keeping secrets. The distant memory of her mother's deathbed flashed painfully through her mind.

She took a seat at the side of the room, grudgingly allowing Matthew to conduct the interview. *It's better this way,* she told herself. *Let Matthew ask the questions. Don't get involved in the past.*

Matthew began their session by praising the Palisades Park model, oohing and aahing over the tiny details like a little kid. He wanted to start the taping with Emmett giving a guided tour of the mini-park for the camera.

"Just show me everything. Talk to me like you would if the cameras weren't here."

Emmett obliged, nervously at first, but gaining confidence as Matthew encouraged him with his enthusiasm about the model. Emmett started at the Hudson Gate, took the cameras around the saltwater pool and down the midway, past the waffle stand, the cigarette wheel and the Caterpillar ride. He pointed out the hole in the fence where the kids used to sneak into the park without paying, talked about what he had seen on the Free Act Stage and eaten in the restaurant. The cameras rolled on the Hurricane, the Tilt-A-Whirl and the Boomerang as Emmett manipulated the rides' moving parts. When they got past the bingo parlor, the Arcade and the intricately carved, carousel, the tour reached the Cyclone.

"How long did you operate the Cyclone, Mr. Walsh?" Matthew asked.

"Just one summer. The last one. I started working at the park when I was sixteen, started as a soda jerk. But the summer after I turned twenty-one, they let me operate the roller coaster."

"Did you enjoy it?"

"Sure."

"Give anyone famous a ride?"

"Lots of the entertainers who came to the park stopped by."

"That must have been fun."

"Yep."

Since they had gotten to the Cyclone, Matthew detected a marked lessening of Emmett's enthusiasm for his subject; the tenseness had developed again.

"You know, last night I was fooling around on the Internet and looked up one of the Palisades Park websites," remarked Matthew, trying to relax Emmett. "They have a section on it where people can write in their memories of the park. One guy wrote that he remembered doing errands for you in return for free rides."

Emmett looked sharply at Matthew, a stricken look on his face.

"That wouldn't have been legal. You're not going to put that in your story, are you?"

"No, that doesn't really have anything to do with our story," Matthew tried to reassure his interview subject. I just thought it was neat when I read it. You know . . . that the guy remembers that after all these years."

"Are we almost done yet?" asked Emmett impatiently.

Matthew sensed from experience that he should get his last questions in now. His interviewee had just about had it.

"I just want to ask a few more questions, Mr. Walsh. About Tommy Cruz. What do you remember about the time he disappeared?"

"I only know what I read in the newspapers and what I heard around town. People were pretty shook up about it."

"Did you know Tommy?"

"Sure. He was a town kid. He spent a lot of time in the park."

"Ever give him rides on the Cyclone?"

"S'pose so."

"Do you remember anything specific about Tommy?"

"Mister, there where thousands of kids who came through that park. After a while, they all seemed pretty much the same."

"Okay, thank you, Mr. Walsh. We can wrap it up here. You can break down, guys," directed Matthew, disappointed that Emmett hadn't given them more to work with. They needed to get some better interviews elsewhere or this segment wasn't going to cut it.

The group climbed the stairs. As they were about to exit the Walsh home, Laura turned to her father. "Pop, I almost forgot.

I want to get that scrapbook you have with the old pictures of Palisades. We might be able to use them in our piece."

When his daughter, with the red photo album under her arm, and her colleagues left, Emmett headed straight to the refrigerator.

66

MATTHEW OFFERED THEIR camera crew a choice. They could break for lunch and then go shoot the Palisades Amusement Park memorial site later in the afternoon, or they could go straight from the interview to the nearby monument, get the video they needed and then call it a wrap, having the rest of the day off to do as they pleased. The crew chose the latter.

Laura was quiet, the corners of her mouth turned down, as she stood in the bitter January cold, watching the cameraman zoom his lens in on the huge rock that was the centerpiece of the "Little Park of Memories." Just in front of Winston Towers building 300 sat a large boulder surrounded by a brick walkway. It was a commemoration of sorts, funded by donations from hundreds of people across the country who all shared the same passion for Palisades.

DEDICATED TO THE MEMORY OF PALISADES AMUSEMENT

PARK, read the bronze plaque affixed to the front of the boulder. HERE WE WERE HAPPY, HERE WE GREW!

Yeah, right, thought Laura.

"Make sure you get the inscriptions on the bricks, too," Matthew instructed the crew. The camera panned over the names of people and families who had paid for the memorial walkway and now were listed permanently in the hardened red clay.

"I was expecting something more," observed Matthew. "This reminds me of a little cemetery plot."

Matthew was right. This little monument was not going to make it visually, thought Laura.

"There is some sort of move to establish a Palisades Park museum," she offered. "Actually, there is going to be a big fundraiser for it at the end of the month."

"Great." Matthew brightened. "Let's see if we can get in and shoot. I'll bet we could get some great sound of park lovers' memories and show how much the amusement park meant to so many people."

Laura nodded expressionlessly.

"You're awfully quiet," said Matthew softly as the crew started to pack up their gear.

"I'm just cold. And I'm ready to call it a day, too." Laura turned her back on Matthew and started toward the car. But the car was locked and she had to wait while Matthew gave the crew their "in-time" for the next day and briefly informed them about what they'd be shooting tomorrow.

As the crew pulled away in their *KEY News* sedan, Laura and Matthew got into his black Saab.

"Want to stop for some lunch?" offered Matthew.

"Sure. Why not?" Laura shrugged.

"Great. I'm starved. This is your territory. Any suggestions?"

"You like hot dogs?"

"Love 'em."

Laura thrust her chin forward. "Straight ahead."

They drove in silence up Palisades Avenue into Fort Lee and pulled into the busy Hiram's parking lot. Once inside, they ordered hot dogs, french fries and a pitcher of root beer.

"This place has been here forever—this and Callahan's, the place next door." Laura motioned out the restaurant window to the companion building, feeling she should make some sort of effort at conversation. "The menus are just about the same, but they're both always packed. They used to be just open-air roadside stands doing most of their business in the warm weather. Then they enclosed everything, so now the locals can get their sodium fixes all year round."

Matthew bit into his steaming frank. "Excellent!" he proclaimed.

Laura played at dipping her french fries into the ketchup.

"Okay. What's wrong?" he asked.

"Nothing."

"Yeah, sure. Nothing. You've been miserable all day. Why don't you tell me what's bothering you?" Matthew reached across the table and placed his warm hand on her cold one.

His touch felt so good and, even as she pulled her hand away, Laura ached to tell him about Gwyneth's will, the call from Detective Ortiz and her worries about her father. But something kept her from unburdening herself. She didn't know if she could trust him.

Laura excused herself as Matthew settled the check. With

Laura gone, Matthew took a vial from his pocket and popped a tiny pill. He had hoped he would get through the whole day without one. *Better luck tomorrow,* he thought as he waited for the calm to settle over him.

67

AFTER WORK, DELIA walked along Central Park West toward the 72nd Street entrance to Strawberry Fields. An icy rain sprayed her face and she pulled the collar of her four-year-old wool coat up around her ears. One of the first things she was going to do with her new funds was buy one of those coats she saw advertised in the magazines. A nice heavy black coat, with thick warm fur trimming the collar and cuffs. A rich lady's coat.

Since she had made the phone call the day before, Delia had been wondering if she was doing the right thing. Her mother, God rest her soul, would be appalled, and would tell her to go to the police immediately and tell them what she had seen. But her mother, who had struggled all her life, thought that it paid to tell the truth. Delia didn't. She was tired of working hard and getting nowhere.

Still, her conscience was bothering her as she waited for the light to change so she could cross the broad avenue. She uttered a silent prayer as she suddenly remembered that it was the Feast of the Epiphany, the day when the Magi brought their gifts of gold, frankincense and myrrh to the Christ child. Delia looked forward to getting her hands on the gold.

The Central Park entrance at Women's Gate was well lit but deserted, save for a devoted jogger who was leaving the park after his run in the inclement weather. Delia stood beneath the streetlight and waited, looking down the avenue at the remaining holiday lights. The sleet was turning to rain.

After ten minutes passed, Delia began to panic. What if no one was going to meet her?

She ventured slowly into the still park, walking to the plaque honoring John Lennon, the assassinated Beatle who had met his death outside the nearby Dakota, his venerable apartment building. She shivered beneath her wet coat.

Looking farther down the darkened path into the park, she could make out a figure sitting huddled on a bench.

"Delia? I'm down here."

Slowly, Delia walked toward the bench. The figure rose.

"Come. Walk with me. I don't want anyone to see us."

Delia eyed the package under the camel-hair-coated arm.

"Why don't you just give it to me here? There's no one around."

"All right, if that's the way you want it."

Delia saw just a flash of the steel blades reflected by the lights on Central Park West as the scissors were plunged viciously into the space between her collar and her neck, and into her jugular vein.

68

AFTER DEBATING ABOUT it all morning, Laura tapped tentatively on Joel Malcolm's opened office door.

"Got a minute?"

"Of course. For you I do. Come on in, Laura." He waved for her to take a seat. "Well, I see you survived the first week with us. And what a week it's been."

Laura smiled weakly.

"What's up, kiddo?"

Twisting her hands in her lap, Laura began uncertainly, "This is going to come out eventually and I thought it would be better if you heard it from me first."

The pleasant lines that Joel had arranged on his face changed to an expression of intense interest. "Shoot."

"Gwyneth named me as a beneficiary of her estate."

"You know this how?" Joel asked calmly.

"Her attorneys notified me by mail."

Why hadn't he gotten any letter? He felt his face grow warm as the reality became clear to him. Gwyneth had not included him in her will. After all they had been through together and after all, he thought, they had meant to one another. She could have left him something to remember her by.

Screw Gwyneth. But, of course, he already had.

"Do you mind my asking what she left you?" he said evenly.

"Pretty much everything."

Joel whistled through his teeth. "Baby, you don't have to work another day in your life."

Laura shook her head in wonderment. "I don't understand this at all. I knew Gwyneth was fond of me, but I never imagined anything like this. I never even met her until I came here to do my internship. And I never really understood why she took such an interest in me."

Joel looked puzzled. "What do you mean, you never even met her until your internship? Gwyneth set up that internship especially for you."

69

MIKE SCHULTZ TOOK the elevator from the Bulletin Center down to the Broadcast Center lobby to meet Detective Ortiz. He planned to talk to Ortiz in the cafeteria, preferring not to bring the detective up to his office where repeated interruptions would disturb their privacy. He was not particularly concerned that Ortiz wanted to talk with him. In fact, he had been waiting for the detective's call.

Once they were settled in one of the Station Break booths with steaming cups of coffee before them, Ortiz got right to the point.

"How would you describe your relationship with Gwyneth Gilpatric, Mr. Schultz?"

"Strained," Mike answered honestly. "I had been her producer at *Hourglass* and I didn't leave under the best of circumstances."

"Tell me about that," Ortiz urged.

Mike recounted pretty much the same story that Joel Malcolm had: the informant who had been identified by drug pushers and his resulting death.

"Did you feel that you had been unfairly singled out as the patsy to take the fall for the foul-up?" Ortiz asked.

Mike shrugged his large shoulders. "Yes and no. While we were editing the piece, I did see Jaime Cordero in the corner of Gwyneth's 'standup,' but he appeared very briefly. When I pointed it out to Gwyneth and suggested we reshoot it, she refused. Her schedule was packed and she said she was just too busy to go back up to East Harlem and shoot another one. She said that no one would notice. At that point, I should have gone to Joel and insisted that we reshoot. But I didn't. My loyalties were to Gwyneth, above the show. That was a mistake." Mike sighed deeply and took a swallow of his coffee.

"But Gwyneth didn't turn out to be loyal to you, did she, Mr. Schultz?"

"No, sir. She didn't."

70

"HE WAS BORN in Puerto Rico and landed his first acting part, the role of the devil, as a first grader in San Juan. As a young man he traveled to New York to study acting and eventually starred in many films, theater productions and television shows. You might know him best as Gomez in *The Addams Family*."

"Who is Raul Julia!" Jade chimed triumphantly.

"Absolutely right!" Laura smiled broadly at her eager student. They were playing African-American *Jeopardy!*—Jade's favorite tutorial project game. Laura liked to supplement the answers with some of her own about Hispanic-Americans and women, hoping to give Jade further role models for achievement.

"Let's do another one!" Jade's eyes danced with enthusiasm.

"Okay. Known as the Mother of the Civil Rights Movement in 1955, this black seamstress refused to give up her seat to a white person on a Montgomery, Alabama, bus and helped to start a movement against segregation."

"Rosa Parks!"

"You forgot to put your answer in the form of a question . . ." Laura prompted.

"Oh, yeah, I forgot. *Who* is Rosa Parks!"

"Correct! You, Miss Jade Figueroa, win the candy bar of your choice."

"Can we go get it now?" asked the happy child.

Laura looked at her watch. Their two-hour Saturday morning session together was just about up.

"Sure. But what about my Spanish lesson? What's my new word for today?"

"Oh, yeah, right." Jade nodded solemnly. She took her reciprocal job as Laura's Spanish teacher very seriously. "The word for today is 'cruz' Do you know what 'cruz' means, Laura?"

"Tell me."

" 'Cruz' means *cross*," declared Jade proudly.

How appropriate, reflected Laura as thoughts of Tommy Cruz's mysterious death filled her mind. Felipe and Marta Cruz had certainly had their own cross to bear.

71

Sunday, January 9

MATTHEW HAD SUGGESTED that they meet Sunday morning for a run in Central Park and then go out for some breakfast and discuss where they stood with the Palisades Park story. Laura was glad that the day, though cold, was clear. She was looking forward to some strenuous exercise to help clear her head.

It was a beautiful place to run. The Manhattan skyline loomed elegantly around the park. And through the now leaf-less trees that framed the Jacqueline Kennedy Onassis Reservoir jogging trails, Laura could see riders exercising their horses on the bridle paths that ran parallel to the jogging route. Bird-watchers and nature lovers were out in force on this brisk winter morning, eager to claim their share of nature's beauty in the now gray and cold city.

As they pounded their way a third time around the jogging track, holding back as the other weekend runners sped past them, Matthew broke their companionable silence.

"Were you going to tell me that you are inheriting big-time from Gwyneth?"

Laura stopped running and tried to catch her breath. "Who told you? Joel?" she panted.

"Of course. Didn't you realize that telling him was tantamount to telling the world?"

"Obviously I should have."

They walked the rest of the way around the reservoir in silence, cooling down from their run. Their warm breath looked like smoke as it hit the winter air.

Laura looked at Matthew, his cheeks flushed and perspiration beading at the temples near his dark hair. He kept his eyes cast downward. *He looks hurt,* she thought.

She could have told him that day at Hiram's or any of the days since. But she hadn't. But now, knowing that he knew, she was relieved. She was attracted to him, wanted to share more with him, but couldn't quite define why she was so hesitant about doing so.

Francheska was always saying that Laura had a problem with men, was afraid to trust them because of her experience with Emmett. Laura didn't need to go to a shrink to tell her that. But maybe she should get some therapy. She had never dated anyone longer than six months, always breaking it off when things started to get too serious. If she did not learn to be more trusting, she would never have any real intimacy with a man.

"I'm sorry I didn't tell you," she said softly. "I meant to, I just didn't."

Matthew took her gloved hand. "Laura," he said softly, "I want to get to know you better, but you don't seem to want that. Why won't you let me in a little bit? Why don't you trust me?

"I'm not going to hurt you, you know," he said gently.

Laura was silent, but slowly her hand went up to her forehead and pushed back her bangs.

"What's that from?" asked Matthew as he squinted at the thin scar.

"My father," she said quietly. And after a slight pause, Laura added, "Let's not get into all the sordid details now, but if I have a problem opening up to men, he's probably the reason why."

Matthew leaned down and softly kissed the marred spot above Laura's brow. Pulling back and smiling encouragingly, he said, "You'll tell me when you're ready. Come on." He smiled. "Let's go get something to eat."

Over waffles, crisp bacon and lots of hot coffee, they sat at an East Side coffee shop, Matthew listening intently as Laura told him about her relationship with Gwyneth and how puzzled she was about what was happening.

"I didn't know that Gwyneth had set up that college internship for me. I had never even met the woman before I arrived at *Key News*. Now she's left me most of her estate. And the police say there were regular entries in Gwyneth's checkbook—of checks made out to my father. It just doesn't make sense. To make matters worse, in addition to an inheritance motive, I had her obituary ready, to boot. So I feel pretty confident that the police are thinking of me as a suspect."

"What does your father say?"

"I asked him about Gwyneth the day we interviewed him out at his house. Remember, when you and the crew were downstairs? He denies knowing her." Laura placed her knife and fork neatly on the side of her plate. "Of course, my father hasn't always been known for his honesty with me."

Matthew was quiet, and Laura thought she may have told

him too much. Why would he want to get involved with someone whose life was so complicated?

"I'm bad news, huh?" she declared with a wry smile.

Matthew reached out and took her hand. "Everyone has baggage, Laura. That's just life."

"You seem pretty unencumbered."

"Don't worry. I have my own demons."

"Such as?"

"Try a drug problem, that I fight every single day."

Laura was flattered and touched that he trusted her enough to reveal himself to her by telling her something so personal and potentially damaging. At the same time, she wondered if it was a death wish to get involved with Matthew Voigt.

72

Monday, January 10

TO: Laurawalsh@key.com
FROM: Russdefilippis@key.com
RE: Palisades Park story

Hi Laura,

We've never met, but I work as an audio editor in the KEY Entertainment Department.

I grew up in Cliffside Park and spent many summers at PAP.

Some of my happiest memories are of the fun we used to have in the park. It was a rite of passage to be tall enough to ride the Cyclone, to see how may times you could ride the Tilt-A-Whirl before you got sick. I remember, as a teenager, spending nights at the Penny Arcade, wearing my father's Eisenhower bomber jacket, commandeering a pinball machine with my cigarette balanced on the edge as I banged away at the flippers. I also remember my old man, in his boxer shorts and argyle socks, waiting at the door for me when I got home, furious at the nicotine stains on my fingers and on my face. And, of course, it was always fun to bring a girl into the photo booth, have her sit on your lap and get four, quick pictures for a quarter.

I'm sure you have lots of good information for your story, but one thing that might not be in your research material is the fact that after they tore down the amusement park, Cliffside Park was infested with rats. They came swarming out of the old rides and buildings near the water and headed for new homes in the surrounding residential neighborhoods.

Late at night, I would awaken to hear the rats scratching in the walls, though it sounded like they were actually in my bedroom. I'd bang the wall and would hear them scurry.

The town Board of Health gave out poison, but at first, not wanting to have the rats die and rot in the house, we tried setting traps. Every morning, my father would wake me and tell me, "Clear the rats before your mother gets up," and I'd dutifully dump two or three fat, slimy rodents into the garbage can. One day my mom was ironing in the living room when a hairless baby rat scrambled across the rug. That set my mother running out the front door screaming.

Eventually, we resorted to the rat poison, putting the powder and pellets into the holes we had to cut in the walls and under the sinks, because, as you probably know, rats always head for water. My mom even had to put a telephone book on top of the closed toilet bowl seat, because the rats were getting in that way, too.

The rat poison finally worked, but not before we had to cut away large portions of the ceilings to get out their rotting carcasses.

Don't know if this will be of any help to you, but I thought you might want to know.

Russ

73

Tuesday, January 11

COVERED WITH AN afghan his mother had crocheted, Ricky Potenza lay sprawled on the living room couch waiting for *Hourglass* to come on. He wanted to see who this "eyewitness" to Gwyneth Gilpatric's death they were promising was. KEY had been promoting the show all week.

He had turned off all the lights, wanting to concentrate solely on the television screen. He was relieved when his mother said she was tired and was going to bed early. Ricky did not want her to watch the program with him. He did not want her watching him. She was always watching him warily, staring at him, trying to figure him out. Didn't she know by now that there was no use in that?

The sand began sifting through the hourglass. Ricky felt the little hairs rise on the back of his neck.

"Good Evening. I'm Eliza Blake, and welcome to *Hourglass*."

Eliza was much prettier and nicer than Gwyneth Gilpatric. He approved of the new host. "Last week, we told you that *KEY News* would be doing its own investigation into the death of correspondent Gwyneth Gilpatric and we promised you that

203

tonight you would hear from an eyewitness to Gwyneth Gilpatric's fatal fall from the rooftop of her New York City apartment building. This afternoon, I interviewed the eyewitness, and what she had to say indicates that Gwyneth Gilpatric did not commit suicide, did not jump to the Central Park West sidewalk. Gwyneth Gilpatric, according to our eyewitness, was pushed." Eliza stared into the camera solemnly. "Tonight, on *Hourglass*, we'll have an exclusive interview with an eyewitness to the murder of Gwyneth Gilpatric."

There is some justice in this world after all, thought Ricky as his lips formed a tight smile. The commercial for a new car that Ricky could never afford, much less get a license to drive, ran on the television screen. Ricky got up and went to the kitchen, poured some ginger ale and grabbed a bag of pretzels from the cabinet. This was going to be entertaining.

74

NOT ONLY HAD Joel forced Kitzi to talk, he had pressured her into allowing the *Hourglass* camera crew into their apartment. Viewers across the country were now peering into the place where she conducted the most private part of her life, her home.

Kitzi cringed when she first saw herself appear on the television screen. Did she really look that old? The day-spa trips to Elizabeth Arden could only do so much. Sitting across from the luminous Eliza Blake certainly didn't help any. In Kitzi's eyes, the contrast between the two of them was sharp and depressing.

Eliza introduced Kitzi, clarifying for viewers that she was the wife of the executive producer of *Hourglass*.

"Now, Mrs. Malcolm, as I understand it, you were supposed to attend Gwyneth Gilpatric's New Year's Eve party?"

"I had planned to, yes," answered Kitzi. "But at the last minute, I didn't feel well. I urged my husband to go on to the party without me."

"So you were here alone all evening?"

Kitzi stroked the miniature gray poodle that sat curled in her lap. "Yes, except of course for Missy here. She kept me company."

Eliza looked down at the little dog and smiled.

"Tell me, then, what happened."

"After Joel left, I went to bed and slept for a while. Until Missy here woke me and wanted to go out for her walk. I take her out every night after the local news is over at eleven-thirty. The cold air must have helped my headache, because after we got back, I felt a little better."

Eliza nodded for Kitzi to continue with her story. "What happened then?"

"At just before midnight, I decided I would go out to the terrace and watch the fireworks over the park."

"Can we go out to the terrace now? Would you show us, Mrs. Malcolm?" Eliza urged.

The two women rose from their seats and the camera followed them through the double doors, out to the terrace. Kitzi walked to the large telescope that stood planted on the terra-cotta tiles.

"I was waiting for the fireworks to begin and decided to see if I could take a look across the park to Gwyneth's apartment. I was curious to see if I'd be able to make out the faces of any of the people at the party."

"Could you?"

"Not really. I could see figures making their way onto Gwyneth's balcony. But her terrace wasn't well lit."

"Please go on, Mrs. Malcolm."

Kitzi gazed across Central Park, gathering her thoughts.

"The fireworks began. They were really quite spectacular, but then they always are as far as I'm concerned. Each burst lit up the sky in the most beautiful way. I looked into the telescope again, wanting to see if I could catch sight of Joel as one of the explosions lit up the terrace."

"Did you? Did you see your husband?"

Kitzi shivered and she wrapped her arms around herself as they stood in the cold January wind that whipped them as they stood on the exposed Fifth Avenue balcony.

"Do you want to go back inside, Mrs. Malcolm?" Eliza asked. "We can finish our interview inside."

Kitzi pushed back the hair that blew across her face. "No. It's all right."

Kitzi pressed her right eye against the telescope's viewing lens and pointed it in the direction of Gwyneth's apartment. Then she stood back from the telescope and gestured for Eliza to take a look.

"I'm looking at the roof," Eliza said puzzledly.

"I know," Kitzi nodded. "The telescope skips a bit upward when you step away from it. That's what must have happened that night. Because when I went back to look after training it on Gwyneth's terrace just minutes before, I saw what you are seeing now, Eliza . . . the roof of Gwyneth Gilpatric's building."

～

Nancy and Mike Schultz sat together in their family room, engrossed in what they were watching.

"Joel has got to be wetting his pants," muttered Mike. "The ratings on this are going to be stupendous."

"Sshhh!" commanded Nancy, leaning forward to better hear the television.

On the screen, Eliza Blake and Kitzi Malcolm were going back inside the apartment. They reseated themselves in the luxurious living room. Kitzi continued with her story.

"I saw two people on the roof. Two figures, really. One I could tell was a woman. She was wearing a long, full skirt that was blowing in the breeze."

"That would have been Gwyneth?" Eliza offered.

"Yes," Kitzi affirmed. "I found out later that she had been wearing a full evening skirt."

"And the other person? Could you tell if it was a man or a woman?"

"Not really," answered Kitzi. "It was just a form."

"What else did you see?" urged Eliza.

"I saw a faint light pass between the two of them."

"What kind of light?"

"I'm assuming it must have been a cigarette lighter. Gwyneth smoked, you know."

"No, I didn't know that," declared Eliza. "Could you make out the faces in the light of the flame?"

Kitzi shook her head.

"And then? What did you see next, Mrs. Malcolm?"

Kitzi called to her dog and the poodle sprang to her lap. She gently stroked its soft gray fur.

"They stood there for a minute or two." Kitzi's voice began to quiver. "And then one figure merged with the other. For a moment, it looked like there was just one person on the roof."

"Did it look like they were struggling?"

"I couldn't tell." Kitzi's hand trembled as she petted Missy.

"Go on, please, go on," Eliza prodded.

"There was a huge burst of light as the fireworks finale began," Kitzi recalled slowly. "And the next thing I saw was the figure with the sweeping, full skirt tumble over the side of the building."

～

At the commercial break, Laura's home telephone rang.

"Are you watching this?" Francheska asked in amazement.

"Of course I am."

"My God! Did you know this was going to be so good?"

"There was gossip about it around the office, but Joel Malcolm wasn't letting anyone but the people actually working on the piece late today look at it."

"Jesus, Laura. Murder! This whole thing gives me the chills. How the hell are you going to move into that apartment? It would creep me out to live there all alone after what happened."

Laura was thinking the same thing.

75

THE MORNING AFTER the *Hourglass* broadcast, Alberto Ortiz wasted no time in talking to Kitzi Malcolm. But when he left her apartment, he knew no more than he had after watching *Hourglass* the night before. Kitzi recounted the same story that she had on the show.

He had upbraided her for not coming forward earlier with what she had seen, but he knew that the fact of the matter was Kitzi would not be punished for holding out. If Ortiz pursued it, Kitzi's son-of-a-bitch husband would get his attorneys in on the act and the most Kitzi would get was a slap on the wrist. *Why bother expending the energy?*

Ortiz stopped at a sidewalk vendor's kiosk and bought a hot pretzel. Looking at his watch, he realized he would have to hurry if he was going to finally interview Dr. Leonard Costello. The doctor had not been at all cooperative in meeting with him, giving one excuse after another. At last, grudgingly, Costello had set a definite time, between the doctor's morning rounds at Mt. Olympia and the start of his afternoon office hours.

As he steered the dark police sedan through Central Park toward Manhattan's East Side, Ortiz wished he was further along in wrapping up the case.

When he arrived at Dr. Costello's office, several patients were already in the sitting room. Nurse Camille Bruno introduced herself.

"Dr. Costello just called. He's on his way. Would you like to have a seat in his office, Detective?"

"Thanks."

"Can I get you a cup of coffee?" the nurse offered cheerfully as she escorted him down the hallway.

"Actually, that would be great," said Ortiz appreciatively. "It's cold out there."

While he waited, Ortiz scanned the framed diplomas and certificates that lined the office walls. Arranged to reassure potential patients, they were impressive. He admired the massive mahogany desk and the top-of-the-line computer that sat upon it.

The office door opened and Camille Bruno entered with coffee mug in hand. An unsmiling Dr. Costello followed.

Costello took a seat behind his desk and, once the nurse left the room, asked brusquely, "How can I help you, Detective?"

He's used to calling all the shots, the arrogant s.o.b., thought Ortiz, immediately disliking his interview subject.

"As I told you a number of times on the phone, I'm working on the Gilpatric murder case."

Costello smirked. "You must have loved last night's *Hourglass,* Detective Ortiz. It must be great to have *KEY News* finding your eyewitnesses for you."

Refusing to rise to the bait, Ortiz deliberately kept his expression from changing. Ignoring Costello's dig, the detective proceeded.

"I understand that Miss Gilpatric was your patient."

"*'Was'* is the operative word there, Detective."

"Can you explain that, please, sir?"

"What's there to explain? Once she was my patient, but at the time of her death, she wasn't."

"And why was that?"

"You'd have to ask her that, Detective." Costello gripped a silver pen in his right hand to steady the tremor he felt beginning. "But, forgive me," he said mockingly, "you can't do that, can you?"

76

WHEN ROSE POTENZA asked Laura if her son could be interviewed at the *KEY News* studios, Laura was only too happy to comply. Though it could be better visually to have Ricky in his home environment, thereby giving the viewer a look into the way he lived, having Ricky come to the studio saved Laura and Matthew and the crew a schlepp out to Rockland County.

The Potenzas arrived early and the camera crew was not quite set up. Laura offered to give them a short tour around *KEY News*. Ricky enthusiastically accepted.

Maybe this will loosen him up a little, make him feel relaxed, thought Laura as she guided mother and son around the labyrinth of hallways that made up the Broadcast Center. As they entered the studio of the *Evening Headlines,* they bumped into Eliza Blake. Laura made the introductions, explaining to Eliza why the Potenzas were there.

"I've been watching you on *Hourglass,*" said Ricky, his face blushing. "I like you much better than Gwyneth Gilpatric. I'm glad she's gone."

"It's nice to meet you, Ricky," said Eliza smoothly, ignoring the cut to Gwyneth. "Good luck with your interview."

Ricky looked puzzled. "Won't you be interviewing me?"

"No. Actually, Laura will be interviewing you. Many times the producers do the actual interviewing. I'll be getting involved later, after a lot of our elements and interviews are already recorded."

Disappointment clouded Ricky's face.

"Don't worry, Ricky." Eliza smiled reassuringly. "You are in very good hands with Laura. At this point, she knows much more about the Palisades Park story than I do. She's really the one that you want interviewing you."

Ricky looked unconvinced, but Laura tried to ignore it as they continued on their tour. She took them through the control room with its myriad television monitors and intricate electronic keyboards that controlled audio, video and special effects. She pointed out the headquarters news desk, the command post for KEY news-gathering around the world, describing the various jobs of the dozen or so people who sat around it. She demonstrated the *KEY News* computer system, explaining how it was used to facilitate the delivery of news at an ever-increasing pace. "I know how to use a computer," Ricky volunteered.

When they reached the anchor platform from which Eliza Blake broadcast the news each evening, Laura suggested that Ricky try out the anchor chair.

"You mean it?" Ricky asked, his face brightening.

"Sure. Go ahead."

Ricky cast his eyes around the studio.

"Don't worry. No one will be watching. They are all busy doing their own things."

As Ricky mounted the anchor platform, Laura reflected at how childlike this middle-aged man was. What Ricky Potenza might tell her could make her piece. She didn't want to talk down to him and insult him as she did the interview, but she was well aware of his vulnerability and fragility. She planned to be very careful.

Matthew was waiting for them when they arrived in the Bill Kendall Room, the interview room named in memory of the legendary news figure who had once anchored the *KEY Evening Headlines* and led *KEY News*. The space was small, a dark curtain draping the wall serving as a background for the shot. Two chairs were arranged facing one another. The one for Ricky sat facing the camera. Laura's sat across from his, but out of camera range.

Rose Potenza looked more nervous than her son did as she watched the microphone being clipped to his shirt. Makeup artist Christina Weisberg delicately dabbed Ricky's forehead with powder, assuring that his skin would not shine in the bright camera lights.

"All ready, Ricky?" Laura asked.

"I guess so."

"You know we're doing a story on Palisades Amusement Park and the death of Tommy Cruz," Laura began.

Ricky nodded.

"Tommy Cruz was your friend, Ricky?"

Ricky nodded again, silently. *Please, God, let him open up. We need some good sound bites,* prayed Laura.

"Can you tell me about Tommy, Ricky?" she urged gently, trying to draw him out.

Ricky cast a look in the direction of his mother. Rose Potenza nodded and smiled encouragement to her son.

"I'm really going to be on television?" he asked suspiciously.

"Yes. If you have something important to tell us."

The foot on the end of Ricky's crossed leg jiggled up and down and a determined expression came to his face.

"Tommy was my best friend."

"Can you tell me some of the things you used to do together?"

"We were in the same class in school. We were in Boy Scouts together. Played football on the same team."

"You had a lot of fun with Tommy?" Laura led him on.

"Yeah, we had lots of good times."

"Ever go to the amusement park with Tommy?"

Ricky nodded.

"What did you do there?"

"We'd go swimming in the pool," Ricky recalled. "We'd try to get there early in the day before all the crowds came."

"That must have been fun."

"Yeah, but the pool got awfully dirty. There would be hot dogs and hair and green gunk floating in it sometimes. Kids used to pee in there, right in the water. They were too lazy to get out of the pool and go to the bathhouse. They said they changed the water every day, but I didn't believe it."

Rose Potenza winced.

"What about the rides, Ricky?" asked Laura, changing the subject. "Did you and Tommy like the rides?"

"Yeah, they were cool, when we had the money to go on them. But once in while the guys who ran the rides would let us on for free."

"Did you and Tommy have a favorite ride?"

"Not really."

"You know, Ricky, my father used to run the roller coaster at Palisades. Did you ever ride the Cyclone?"

The man uncrossed his legs and sat up stiffly in his chair. His knuckles whitened as he gripped the edges of the armrests.

"Ricky?"

"I was afraid of the Cyclone," he answered shortly.

Laura sensed Ricky's tension and didn't want to exacerbate it, especially since she hadn't gotten to the questions she most wanted to ask him.

"I'd like to talk a little more about Tommy if we could, Ricky. About the time when he disappeared. That was the last summer that Palisades was open, wasn't it?"

Ricky nodded.

"Just before school started?"

He nodded again.

"Do you remember the last time you saw Tommy?"

Ricky stared piercingly at her.

"Ricky?"

He pulled the microphone from his collar. The interview was over.

77

OVER A SCOTCH on the rocks, Francheska listened as Leonard spewed out his story of what a tough day he'd had. Though Leonard was trying not to show it, Francheska could tell that the visit from the detective worried him.

"I've got nothing to hide," he declared. "Let that dick dig all he wants."

At another time, Francheska would have gone to him, circled her arms around him and distracted him with a long, deep kiss. But not tonight.

Maybe he wouldn't really care that much when she told him that they were through. But she had given special attention to getting ready for tonight. She wanted him to be fully aware of what he would be missing without her in his life.

"Come here, baby." Leonard patted the cushion on the sofa beside him.

Francheska approached, her skin radiant in the glow of the candlelight that lit the room. Her black hair fell softly on her cashmere sweater. She took her place alongside him.

"You smell great, baby." Leonard leaned forward to nuzzle her neck.

If she allowed him to get started, she would never tell him, she thought, pulling away.

"Hey! What's wrong, sugar?" Leonard inquired sweetly, but Francheska knew his short temper would flare quickly if she continued to hold out.

"I don't want to do this anymore, Len."

Leonard stared at her uncomprehendingly. "Don't want to do *what* anymore?"

"This!" Francheska gestured widely. "Living like this, being a mistress, your mistress. I don't like all the lies and stolen moments and lonely nights. I'm tired of feeling like trash. I'm not going to do this anymore. It's over, Len."

"Oh, come on, Francie," he urged. I know it's been rough lately, with the holidays and all. I'm sorry that I've had to spend so much time at home with the kids, but I thought you understood that."

"Of course I understand that. And you should be with your kids, and your wife, too, for that matter. But I want more, need more, than you are willing to give. I want kids of my own someday, and much as I've hoped and prayed and wished it would be otherwise, I know you are not going to be my children's father. I have to get out of our relationship, Leonard. Get out and move on. Make a decent life for myself. I've made up my mind."

Without a word, Leonard rose from the sofa, walked to the hall closet and pulled out his coat. As he opened the front door, he turned to her.

"You'll change your mind, Francie. You'll see. It's a cold, hard world out there. You just better hope that when you come crawling back, I still want you. And it will be only on my terms."

"I'll be out by the end of the month," called Francheska, tears welling in her eyes, as the door slammed shut behind him.

78

Thursday, January 13

"THINGS WERE GOING pretty well there, until you asked him about the Cyclone," Matthew observed as they screened the tape of Laura's interview with Ricky Potenza recorded the day before.

"Yeah," answered Laura dejectedly. Unrealistically, perhaps, she had been hoping to get Ricky to open up about the time of his friend's disappearance. How conceited of her to think she could succeed where so many professionals had failed. But even more upsetting to her than the lack of good sound bites was the nagging suspicion that the mention of her father might have been what had caused Ricky to shut down.

The tape finished running and their editor announced that, if they did not have anything else for him right now, he was going to lunch. Alone in the semidark editing booth, Matthew and Laura discussed the elements they had at this point for their story.

"We've shot Ricky, your father and his miniature playground, and the monument in Cliffside Park. We've got the old black-and-white film of the park from archives. I'm getting tapes of various songs about Palisades Park. And we have permission to shoot at that fund-raiser in two weeks."

It was a start, but not enough to make an *Hourglass* story, and they both knew it.

"I haven't made much progress with the Cliffside Park police," Laura said glumly. "There is no one left on the force there who worked on the Cruz disappearance. The ones who are there now don't want to comment on the latest developments in the case. But I'm going to try to track down a retired cop that I saw quoted in some of the newspaper articles from that time."

"Good," said Matthew firmly. "Anything I can do to help on that score?"

"No, thanks. I can do that, but I'll let you know if I need anything."

"What else?" Matthew mused, staring at his notepad and chewing the end of his pen.

"We need to get Tommy Cruz's parents to talk to us."

"You want me to try to set that up?" offered Matthew.

Laura considered before answering. "It would probably be better if I called the Cruzes. Since I'm a hometown girl and all."

"Fine, but is there anything you are going to let me do? Or do you want to do this piece all by yourself?"

Matthew smiled, but Laura thought she detected some annoyance in his voice.

"Feel like going through that old scrapbook that my father gave us and looking for any pictures we could use?" she suggested.

"Sure, I think I can handle that." He capped his pen and abruptly left the editing room.

79

MATTHEW UNSCREWED THE amber plastic vial and emptied out a small pill, swallowing it with a swig of the unfinished cold coffee that sat in the paper cup on his desk. He hated himself for doing it.

Was it just his imagination, or was Laura treating him differently since he had confided in her about his drug abuse?

It had all started so innocently. He had only been at *Hourglass* a short time when one of the stories he was working on began keeping him up at nights. It was that Cordero story. They were trying to meet an impossible deadline. Gwyneth had become a screaming harpy, Joel wouldn't let anyone get a word in edgewise, barking at everyone who came near him, and even Mike Schultz, usually a sweetheart of a guy, had begun losing his temper at the drop of a hat.

Matthew had mentioned to a friend how toxic the anxiety was becoming and that losing sleep at night only made him more anxiety-ridden during the day. He was worried that he would lose his job. It was then that he got some "friendly" advice—a small vial of Valium. He was told, "These will calm you down, and when the piece airs during February sweeps, you'll be back to your old self."

Only that didn't happen. After just a few weeks, he was hooked—it seemed that he couldn't even manage waiting for the subway in the morning without popping a five-milligram tablet on the subway platform. Now, three years later, and almost twelve sweeps periods later, he was trying, without much success, to quit.

But Gwyneth's murder had everybody jumpy. And this Palisades story had him as anxious as ever. His attempts at romance with Laura seemed to be going nowhere.

Matthew tried to be philosophical—again.

Hey, it was no sin to be anxious, was it? Everyone experienced anxiety at one time or another, didn't they? Who didn't have sweaty palms during a job interview or have butterflies in the stomach before a speech?

And, God knew, the profession he had chosen had more than its share of stress. Deadlines, competition, exacting standards. Anyone in his right mind would be worried about the repercussions of getting the facts wrong in front of millions of television viewers.

Working for Joel Malcolm just twisted the tourniquet tighter. The relentless demand for stories hit out of the ball park time after time after time. Not even Sammy Sosa could hit a home run every time at bat.

He wondered how many of the other *Hourglass* producers were taking drugs. He knew he couldn't be the only one who took Valium to relax.

But Matthew's problem was that his use had gotten out of hand. He'd become addicted. He was clever enough to have arranged to get prescriptions from three different doctors, so none of them realized the scope of his dependency. He only submitted the bills from one set of prescriptions, so the *KEY News* HMO never red-flagged the pharmacies he used.

He was trying to stop. At first he went cold turkey. But the withdrawal had been a nightmare. He couldn't sleep, couldn't eat, the headache was blinding. He'd had a story that was near air, and, panic-stricken, he'd popped the pills again.

There was never a good time to stop. There was always some other stressful situation that had to be dealt with and the Valium made it bearable.

Yes. Much better. It was kicking in now.

80

THE GNAWING WORRY had been intensifying over the past two days.

What if Kitzi Malcolm hadn't been telling the truth during her Hourglass *interview?*

She said that she couldn't see faces. Couldn't tell if the figure on the roof with Gwyneth was a man or a woman. But what if she was lying? What if the light from the fireworks had illuminated them as they stood on the freezing rooftop?

Would there have to be a third murder?

The newspapers and television hadn't reported anything about a woman's body found hidden deep in the thicket in Central

Park. So far so good. Sooner or later, though, Delia's body would be discovered.

That would be a great addition to the Hourglass *series. Gwyneth Gilpatric's maid found murdered!*

Killing Kitzi would be more difficult, but not impossible.

81

BEFORE SHE LEFT the office for the day, Laura dialed her father's number.

"Hey, Pop. It's me. Just checking in. How's it going?"

"I'm fine, Munk. How are you?"

"Okay," Laura answered, holding the phone against her shoulder as she replaced her shoes with sneakers for the walk home. "Working hard on this Palisades Park story."

There was no answer from Emmett.

"Know who I interviewed yesterday? Ricky Potenza," Laura continued. "He was Tommy Cruz's best friend."

"Did he tell you anything you didn't know?"

Laura thought she detected a slurring of her father's voice. She cringed.

"No. Not really, but we still have some time left to work on our other sources. I'm praying that we can find out what happened to Tommy Cruz before this piece airs."

Silence on the telephone line.

"Pop?"

"Yeah, Munk?"

"What's going on? Why are you so negative on me doing this story?"

A deep sigh filtered through Laura's earpiece. "I told you at Christmas, Laura, I think you should let what happened lie. What good is there in digging all this up?"

"Try a little piece of mind for the Cruzes. How about that?" Laura answered, annoyed. "Did you ever think that it might bring some closure for them, to know what really happened to their son?"

"Come off it, Laura. Helping the Cruzes isn't your main aim here." Laura could hear the anger in his voice. "Get off your high horse. You want a story that you think could be sensational. You want to impress all your *KEY News* buddies. Miss Big Hotshot Producer solves a thirty-year-old murder mystery."

Laura was taken aback and hurt by the venom in her father's voice.

82

EMMETT FELT LIKE a noose was tightening around his neck.

Alerted by the New York City police, a Cliffside Park detective had come to the house this afternoon to ask about the checks that Gwyneth had written out to him over the years. There had been no sense in denying them. Something like that was easily traced.

"Gwyneth Gilpatric and I were old friends," he had told the detective. "After my wife died, I kind of fell apart and Gwyneth took it upon herself to help me out. She was very loyal."

"And very generous," added the detective, but he seemed to accept Emmett's explanation. It had the ring of truth. Among those who had lived in Cliffside Park for a long time, it was fairly common knowledge that Emmett Walsh had a drinking problem. Over the years, he had floated from one job to the next. People had wondered how he managed to hold on to his house and send his daughter to an expensive private college.

When the detective left, Emmett opened a beer and hoped that that would be the end of it. But two hours and a six-pack later, Laura called, with her news of Ricky Potenza.

He had lived in fear for years of Ricky coming forward,

never dreaming that his own daughter would one day be urging Ricky to tell what he knew.

Emmett crushed the aluminum beer can and tossed it at the barrel of empties. *Missed.*

The past was closing in on him from all sides.

83

Friday, January 14

FRIDAY MORNING, LAURA made a trip upstairs to the *KEY News* library. The clippings that lined hundreds of yards of shelves were a treasure trove of information.

Years before the arrival of the computer, with its accompanying easy access to thousands of sources of information around the world, *KEY News* librarians had sat at their desks and quietly scanned the pages of newspapers and magazines. They cut out articles of interest and filed them in manila folders, keeping a running historical account of various people and subjects. The electronic age made the librarians' searches less necessary, but the clipping files were still updated.

Laura cruised the stacks until she found the PALISADES AMUSEMENT PARK file. She pulled it from its high shelf and carried it to a desk near the library window.

Bright, clear morning sunlight streamed in, bleaching out the faded, yellowing newspaper articles. Laura turned the clippings carefully until she found the one she was looking for.

A Cliffside Park police officer named Edward Alford was quoted in the story on the disappearance of Tommy Cruz.

Laura xeroxed the clipping, returned it to its pale yellow folder and refiled it in the *P* section on the shelf. She was about to go back to her office when she impulsively stopped two aisles over.

GATES, BILL.

GIFFORD, FRANK.

GIGANTE, VINCENT "THE CHIN."

GILBERT AND SULLIVAN.

Laura flipped through the files. GILPATRIC, GWYNETH.

She stood in the aisle, scanning the stories and pictures. The file had already been updated with newspaper accounts of Gwyneth's death. Laura dug deeper into the file. The last item was a then-dark-haired Gwyneth Gilpatric's high school yearbook picture. The one Laura had used in her obit.

84

Saturday, January 15

LAURA WAS READY for it when the weekend finally came. It had been an intense week and she was glad to have the break. Spending Saturday morning with her delightful Jade was just what the doctor ordered.

As they worked on math problems together, Laura observed her bright little student. *What a good mind she had!* Laura hoped that they would continue their relationship through the years and that she could help to ensure that Jade would develop her full potential.

Now that she would have more money than she ever dreamed of, Laura realized that she could assist Jade with more than her time. As important as her physical and mental input could be to the child, when push came to shove, Jade would need cash if she was going to go all the way with her education. How wonderful to be able to provide that!

Watching Jade concentrate on the arithmetic worksheet, Laura remembered back to the time when she was applying to colleges. She had been so worried that Emmett would not be able to afford anything but a community college. But, to his credit, her father had told her to apply to any university she wanted. They would find the money, he said.

When the acceptance letter arrived from Holy Cross, she had held her breath as she presented it to him, knowing that the tuition and room and board cost more than Emmett earned in a year. So focused was she on her own youthful dream that she pushed from her mind the question of how Emmett was going to manage to pay when her father told her she could go to Holy Cross.

Now Detective Ortiz's questions were forcing her to look at the situation she had been happy to ignore. Though her father denied it, Laura's gut told her that Emmett had been getting the checks from Gwyneth. That would explain why, though he was often out of work, there had always been food on the table and heat in the house. That would explain why she had been able to go to summer camp for a few weeks each summer. That would explain how she had a new coat each winter as she spurted through her adolescent growth in the years after her mother died. That would explain the expensive watch as a college graduation present.

But why? Why would the famous Gwyneth Gilpatric send money to Laura's alcoholic father? What was the connection between them?

Jade proudly presented her completed math assignment for Laura to check.

"One hundred percent right!" Laura exclaimed. "Good job!"

Jade beamed in the glow of her mentor's praise as Laura put her arm around the child's shoulder and hugged her. Laura was growing to love Jade. She suspected that she was getting as much of an emotional payoff from their relationship as Jade was benefitting mentally from their time together. It felt good to help someone, to make some sort of difference in a young person's life.

As they got ready to play African-American *Jeopardy!*, Laura's thoughts turned to her conversation with Joel Malcolm. Though Laura had been completely unaware of it, Gwyneth had arranged for Laura to intern at *Hourglass*. Unknowingly, Laura had been helped by Gwyneth Gilpatric for many years. And Gwyneth Gilpatric had made sure that Laura would be taken care of for the rest of her life.

Why?

85

MAXINE BRONNER WAS practicing Mozart's Sonata No. 1 on the piano when the ringing of the telephone interrupted her. She answered resignedly, expecting another one of those nuisance calls from somebody trying to sell something. Replacement windows, a home security system, another magazine subscription.

She was pleasantly surprised when she heard the caller's voice.

"Laura! How good to hear from you, dear."

"You may not think so when you hear that I want something

again." Laura laughed uneasily. "I'm trying to track down a policeman who worked on the Tommy Cruz case. I've tried information and there is no listing for him. The Cliffside Park police won't give me any information on his whereabouts, either. I was hoping that you might know him. His name is Edward Alford."

Maxine recognized the name immediately. "Yes. I know Eddie Alford. His wife, Dorothy, and I used to play bridge together."

Pay dirt. "Do you have their number?" Laura asked excitedly.

"They moved to Florida a few years ago," Maxine mused, as she pulled the telephone extension cord and crossed the kitchen to her small desk there. Picking up her worn leather address book, she opened to the first page. "Yes. Here it is. Alford." She recited the telephone number. "I don't think Eddie would mind you calling. He's a terrific man."

Laura was uncomfortable about taking further advantage of her relationship with her former teacher, but she asked her next question anyway.

"Do you have the Cruzes' phone number, too?"

86

Sunday, January 16

"MAN! I CAN'T believe this is all yours!" Francheska shook her head in amazement as Laura escorted her through the rooms of Gwyneth's apartment.

"I can't either."

They reached Gwyneth's bedroom. The walls were covered with hand-painted silk; an eighteenth-century French Aubusson was spread on the floor. A high-canopied bed dominated the room, its mahogany posters decorated with intricately carved birds, butterflies and stalks of wheat. Braided pillows festooned the headboard and custom linens beckoned invitingly.

"Are you actually going to sleep in that thing?" asked Francheska.

"Pretty intimidating, isn't it?"

"Actually," said Francheska, plopping herself on the bed, "it could be pretty cool to do it in here. Think Matthew will like it?" she asked with a devilish gleam in her eye.

Laura grabbed one of the pillows from the bed and flung it at her friend.

"You know, Francheska," began Laura, taking a seat in a

tufted armchair beneath yet another window that opened onto Central Park, "this place is huge. There's another bedroom—in fact, three other bedrooms—any one of which could have your name on it."

Francheska stared at her.

"Come on, Francheska. Now that you've finally given the long-overdue dump to the doctor, why don't you come back and be my roommate again? You'd be doing me a favor. I don't want to live in this place all by myself."

"I don't know, Laura," Francheska answered uncertainly. "This place gives me the creeps after what happened here." She pulled nervously at the pillow's braiding.

"Look. I don't know if I'm going to keep this place or not. It's not really my style, but then again, maybe I'll become accustomed to it," said Laura, grinning. "But in the meantime, you need a new place to live and I need some company. The building security is good. We'll be here together. There isn't anything to worry about."

"That's what Gwyneth thought, too."

Laura persevered. "Will you at least think about it?" she implored.

"I will, Laura. And thanks for asking me. You're a real friend."

Later, as they took the elevator down on their way to find somewhere to go for Sunday brunch, Francheska turned to her friend.

"You're going to need help with this place, Laura. Are you going to keep that maid on?"

"I suppose so, but I haven't been able to get Delia on the phone all week."

87

Monday, January 17

THE *HOURGLASS* OFFICES were even tenser than usual on Monday morning. With the broadcast scheduled to air the next evening, everyone on the staff knew that Joel Malcolm was desperate for something new to report on the Gwyneth Gilpatric murder. Laura holed up in her office, trying to stay out of the executive producer's line of vision.

Alone at her desk, she tried to psyche herself up before placing the phone call she knew she had to make. Emmett's harsh words haunted her because she knew there was some truth to them. She wanted to figure out what had happened to Tommy Cruz at least as much to further her professional reputation as to set the poor kid's parents' minds to rest. She wasn't proud of it, but that was the selfish fact of the matter.

Ambition was such a complicated thing. It propelled you forward, making you push and accomplish. But the repercussions were not always positive. Sometimes you could not foresee how others would be affected, for better or worse.

Laura didn't want to hurt anyone, but even if she wanted to turn back now, she couldn't.

A tap on the door signaled Matthew's arrival. The smile on his face disappeared as he caught sight of Laura's.

"Why so glum?" he asked.

"I'm about to call the Cruzes and harangue them for an interview. I hate this." Laura sighed and buried her face in her arms on top of her desk.

"I'll do it if you want," he offered.

Laura looked up, sorely tempted to take him up on it. No, that would be the coward's way out.

"Thanks, Matthew, but I have to do this myself."

88

MARTA CRUZ HUNG the telephone receiver back on the wall and gently eased herself into a chair at the kitchen table.

Would this nightmare never end?

She could tell Laura Walsh had been uncomfortable during their conversation, but not uncomfortable enough to put off their interview.

Laura said she realized how painful it would be for them, but how could she truly know? Only another parent who had lost a child could know their pain. One could learn to live with it, but it never, ever went away.

Rousing herself, Marta went to the refrigerator and pulled

out the peppers to stuff for Felipe's dinner. As she scooped the seeds from the green shells, she wondered what, if anything, was to be gained from talking to Laura Walsh.

Felipe and she had promised one another that, now that they had found Tommy, they would really try to put it all behind them. They must go on with the rest of their lives as best they could. Why bring it all up again, why rip off the thin scab? They needed to heal.

But what if, as Laura had suggested, their recollections could finally help to solve the mystery of what had happened to their son? What if there was some animal out there who could still be hurting children? Didn't she and Felipe have a responsibility to do anything they could to bring a monster like that to justice and keep him from harming another child?

Marta peeled a yellow onion and, as she sliced it, she began to cry. A good excuse for tears.

89

THE BASKETBALL SCORES were being given at the end of the eleven o'clock news and Kitzi couldn't care less. As Kitzi pulled her fur coat from the hallway closet, Missy eagerly scampered to the front door. Kitzi hooked the leather leash to the dog's collar.

As she rode down the elevator, Kitzi wondered how late Joel would be tonight.

His secretary, Claire, had called to say that tomorrow night's broadcast was far from ready and that Joel didn't know when he'd be home.

Kitzi doubted Joel had even bothered telling Claire to call her. The sweet woman had been privy to the way Joel treated his wife. Knowing that her boss was not always considerate, Claire may have taken it upon herself to let Kitzi know that her husband would be quite late.

Missy's short legs trotted across the sparkling lobby. The doorman called out a greeting.

"It's cold and icy out there, Mrs. Malcolm. Be careful, ma'am."

Kitzi nodded and went out into the frosty night.

90

THAT SHOULD DO IT.

Thank God people were creatures of habit. Though Kitzi had lied on national television when she said she always walked the poodle herself. The last three nights she *hadn't* walked her dog. Her killer had the cold and hacking cough to prove it.

Of course, the cigarettes didn't help any.

Waiting in the bitter January night, watching for Kitzi to come out with Missy, the little gray poodle that had sat on her mistress's lap on *Hourglass*. Watching as Kitzi's mink-swathed figure carefully picked its way over the patches of ice on the Fifth Avenue sidewalk and turned down the quiet side street, the poodle straining on the leash.

Crossing over the broad avenue and following the target, gripping the box cutter hidden, smooth and warm, at the bottom of the deep pocket of the camel hair coat. Walking briskly to catch up with the prey.

Kitzi's panicked eyes as she realized what was happening to her.

But now it was done. The eyewitness could give testimony no more.

There was no reason to kill the tiny, fluffy dog.

91

Tuesday, January 18

THE SHRILL RING of the telephone pierced the darkness, awakening Joel from a fitful sleep. He flipped on the lamp on the bedside table. Three A.M. He'd only gotten to bed an hour ago.

There was no sign of Kitzi beside him. But that didn't trip

any warning signals in his mind. His wife had been sleeping in the other room for months. Tonight, when he got home from the Broadcast Center, he had left the firmly closed guest room door unopened. He hadn't wanted to sleep with her, either.

The phone continued its insistent bray.

"Yes."

"Mr. Malcolm, sir. I'm sorry to disturb you," said the overnight doorman nervously.

"Who the hell is this?" Joel asked irritably.

"It's Toby, Mr. Malcolm. Toby, the doorman."

"This better be good, Toby," growled Joel.

"Mr. Malcolm, I think you better come down here, sir. There's been a . . ." the doorman's voice trailed off, as the sound of a small dog's barking drowned out Toby's tentative explanation.

"Speak up, man, what is it?"

"An accident, Mr. Malcolm. There's been an accident. Please come downstairs right away."

92

IT WAS THE talk of *KEY News*.

Kitzi Malcolm's body had been found in an alley around the corner from her Fifth Avenue apartment by a passerby who had responded to the incessant yapping of Kitzi's poodle.

But even more dumbfounding to the news staffers was the word that spread through the Broadcast Center: Joel Malcolm was ensconced in his *Hourglass* office, masterminding tonight's broadcast. Even the most driven of the newshounds were astounded that Joel was at work only hours after his wife had been killed.

Somehow, Joel had had the presence of mind to call the *KEY News* assignment desk and order them to send a camera crew right away. In the *Hourglass* editing rooms, videotape of the crime scene was scrutinized shot by shot. Laura and Matthew were pulled from working on their Palisades Park story to help.

The tape that rolled on the monitor before them was mesmerizing to Laura. Obviously, it was still dark when the crew had arrived, because she recognized that the narrow alleyway was illuminated with the crew's bright, battery-powered lights. A yellow police crime-scene tape cordoned off the area. On the videotape, Laura could hear a voice she recognized barking commands.

"What do you mean, the cameras aren't allowed in there? It's my goddamned wife. I have the right to document this. I demand it."

Obviously the police weren't budging, because next she heard Joel instruct the cameraman to try to zoom in as best he could, down to the back of the alley. Laura watched as the camera shot went in closer.

Police officers and detectives were gathered near a heavy green Dumpster parked deep in the passageway. The camera panned down. There at the bottom edge of the Dumpster, a few feet of bright yellow plastic sheeting protruded, covering Kitzi's body.

Laura heard Joel's voice again.

"They can't keep me from going in there. I'm her husband."

The camera changed focus again, pulling back to follow Joel as he strutted up the alleyway. He went directly toward the waterproof covering and, before the police realized what was happening, he pulled back the sheet.

Laura heard the cameraman utter, "Holy Christ!" even as he zoomed in his lens to capture a shot of Kitzi Malcolm's head.

Laura felt sick to her stomach. "Stop the tape," she whispered to the editor. Kitzi's bloody neck was freeze-framed on the monitor screen.

"That man is an animal!" hissed Matthew, and he patted at his jacket pocket to reassure himself that what he needed was there.

93

LOCKING HER OFFICE door behind her, Laura headed for the telephone and automatically checked her voice mail.

"Laura? It's me, Francheska. I've been thinking about your offer to come live with you, honey. And if the invitation still stands, I accept. I want to be out of here by the end of the month and I could never find my own place by then. Thanks, sweetie. Call me when you can. *Adiós, amiga.*"

Laura punched the numbers of the telephone pad. Finally, some good news.

Francheska picked up on the second ring.

"*Mi casa es su casa, mi amiga.*"

"*Gracias, gracias, gracias,*" her friend said with a laugh. "The time you're spending up in East Harlem is really helping your Spanish, I see."

"Don't laugh. After what's going on around here today, I might get out of this perverse business altogether and go get a teaching job up there."

"Honey, you have so much money now, you can do whatever your little heart desires."

"True enough," Laura admitted. "You won't believe the latest lunacy here." She groaned, describing for Francheska the videotape she had just watched and Joel's role in getting it.

"What a twisted guy. But I know I'll be sure to watch the show tonight."

"That's the problem, Francheska. You'll watch and so will millions of other Americans. The ratings will be through the roof. And the beat goes on."

94

"YOU SHOULDN'T BE alone tonight," Matthew had insisted. "Why don't you come over to my place and we can watch the show together? I'll order in a pizza, we'll drink a few beers and we can commiserate about how we make our sordid living."

Laura agreed with little hesitation.

She stopped at her apartment to shower and change. She felt dirty, tired and scared.

Gwyneth's murder, followed by the murder of Kitzi Malcolm, the eyewitness. Laura's body felt cold beneath the hot shower spray. Thank God Francheska had agreed to come live with her. After all that was happening, she didn't know if she could move into that apartment alone. Her tiny place here in the Oliver Cromwell suddenly seemed so safe, the Pilsners such comforting, if unknowing, neighbors.

She toweled off and pulled on a navy turtleneck, her favorite pair of jeans and a pair of thick white cotton socks. She was too tired to bother with makeup. Matthew would just have to take her or leave her, au natural.

Hailing a cab in front of her building, she instructed the Hispanic driver to take her to Matthew's East Side address. As they drove through Central Park, she noted the driver's name on the taxi license affixed to the back of the front seat.

José Rios. *Joe Rivers,* mused Laura, smiling to herself, as she thought of Jade and their informal Spanish lessons. She was grateful that she had Jade in her life, something outside of her work on which to focus her attention. She needed more balance in her life.

Possibly Matthew could be that balance. If she would only let him.

Matthew had the pizza waiting when she arrived. They ate and drank and laughed, making macabre jokes about Joel and *KEY News* as the time passed until *Hourglass* was scheduled to begin.

Laura looked at her watch. "Where's the remote control? It's about to start."

A devilish expression came to Matthew's good-looking face. "What?"

"Want to be wicked and rebellious?" he tempted.

Laura waited.

"Let's not watch the damned show." His eyes twinkled merrily.

Laura laughed. "Come on. You're kidding, right?"

Matthew paused to consider. "No, I'm not. We've seen everything already. Why put ourselves through it all again? Plus, the idea of daring not to watch Joel's ratings masterpiece appeals to the heretic in me." Matthew walked across the room and took a seat next to Laura on the sofa. "Besides, I can think of a much more worthwhile way to spend our time."

He leaned forward and gently kissed her mouth. Pulling back, he looked into Laura's face and stroked her shining blond hair. "You're even more beautiful without your makeup," he whispered. He pushed back the bangs and kissed the scar on her forehead. "What do you say, Laura? Do we watch the show or not?"

Neither one of them thought about the remote control again that night and, by the time morning came and Matthew held her in his arms, Laura had told him a good deal about her life growing up with Emmett.

95

Wednesday, January 19

A PUSH OFF a rooftop, a pair of scissors to the jugular vein, a box cutter to the neck. How easy it was to find the tools to kill! All one had to do was pay attention and keep one's eyes open. The media was full of great ideas.

Just this morning, the newspaper ran a story about a high school student who was killed after unsuspectingly drinking a glass of Mountain Dew laced with GHB, the "date rape" drug. "Liquid G," as it was called, was a highly addictive chemical compound that depressed the central nervous system. Because GHB could render someone unconscious or unable to remember what happened next, the drug was being used by sexual predators across the country who put it into women's drinks.

The newspaper article reported that GHB, gamma hydroxybutyrate, was colorless, odorless and virtually tasteless. While small quantities of the drug produced a temporary euphoria or hallucinations, larger quantities caused unconsciousness or even respiratory failure and death. The drug could be lethal even in tiny doses, especially if it was poorly prepared. After ingesting her drink laced with Liquid G, the sixteen-year-old girl in the story went into a coma and died.

The drug broke down quickly in the body and was extremely difficult for laboratories to detect.

Perfect.

And finally, thank you very much, the police toxicologist quoted in the newspaper story said that GHB was easily made by people who got the recipe off the Internet.

Hi ho, hi ho. It's off to the Web we go!

Just in case.

96

HE HAD BEEN avoiding the chore of looking through Emmett Walsh's scrapbook, but after last night, he felt he really should get to it. Though he had not voiced his concerns to Laura, he was really worried about the Palisades Park piece. They just didn't have enough good material. Matthew hoped that there would be something in the scrapbook they could use, but he was not counting on it.

He carefully studied the photographs that were pasted onto the heavy black paper pages. There were pictures of the Cyclone taken from every conceivable angle. Laura's dad really must have been in love with that old roller coaster.

Funny, from the little he had observed, Laura seemed so very different from her father. She looked nothing like him, either. She must have taken after her mom.

Matthew continued to flip through the scrapbook pages. Emmett had been a real pack rat, saving matchbook covers, discount coupons, ride tickets and bumper stickers. Maybe the graphics department could work up something with them. Matthew marked the page with a yellow Post-it note.

Toward the end of the scrapbook there were more pictures, several of the Free Act Stage with performers on it. He easily recognized Diana Ross and the Supremes and the Jackson Five.

On the last page was one final picture of the roller coaster with a young man and woman standing arm in arm in front of it. Squinting, Matthew was certain that the dark-haired guy was a youthful Emmett. The female had dark hair as well, long and parted in the middle. If that was Laura's mother, where had Laura gotten the blond hair from?

He'd have to ask her about that. There was so much he wanted to ask Laura.

97

Thursday, January 20

ON HER WAY to work Thursday morning, Laura stopped in the laundry room and tacked a notice on the bulletin board advertising most of the contents of her apartment for sale. Her clothes, her books, her computer and her framed pictures and prints were just about all she planned to take with her when she moved.

She wished she had been able to contact Delia to tell her that she and Francheska were coming on Sunday to move in some of their stuff. But it looked like Delia had taken off. Laura couldn't really blame the maid. After reading what Gwyneth had left Delia, Laura figured she must be pretty disgusted.

Walking briskly down Broadway, Laura stopped and bought a dozen yellow roses from a Korean grocer. A big six dollars. She could afford to splurge. She still could not imagine that she would never have to worry about money again.

But if there wasn't one thing to worry about, there was another. That was just life, she reflected. The deadline for the Palisades Park story was looming and it was still far from completion.

Tommy Cruz's parents still had not gotten back to her about

an interview and she had not wanted to press them. But she had to call them today and get their answer.

She still had not gotten hold of that retired cop in Florida to get his memories of the case.

And the worry that her father may have been somehow involved in what had happened way back then bothered her most of all.

Thank God she had Matthew working with her on this.

98

"COME ON, I'LL take you to lunch. We have something to celebrate!" Laura smiled brightly as she stood in Matthew's office doorway.

He looked up from his desk with pleased surprise. "Let me guess. Our evening together?"

"Sshhh!" Laura advanced into his room. "We don't need the office knowing our business," she whispered.

"I wouldn't mind." He smiled. "In fact, I'm pretty darn proud of it. Besides, sooner or later, everyone knows everything about everybody around here."

"Well, let's just keep this to ourselves for as long as we can, okay?" Laura touched the sleeve of Matthew's shirt, feeling his strong shoulder beneath.

"Okay, if that's the way you want it," he agreed, forcing

himself not to pull her down into his arms. "But if it's not us you want to celebrate, what is it?"

"I heard from the Cruzes," Laura answered excitedly. "They've agreed to the interview! It's all set for Monday morning."

99

MIKE SCHULTZ ORDERED a cheeseburger and an extra-large order of fries from the Station Break grill. *Screw the doctor's orders.*

He paid for his lunch and searched the crowded cafeteria for an empty table, spying one in the corner. Usually he brought his lunch upstairs and scarfed it down at his desk, amid at least a half dozen interruptions. But not today. Today he needed to sit quietly and relax for twenty minutes.

It was not going well at home. He was worried about Nancy. She was so negative and down all the time, and it was getting to him.

Yeah, they had some financial problems. But nothing they couldn't work out eventually. They had three great kids. They were all healthy. That was all that really mattered, wasn't it?

He was losing patience with his wife. When he came home after a stressful day at the Bulletin Center, he wanted their home to be his refuge. Instead, he would find Nancy complaining about her day and all she had to do but had not accomplished. He wanted to shake her.

Why was she so unhappy?

He had a few comp days coming to him. Maybe he could book a flight to Florida and they could get away together for a long weekend. Just the two of them.

He knew that Nancy would say they couldn't leave the kids. So he would have to arrange that, too. He would call the mothers of each child's playmates and ask if they would take one of them for a couple of days. The Schultzes could reciprocate later.

Yeah, a few days relaxing in the sun might do their marriage a lot of good.

Mike munched on his cheeseburger, making plans, and did not notice as Laura and Matthew approached from across the busy lunchroom.

"Hi, Mike," Laura greeted him. "Mind if we join you?"

Mike gestured with his large hand to the seats across from his. "Please do."

As Laura and Matthew slid their trays onto the table, Mike laughed. "You guys must be going berserk up there with all that's happening."

His lunch companions groaned in unison.

"How's Joel holding up?" asked Mike, dumping a cluster of french fries into ketchup and popping them into his mouth.

"Pretty damn well, for a guy whose wife was just murdered," answered Matthew grimly. "You know how it is, Mike, the show must go on." Matthew shook his head in disgust.

"Yeah, what's going on with that anyway? Anything new on Kitzi's murder?" Mike asked.

"Nothing that I know of." Laura opened a packet of mustard. "But you can bet Joel will pull out something before next week's *Hourglass*."

Mike sighed heavily. "Man, as much as I detested the way Malcolm treated me, it was a blessing in disguise that I got fired from that show. Gwyneth and Joel did me a favor."

"You never did tell me what happened there, Mike," urged Laura. "And I didn't want to ask you."

Mike nodded toward Matthew. "He can tell you, can't you, Matt?" Not waiting for Matthew's response, he added, "It was all pretty sickening." Mike rose with his plastic cafeteria tray. "I've got to get back upstairs."

100

Friday, January 21

RETIRED POLICE OFFICER Ed Alford was unpacking the clothes from his suitcase when the telephone rang in his Ocean Ridge, Florida, condominium.

"Hello?"

"Hello, Mr. Alford?"

"Speaking."

"Mr. Alford, my name is Laura Walsh. I'm a producer at *KEY News*. And I'm working on a story that I'm hoping you can help me with."

Alford looked out the bedroom window at his prized view of the Intercoastal Waterway. "What's the story?" he asked brusquely. He wasn't going to commit to anything until he heard what she wanted.

"It's a story on the disappearance of Tommy Cruz. After thirty years, his body was recently found."

"Yeah. I heard."

"I understand you worked on that case?" Laura led.

"That's right."

"Well, we'd like to interview you for *Hourglass* about that time. Your impressions, memories, that sort of thing."

Alford twisted the phone cord. "I don't know," he began uncertainly. "What are the Cliffside Park police saying?"

"Not much," Laura said truthfully. "They say they don't want to comment on an ongoing investigation."

"That makes sense, doesn't it, Miss Walsh?"

Laura ignored Alford's question. "We'd be asking you about what happened back then. What the police thought at the time."

"I could only speak for myself. I could only say what I thought."

"That would be fine," Laura answered hopefully. "What *did* you think then?"

"Obviously we couldn't prove it at the time. But after many interviews with his parents, neighbors and teachers, I knew that boy was no runaway—my gut told me that Tommy Cruz died at Palisades Park. I was sure of it."

"Would you be willing to say that in front of a camera?"

Alford paused to consider. *Why not? That wouldn't hurt the present investigation any.*

"You'd have to interview me down here. My wife and I just

got back from up there, visiting my son and daughter-in-law and the grandkids on Long Island."

So that's why she hadn't been able to get hold of him all these days, she thought. Too bad she hadn't known he was up north.

"Fine, Mr. Alford. We'll come to you."

101

NANCY SCHULTZ STIRRED the Campbell's chicken noodle soup in the pot on the stove and thought she would go out of her mind.

Brian was home again from school with a cold. Last week it had been Aaron. And if experience was any guide, next week Lauren would get it.

She loved her kids. Of course she did. But being cooped up in the house all day was really getting to her.

Nancy looked out the kitchen window at the winter grayness outside. Maybe she should agree to Mike's suggestion and take the trip to Florida. He was right. Mike needed a break from the stress at work. And she needed a break from mommying.

As if on cue, Brian called plaintively from the family room where he lay snuggled under a comforter watching television.

"I'll be right there, sweetheart," she answered with a sigh.

She arranged the bowl of soup, a paper napkin and a spoon on a tray and carried it to her son.

"I'm bored, Mom," Brian complained, his six-year-old voice thick with congestion.

"Eat your soup, honey. It will make you feel better."

"I want to *do* something. Something fun," he insisted.

Great. Now she had to play another endless game. Her mind was atrophying from disuse.

"Tell you what," said Nancy resignedly, as she went to the toy cupboard. "You finish all your soup and then I'll play the Casper the Friendly Ghost game with you."

It was Brian's favorite.

102

Saturday, January 22

JADE'S MOM HAD called to ask if Laura could reschedule their tutoring session for Saturday afternoon, rather than in the morning. Laura agreed, putting the time to good use, getting boxes at the grocery store and packing up her books and pictures before she left to go uptown.

Jade had gone to a birthday party and was wired after two hours of sugar. She couldn't concentrate on her math problems, so Laura switched to African-American *Jeopardy!*

"When he was young he was teased because his mother wasn't married when he was born. In 1971, he organized Operation PUSH, an organization that fights for equality for all. He has tried to win the Democratic nomination for president of the United States, but you may know him for his Rainbow Coalition."

"Who is *Jesse Jackson!*" yelled Jade.

"Ssshh, Jade. You don't have to shout. But you're right."

"Another one, Laura. Let's do another one." Jade was obviously enjoying herself.

"Okay," agreed Laura, flipping through her cards. "Here's one. He started his baseball career in the Negro Leagues, at the time when black players were not allowed to play with whites. But he ended up playing for the New York Giants and the New York Mets. He got to be known as the 'Say, Hey Kid.' "

Jade frowned. She did not know the answer.

"Who is *Willie Mays?*" Laura supplied the question.

Jade became uncharacteristically sullen.

Laura checked her watch. Still more than an hour until Myra came to pick Jade up. She could see that they weren't going to get anywhere today with schoolwork.

"Hey, want to go on a field trip?" Laura suggested.

Jade perked up. "What sort of field trip?"

Laura thought fast. "How about we take a walk around your neighborhood and you can give me a tour?"

"You mean I'll be a tour guide?" asked Jade with some excitement.

"Yep. Want to?"

They donned their parkas, scarves and gloves and Jade led

the way from the East Harlem Tutorial building to the dingy block outside. Remnants of snow at the sidewalk's edge were crusted with black soot. Litter was strewn carelessly on the path before them. A police car rushed by, siren blaring.

Some tour.

They walked west on 106th Street, Jade reciting who she knew that lived in some of the tired apartment buildings and flaking brownstones. A mangy-looking mixed-breed dog wandered alone and without a collar. Laura steered Jade to the other side of the street.

As they neared Lexington Avenue, Laura thought they should turn back.

"Let's just go to Central Park," urged Jade. "Then we can turn around."

They walked along the next block, Laura feeling relieved that the neighborhood was noticeably better. Before they reached Park Avenue, they came to a big red-brick church crowned with three giant arches. ST. CECILIA'S, announced one of the signs out front. PARROQUIA STA. CECILIA, trumpeted another. Laura read the two sentences—one in English, the other in Spanish—inscribed below the cross on the signs: HOW GOOD GOD HAS BEEN! and ¡QUE BUENO HA SIDO DIOS!

"Want to go inside?" Jade offered. "Mom and me go here sometimes."

"Mom and I," Laura corrected instinctively, as they pulled open the heavy front door, passing by a homeless man muttering to himself as he sat beneath one of the arches.

Just about a dozen people sat scattered through the pews. Though she was ashamed at how long it had been since she had attended Mass, Laura recognized immediately that the priest at the altar was well into the celebration of the Eucharist. Moving quietly up the aisle, Jade and Laura easily found an empty pew and knelt along with the other worshippers.

Laura felt soothed listening to the congregation make their rhythmic responses as the priest snapped the large white wafer into bite-sized pieces.

"*Cordero de Dios, que quitas el pecado del mundo, ten piedad de nosotros.*"

"*Cordero de Dios, que quitas el pecado del mundo, ten piedad de nosotros.*"

"*Cordero de Dios, que quitas el pecado del mundo, danos la paz.*"

Laura felt satisfied as she mentally translated the Spanish words.

"Lamb of God, you take away the sins of the world, grant us peace."

"*Cordero de Dios.*"

103

A MOVIE AND a good Italian dinner. To Laura, it was a perfect Saturday night date. If it was with the right person.

"Let me help you move your stuff in tomorrow," Matthew urged as they lingered over espresso.

Laura agreed readily, more for the opportunity just to be

with him than for the physical assistance. "We better watch out, though," she said with a laugh, "or we're going to get sick of one another."

"Not on my end, I won't. You're good for me, Laura." Matthew gazed at her lovely face framed with the soft golden hair that glowed by the light of the candle in the center of the table. He was well aware of the fact that he hadn't taken a Valium all day. Breezily, he handed the waiter his American Express card.

"Ready?"

"Um-hmm."

The night was unseasonably warm for late January and they strolled, hand in hand, past glittering Lincoln Center, the Marc Chagall murals adorning the Metropolitan Opera House. How lucky they were to have all this around them!

Impulsively, Laura turned to Matthew. "Want to see my new apartment?"

His contented face spread into a wide smile. "I'm dying to."

They held hands as they strolled out of the park and made their way to Laura's elegant new address.

Matthew whistled softly through his teeth as they got off the elevator and walked directly into the large foyer. A chandelier with a hundred gleaming crystal prisms lit their way to the living room.

Illuminated by the beautiful wall sconces and porcelain lamps all carefully set on timers, the rich red and blue hues of the sweeping Persian carpet covered most of the parquet floor. A carved red Oriental screen dominated one wall, a Matisse cutout hung on another. Plush furniture was expertly arranged throughout the room.

"Jesus," Matthew whispered. "The night of the party, it was

so crowded in here, I really didn't get a chance to take this all in."

"Unbelievable, isn't it?" asked Laura. "And so not-me."

"Maybe you'll get used to it?" Matthew offered.

"I don't know." Laura shrugged uncertainly. "But I do know one thing I wouldn't change."

She took his hand and led him to the windows and, together, they gazed at the jeweled skyline.

It was the first night Laura spent in her new home. She wasn't afraid at all.

104

Sunday, January 23

WHEN FRANCHESKA ARRIVED early Sunday afternoon, Laura and Matthew had already made two trips back and forth from Laura's old apartment. They were unpacking books onto the library shelves when the doorman announced that Miss Lamb was coming up.

As Laura introduced her best friend to Matthew, he studied Francheska's face with puzzlement.

"You look familiar," he said slowly. "Have we met some-where?"

"I don't think so." Francheska smiled. "I think that I would remember you. It's so nice to meet you, Matthew. Laura has told me a lot about you."

Matthew suddenly realized that Francheska was struggling under a heavy load, so he took the video monitor from Francheska's arms. "Here, I'm sorry, let me take that for you. Where do you want it?"

"All our computer stuff is going into the library," called Laura as Matthew went down the hallway.

"He's cute," Francheska whispered when Matthew was out of earshot. "How's it going between you two?"

"So well, I can't believe it."

They heard Matthew's footsteps approaching.

"Well, I've got to go," said Francheska, heading to the door. "I'm going to leave you two alone." She winked at Laura.

"Don't be ridiculous, Francheska. Stay," urged Laura. Matthew seconded it earnestly.

"No, really, I have things to do. It was great meeting you, Matthew. Talk to you later, Laura." And she was gone.

They went back to the library to finish unpacking. "I know her face from somewhere. Francheska Lamb," he mused, coming up empty.

"She used to model," Laura suggested. "Maybe you saw her in some ad or something."

"Yeah, maybe that's it."

105

TAKING ADVANTAGE OF the unusually warm January afternoon, Roger Chiocchi decided to take his six-year-old daughter Catherine to Central Park for a little exercise. As they left the apartment, he grabbed a Frisbee from Catherine's toy box.

Catherine was such a serious little soul, he reflected, as he held her small hand tightly in his. She needed to get out and run around more, laugh and play outside like he did when he was kid. Of course, he hadn't grown up in the city.

They crossed Central Park West and entered the park at Women's Gate, the 72nd Street entrance. Many other parents had the same idea he'd had. The park was crowded with families, Parego strollers and leashed dogs.

"Let's go see if we can find an empty spot where we can throw our Frisbee," Roger encouraged. The little girl followed along gamely. They finally reached an open place where the ground looked reasonably dry.

Roger demonstrated for his daughter the flick of the wrist that would make the plastic disc fly through the air. But Catherine

was better at running after the Frisbee than throwing it. Undaunted, he kept trying until, gradually, Catherine started to get the hang of it.

"Okay, sweetheart," called Roger as he backed up several yards. "I'll throw it to you and see if you can catch it."

He sailed the Frisbee toward his daughter and would forever curse himself for misjudging and flinging it too hard. The yellow disc sailed over Catherine's head and flew deep into a thick bramble.

"I'll get it, Daddy," called Catherine eagerly as she ran to find the downed Frisbee.

"Wait, honey. Let me get it. There are thorns in those bushes."

But the child ignored her father's command. Reaching the bushes before him, she got down on her knees to search for her toy.

Roger would never forget his child's scream as she found a booted human foot.

106

HER APARTMENT WAS quiet and still. But as Francheska entered, she noticed uneasily that the hallway closet was ajar. She could have sworn she had closed it after she took out her coat when she left to go to Laura's.

She switched on the lamps in the living room. Everything was as she had left it.

Francheska went to the refrigerator and poured herself a glass of orange juice. Stopping by the bar to lace the drink with a little vodka, she headed for the bedroom.

The closet doors were open there, too.

Leonard had been here.

Her heart pounded. She hadn't heard from him since she announced she was leaving, nor had she called him. She didn't want to see him, didn't want to lose her resolve.

She wondered if he had noticed that some of her clothes were missing. If he had, he must have been surprised, because she knew he didn't think that she was really going through with it. But she was, she thought with satisfaction. She was finally doing it and she was proud of herself.

The front buzzer rang. She didn't answer, but walked back into the living room and waited.

She heard the key enter the lock, watched as the doorknob twisted, and waited to speak as the door slowly opened.

"Hello, Len."

He was caught unawares, a startled expression on his face.

"Where have you been? I've been looking for you."

Francheska pulled a cigarette out from the pack she had left on the table, lit it and exhaled slowly. "I don't have to tell you where I go or what I do anymore, Len."

"Oh, baby, put out that cigarette. You know it's not good for you or for those great looks of yours. Come on, now. Haven't we gone far enough with all this?"

As he approached her, Francheska smugly noticed that Leonard's hand was shaking. Good, he was upset. She was glad that he was hurting, too.

She took another draw on her cigarette. "If you really want to know, I started moving into my new apartment today."

Leonard's eyes widened, but then he caught himself and laughed meanly. "Sure, Francheska. And where are you getting the money to pay for this new place?"

"I'm moving in with Laura. Moving into Gwyneth Gilpatric's apartment. And as you know, Gwyneth's place makes this one look like a dump."

Leonard's rugged face darkened with rage. He moved toward her, spitting his words. "No one treats me like this and gets away with it, Francheska. No one, especially not you. You are mine. You are going to regret this. I swear you will."

Francheska watched as a vein at Leonard's temple pulsated, and she listened to his angry voice as he delivered his final vicious blow.

"Go ahead, Francheska. Go ahead and try it out there. But you'll come crawling back, I know you will. Because you'll always be someone's 'other' woman. You're not the type that men want to marry. And guess what, sweetheart? You won't always be so beautiful. I know what you're going to look like in ten or twelve years. I can tell from your bone structure. I've seen it dozens of times. Your face will fall," he hissed. "In fact, I've already noticed that pretty neck of yours getting thicker."

Leonard turned and left the apartment, slamming the door callously behind him, leaving Francheska curled up and weeping on the red sofa.

107

Monday, January 24

MATTHEW HAD OTHER *Hourglass* business to attend to and Laura was glad to be interviewing Felipe and Marta Cruz by herself. She wanted to do this on her own, not have Matthew thinking he had to babysit her all the time.

It wasn't that she didn't appreciate the care and attentiveness he was showing her at work. She did. But if their relationship was to be one of equals, she had to earn his respect by holding her own as a competent professional.

Another reason she was glad that Matthew was not coming along on the interview was that she wanted the opportunity to stop afterward and speak to her father in person.

She would have the camera crew drop her off and she could take public transportation back into the city later.

Felipe Cruz greeted them politely at his front door and invited them into his home. Marta Cruz was waiting solemnly in the modest but immaculate living room.

How hard this must be for them, thought Laura as the crew unpacked and set up the gear. She admired their quiet courage as the couple waited patiently to begin.

"Thank you so much for talking with us, Mr. and Mrs. Cruz."

"We hope this will do some good, Laura," answered Felipe softly.

"First of all," began Laura, "I've spoken with a police officer who worked on the case at the time of Tommy's disappearance. Edward Alford. Do you remember him?"

The couple nodded earnestly. "Of course we remember Officer Alford," answered Marta. "He was very kind to us. I know he worked hard to find Tommy for a very long time. Even when, over the years, there was no word on our Tommy and it seemed everyone else had forgotten, Officer Alford would call us from time to time. He wanted to check and see how we were."

God, what these people had been through! Laura tried to show no emotion as she continued.

"Officer Alford told me that he never believed that Tommy was a runaway. That yours was such a loving family and that you were such devoted parents that he just didn't buy the theory that Tommy had run away from home."

Felipe nodded gravely. "It hurt when everyone was saying that Tommy might have run away. We knew our son. He was a good boy. He would never run away from us." Felipe looked over at his wife and, seeing the tears welling up in her brown eyes, took her hand.

"It was Officer Alford's theory that something happened to Tommy in the amusement park," stated Laura.

"We know," whispered Marta. "He told us that's what he thought."

"What do you think?" pressed Laura.

"We don't know what to think," answered Felipe, anguish in his voice. "And what does it really matter? Our boy is dead. This we know now for sure."

Laura stared at her notebook and tried to compose herself. She wanted to wrap up the interview and not cause these poor people any more pain. But she knew, for the good of the piece, she had to ask a few more questions.

"Do you know how the investigation is going now? Have the police told you that they have any new leads?"

Felipe and Marta looked at one another.

"The police tell us not to talk about anything new while they continue their investigation," answered Mr. Cruz.

Marta dropped her husband's hand. "Felipe, the police have not solved this case in thirty years. What makes you think that they are going to solve it now?"

She rose and walked to the well-polished maple hutch that hugged the wall. Pulling open a small drawer, she took something from it.

"Marta!" her husband warned.

"I am sorry, Felipe. In over forty years of marriage I have never disobeyed you," she said resolutely. "But if I can help find the person who hurt our Tommy, I must do it. I owe it to the other parents."

She handed Laura the glossy paper.

"It is a picture of a necklace they found with Tommy's body. The police say they think it might have fallen from the neck of someone as they buried him. I begged the police for this picture. I want to have anything that is part of what happened to my Tommy."

Laura studied the picture of the cross and chain. It was quite unique. Her chest tightened as she realized that she had seen one like it before.

108

THOUGH KITZI MALCOLM'S murder near her Fifth Avenue apartment was under the jurisdiction of another precinct, Alberto Ortiz had been sharing information with the East Side homicide squad, and they with him.

Delia Beehan's murder, committed just a few blocks from the Gilpatric apartment, was being handled by the Central Park precinct.

A crumpled credit card receipt bearing her signature was found in the pocket of Delia's frayed winter coat, along with a set of keys that Ortiz was certain would open Gwyneth Gilpatric's apartment.

Though Ortiz's recognition of Delia's body was certain enough, they were looking for her next of kin to make the positive ID. So far, they were coming up empty.

Ortiz flipped through his notepad until he found the information he was looking for. He picked up the phone and called *KEY News*.

109

THE INTERVIEW CONCLUDED, the crew loaded their gear into the trunk of the car parked in front of the Cruzes' house and Laura pulled out her cell phone.

There was no answer at Emmett's.

Next, she checked her voice mail.

"Miss Walsh? Detective Alberto Ortiz. Will you call me, please? It's urgent." He left his number.

Dreading what she would hear, she stood in the cold wind and forced herself to call him back, her face darkening as she listened to the detective's matter-of-fact words.

"I'll be there in about an hour," she answered, closing her cell phone and slipping it into her pocket.

"Where to next, Laura?" asked the cameraman as they got into the car.

"Back to the Broadcast Center," said Laura grimly. "But I have someplace I want you to drop me off on the way."

110

IT WAS MIDAFTERNOON before Laura, pale and exhausted, returned to the Broadcast Center. She headed straight to Matthew's office.

"Hey, stranger!" He smiled welcomingly. "Where have you been?" His pleasant expression turned to one of deep concern as he assessed her. "What's wrong? What happened?"

She sank into a chair and slowly unbuttoned her coat. "I was just at the morgue."

"What?"

"I just identified Gwyneth's maid. Delia Beehan. She was found dead yesterday in Central Park."

"God, Laura, that must have been awful for you." Matthew took her cold hands in his and rubbed them gently. "I'm so sorry, sweetheart." He lifted her trembling hands and held them to his lips.

She had been holding back the tears the whole cab ride back from the morgue, but now, with the tenderness of Matthew's touch, they began to flow. He took her in his arms and held her as she sobbed, whispering that everything was going to be all right.

"Look at it this way," he said, trying to joke her out of her despair. "Now Joel has his lead for tomorrow night's show."

111

"Why don't you just quit that damned job?" Francheska demanded. "It's just too stressful and you don't need it with all that's been happening. God knows, Laura, you certainly don't need the paycheck."

Francheska had arrived early, pulling a large wheeled suitcase containing more of her possessions. She found Laura in the kitchen, staring morosely into her morning coffee.

"Oh, Francheska, quitting my job isn't the answer. That wouldn't solve anything," she said with resignation. "Three women, all connected in some way to me, have been murdered."

"All connected to *Gwyneth Gilpatric*," Francheska corrected. "I'm telling you, Laura, get out of that crazy TV world. It's not healthy."

"I've got to get to work," declared Laura firmly, wanting to end their conversation. She rose with her cup and dumped the rest of the lukewarm coffee into the sink. "And what are *you* going to do today?" she asked sarcastically.

That was cruel. Laura regretted her words and her tone as soon as she asked the question. Francheska was struggling with leaving Leonard. There was nothing to be gained by reminding Francheska of her aimlessness.

But if Francheska was hurt, she didn't show it.

"I'm going to bring more of my stuff over. I should be sleeping here by next week, as soon as I get back from visiting my parents."

"Good," pronounced Laura, giving her friend a hug. "I can't wait. It's going to be great being together again."

As she walked from the kitchen, she turned. "And don't forget. You promised that you'd come with me to the Palisades Park fund-raiser tomorrow night."

Francheska groaned with exaggeration. "Do I *have* to? My flight to San Juan is the next morning."

Laura smiled, the first since yesterday. "Yes. You *have* to. I told Emmett you were coming. He's so proud that his mini-park is the centerpiece of the fund-raiser. You can't disappoint him."

112

WHEN RICKY POTENZA showed his mother the ad in the newspaper for the Palisades Park Museum fund-raiser, she had been flabbergasted when he said that he wanted to attend.

He had been very quiet since they had gone to *KEY News* for Ricky's interview, though that was not unusual. Rose admitted to herself that she had been hoping for some sort of breakthrough, but once again, it was not to be.

What surprised her now was Ricky's insistence that he wanted to go to the fund-raiser. Was that a good sign? Was Ricky, on some level, trying to come to terms with his childhood—a childhood made up of many hours spent at the amusement park?

It was worth a try. She could manage to pay for the tickets with the money she had been carefully putting aside each month. If it would help her son, who seldom showed enthusiasm for anything, she would gladly forgo the bus trip to the Poconos with her church group she had been saving for. Anything to help Ricky.

Please, God, let him get well.

But even as she prayed, Rose prepared herself for the cold reality that her prayers would most likely remain unanswered.

113

DELIA BEEHAN'S DEATH would lead on *Hourglass* tonight and Laura wanted to have nothing to do with the production. With the Palisades Park story set to air in just one week, Laura had her excuse.

She headed for the library and the clipping files.

Pulling Gwyneth's folder from the shelf, Laura rummaged to the back of it until she found what she was searching for.

Gwyneth Gilpatric's high school yearbook picture.

Squinting, she studied the necklace that hung from Gwyneth's young neck. The distinctive marcasite cross was the same as the one that Marta Cruz had shown her.

What does it mean? she asked herself. Gwyneth Gilpatric couldn't have buried Tommy Cruz. That was impossible to believe. She tried to push the thought from her reeling mind.

But she couldn't.

It would be impossible to believe, except for Emmett. Gwyneth's relationship with her father, signaled by the checks she wrote out to him, tied Gwyneth to her father and his beloved Palisades Park. And if Gwyneth was somehow connected to Tommy Cruz's disappearance, that could mean that Emmett was, as well.

Had Gwyneth been sending her father money to keep his mouth shut?

Laura turned the newspaper clippings carefully, not sure what she was looking for. She studied a picture of Gwyneth receiving a journalism award, showing a confident professional at the top of her chosen career.

This was not a woman who would be involved in a murder.

She was about to close the file when she came to a story about Gwyneth attending the funeral of the source for one of her *Hourglass* stories. Because she hadn't thought it important enough in the whole scheme of Gwyneth's biography, it was a story that Laura had just glanced at as she researched for her obit. Now she realized that this was the story that Mike Schultz had lost his job over.

Laura read with fascination, now, the description of the funeral for Jaime Cordero, the young Hispanic man who had bravely come forward to expose the drug dealing in his East Harlem neighborhood and who had been brutally and grossly murdered for his reward.

The picture showed Gwyneth Gilpatric with arms outstretched toward Jaime Cordero's weeping mother. Holding Mrs. Cordero's right arm was a younger woman, her head bowed and a black-leather-gloved hand held up to her face; though partially hidden, just enough of the young woman's face presented itself to the camera's unflinching gaze.

Laura's eyes focused on the figure at the side of the photo. She read the caption beneath the picture, again and again.

> KEY News *correspondent Gwyneth Gilpatric comforts Juanita Cordero, the mother of slain East Harlem hero Jaime Cordero. Mrs. Cordero's daughter, Francita Cordero, at left, supports her mother.*

Francita Cordero.
Cordero de Dios.
Lamb of God.
Francheska Lamb!

114

"I KNEW I had seen her somewhere before!" exclaimed Matthew as Laura showed him the newspaper article from the clippings file she had smuggled out of the library. "It was at the Cordero funeral!"

Laura shook her head in amazement as she stared at Francheska's grainy face. "I don't understand. Why didn't she ever tell me? I thought we were so close. . . ." Her voice trailed off in disappointment.

Matthew remained silent. This was for Laura and her friend to work out.

"Hey. I firmed up the interview plans with Officer Alford today," Matthew offered, trying to distract her. "I'll fly down on Friday."

They had agreed that Matthew would go to Florida to do the interview while Laura would remain in New York to oversee things as their deadline drew near.

"Great," she said glumly as she remembered the other thing she had found in the clippings file.

She told him of the necklace found with Tommy's body and showed him the high school picture of Gwyneth.

"They match."

Matthew whistled softly through his teeth. "You buried the lead!"

He studied Gwyneth's picture intensely. Then he pulled the red scrapbook from his cluttered bookshelf. Opening the album from the back, he squinted at the picture of Emmett Walsh and his girl standing arm in arm in front of the Cyclone. The girl with the long dark hair, parted in the middle.

Another match!

115

EASY ENOUGH.

The small cardboard shipping carton was wrapped in brown paper when it arrived in the afternoon mail. No one could guess its contents.

It was shipped by first-class postage. There was no need to sign for the package.

The contents: a sealed, tamper-proof plastic container, a measuring spoon and instructions. There was a warning:

> GHB can be dangerous when used improperly or when mixed with other depressants. Combining a normal dose of GHB with alcohol can trigger an overdose reaction of unrousable sleep. GHB has been attributed to deaths in the U.S.

But mixing GHB with alcohol was not necessary for the result to be lethal. The teenager in the newspaper article had just been drinking Mountain Dew.

All the dosage information was printed in the instructions. Exactly how much of the powder to measure out. Just like following a cookbook recipe, just like baking a cake.

A recipe for death.

116

FRANCHESKA WAS SURPRISED to open her apartment door and find Laura standing in the hallway.

"Hey, girlfriend." She smiled welcomingly. "Come on in."

Laura walked through the doorway, a solemn expression on her face. Without taking off her coat, she got right to the point.

"Why didn't you tell me, *Francita*?" she implored. "Why didn't you tell me about your brother?"

Francheska's face went ashen. She turned and walked into the kitchen, leaving Laura to follow her.

"Want a drink?" she asked, dropping ice cubes into a glass.

"No. I do not want a drink. I want to know why you didn't tell me. I thought we told each other everything. And this—this is so . . ."—Laura searched for the word—"*huge*! You lost your brother, Francheska, in a most violent, horrible way. I just can't understand why you never confided in me about it."

"Some things are just too painful to talk about, Laura," she said softly.

"Even to me, Francheska?"

"To anybody."

"But I'm not anybody. I'm your best friend."

"I'm sorry, Laura. I just wanted to put Jaime's death behind me. Sometimes Leonard would catch me crying in bed and ask me what's the matter. But this was something I just couldn't share. Can't you understand that?"

Laura stood in silence. Yes, she could understand that. While she didn't know what it was like to lose a brother, she remembered all too well what it had been like to lose a mother. It was still hard to discuss. However, she had talked to Francheska about it several times. It hurt to think that Francheska wasn't able to share her own painful loss.

"And changing your name? What was *that* all about?"

Francheska shrugged. "My parents were moving back to Puerto Rico, wanting to get away from what had happened here. God only knew if those drug animals were going to come after the rest of us for what Jaime did. I was trying to start a modeling career. 'Francheska Lamb' sounded better to me than 'Francita Cordero.' I wanted to make a fresh start with a new name. It's no crime. People do it all the time."

117

Wednesday, January 26

AS SHE ARRIVED at *Hourglass,* Laura ran right into Joel Malcolm.

"Have you seen the overnights for the show last night?" he enthused. "They are through the roof!"

"Congratulations." She smiled weakly.

"Puts the pressure on you, kiddo. That piece of yours better be great next week to kick off sweeps. I'm depending on it. Don't disappoint me."

Laura watched Joel's back as he turned and strutted down the hallway. How would he feel if it turned out that Gwyneth was responsible for Tommy Cruz's death?

Probably not that badly, she decided. Because the broadcast of that sorry story could make ratings history.

118

LAURA WORE THE same blue velvet dress she had worn to Gwyneth's New Year's Eve party as she stood in the entryway of the Palisadium, the restaurant chosen as the spot for the fund-raiser for the museum to honor the amusement park that had once stood nearby. Built atop the cliffs of the Hudson, the restaurant's glass walls offered a twinkling, breathtaking view of Manhattan on the other side of the river.

From what Laura could see, the fund-raiser was going to be a big success. The restaurant was already packed, with a steady stream of people still arriving, a few of whom she recognized. Joel Malcolm had schlepped out from the city. Maxine Bronner and her husband, Alan, were there. Even Ricky Potenza and his mother had come.

Emmett's miniature amusement park was displayed prominently at the middle of the dining room. Her father stood beside it proudly, beaming in the praise of the partygoers as they pointed out the rides and attractions they remembered so vividly.

How sweet this night was for Emmett! How bitter it would be later, when she confronted him about what she now more than suspected.

Laura felt a tap on her shoulder and turned to see Mike Schultz.

"What are you doing here?" she asked in surprise.

"I dragged Nancy out. She didn't want to come, but I forced her. We've got to get out more and have a little fun. Both of us used to go to Palisades when we were kids and I thought, why not come to this?"

"Where's Nancy?"

"In the ladies' room."

"Well, tell her I'll catch up with her later," said Laura. "I have to get some work done. Matthew is already in there rounding up interviews and I should be helping him."

Laura and Matthew canvassed the party with their camera crew, eliciting memories and stories from the happy attendees.

"We're getting some great stuff," yelled Matthew above the din of rock-and-roll oldies and Palisades Park songs that blared from the sound system.

"Thank God," called Laura.

As they continued through the crowd, Laura spied Francheska talking to some man at the bar. She groaned inwardly as she recognized him.

What the hell was Leonard Costello doing here?

119

IT WASN'T WORKING.

When he called her this afternoon, she had seemed happy to tell him that she was going out tonight. Proud to say that she was going to a fund-raiser with Laura Walsh and her television crew. Getting on with her life, she called it. A life that would be interesting and just fine without him.

Getting a ticket at the last minute, Leonard had hoped that by his coming to the party, Francheska would see how much he cared about her, and that he could talk her into staying with him. But she wasn't having any of it. Francheska was excited about the prospects of living in luxury with her best friend, was glad to be making a new start.

Looking over Francheska's shoulder, Leonard saw Laura, with microphone in hand, listening intently as some heavy, balding guy went on and on about the silly amusement park.

Silently, Leonard cursed Laura Walsh. If not for her, Francheska would be staying with him, right where she belonged.

120

A COKE WAS ordered from the bartender and carried to a corner of the crowded room. As dancers gyrated to the pulsating sixties music, no one noticed as the white, slightly lumpy powder was poured into the dark drink.

A harried waiter was asked to deliver the soda to the blond woman in the blue dress. The one who was working so hard with the camera crew.

121

LAURA FELT A tug on her sleeve.

"I'm going home now," Francheska called in Laura's ear. "My flight is early and I haven't even packed yet."

"I can't leave. We haven't finished shooting."

"That's all right. I have a ride."

Laura shot her friend a disgusted look. "Please don't tell me you're going back with the doctor. I saw you two with your heads together over at the bar."

"No, don't worry, honey," Francheska said triumphantly. "I told Leonard to take a hike. But I met your boss. Joel is giving me a ride back to the city."

Laura groaned. "Francheska, he's a leech, too. Watch out, will you?"

"Don't worry. I'm a big girl. I can take care of myself."

122

THE COLA TASTED a bit salty, but Laura had swallowed it down thirstily. Fifteen minutes later she began to feel slightly nauseous.

They were almost finished, just another interview or two, so they would have lots of material to choose from when they edited.

As she got the spelling of the name of another interview subject, the room began to spin dizzyingly. She reached out to grab hold of Matthew's arm as she fell to the floor.

123

Thursday, January 27

EMMETT SAT IN the emergency room waiting area at the Palisades Medical Center and prayed.

Please, God. Please, don't take Laura from me, too.

Though why God should answer his prayers now, he did not know. He hadn't been a faithful servant.

Laura's friend Matthew approached solemnly, a cup of coffee in his outstretched hand. "Here, Mr. Walsh, drink this."

Gratefully, Emmett took the coffee from him. "Thank you for caring about my girl," he said simply.

"She'll be all right," Matthew whispered, taking hold of the older man's arm. "I know she will."

The minutes dragged by and, as they waited together for some word on Laura's condition, Emmett made his vow.

If Laura comes out of this all right, I swear, I will tell all about what happened that night at Palisades Park. Dear God, I promise I will.

124

LAURA LAY ON the gurney in an unrousable sleep, unaware of the commotion going on around her still body.

She did not feel the cold tube snake down her throat, would not remember what it felt like to have her stomach pumped. She did not see the thick, grainy charcoal mixture that was delivered deep inside to soak up the toxins within her.

It was the harsh cough that she would first hazily recall, as the tube was pulled painfully through her esophagus. It hurt to breathe, her chest tender and bruised, she would later learn, because of the CPR Matthew had administered.

She felt tired. So very, very tired. All she wanted to do was sleep.

125

FRANCHESKA STRAPPED HERSELF into her seat as she felt the gentle roll of the airplane pulling away from the La Guardia terminal. She was not really looking forward to the trip in front of her.

The anniversary of Jaime's murder was coming up and she didn't want her parents to be alone. She knew that her presence would be a comfort to them.

They were such good, simple people, never showing anger at the horrible way that Jaime had died. They accepted his death, believing that their son was a hero.

She wished that she possessed her parents' deep religious convictions, their belief that God worked in mysterious ways that human beings could not always understand.

It would be so much easier that way.

126

IT WAS LATE afternoon when Matthew escorted a weakened Laura home to her new apartment. Both Matthew and Emmett had been furious about the hospital's refusal to keep her longer. But that was the way things were in the new world of managed health care. Treat 'em and send 'em home.

The ER doctor suspected that GHB, the so-called date-rape drug, had been added to Laura's drink. The chemical compound broke up quickly in the body and was extremely difficult to trace. Very few laboratories in the tristate area had the equipment to detect GHB, and Palisades Medical Center's lab was not one of them. But physicians around the country had been alerted to the increased use of the drug as more and more cases were wheeled into emergency rooms everywhere.

Matthew and Emmett, listening to the doctor explain his suspicions to Laura, were appalled and deeply frightened at the realization that one of the several hundred people at the fund-raiser had tried to kill her.

The hospital had alerted the Cliffside Park police of its suspicions. The police would go over the list of ticket-buyers and would question the Palisadium staff who worked the party. But the police acknowledged that many of those who came to the fund-raiser had paid the admission fee at the door and might therefore never be tracked down.

It was when the police officer asked Laura for a list of the people she actually knew at the fund-raiser that she became truly terrified.

"You think it was someone who knows me?" she asked fearfully.

"It usually is, in a case like this, miss," the officer replied. "Someone just didn't walk around willy-nilly and, out of the blue, pick *your* drink to poison."

Emmett had tried to convince Laura to go home and stay at his house, but Laura had insisted that she just wanted to go back to her apartment and sleep in her own bed.

Now, Laura gingerly undressed, her body sore and aching. Her throat was dry. The doctor had explained that she would feel dehydrated for a few days.

"Would you mind making me some tea before you go?" she asked Matthew as she slipped gratefully between the clean, crisp sheets.

"Yes, I'll be happy to make the tea, but I'm not going," he said as he stroked her soft hair. "I want to stay with you."

"Matthew, please don't give me a hard time, and don't baby me. I don't have the energy to fight with you. You have to go. You have to do that interview with Ed Alford in Florida tomorrow."

"Screw the interview. I'm staying with you," he insisted.

"Look. All I'm going to do is sleep. That's all I want to do. I just want to be left alone to rest. If you stayed, I'd be feeling like I have to get up and talk. Really, I'll be fine by myself. No one is going to get to me here. This building is totally secure," she declared, sounding braver than she felt. And besides, I want you to go and get that interview. We need it for our piece."

127

"LOOK, IT'S NOT a good idea to give my name," the raspy voice whispered. "But it's something you should check out, Detective Ortiz. Have the feds go with a search warrant to the Internet service provider 'PDQ.com,' and find out who pays the monthly bill for Casper's Ghostland. It may be a long shot, but it might help you figure out who killed Gwyneth Gilpatric."

After the caller hung up, Ortiz checked. The call had come from *KEY News.*

128

Friday, January 28

AN INCH OF powdery white snow fell as Emmett stood outside the Cliffside Park Police Station, not wanting to go in.

But he had to. He had made a promise, and for once in his life he was going to keep it.

What would happen to him, he did not know. He didn't even really care anymore.

Laura was all right. That was all that mattered.

He stamped the snow from his feet as he pulled open the heavy steel door and walked up directly to the police desk.

129

LAURA AWOKE TO the ringing of the telephone.

"Hello?" she answered groggily.

"Laura? It's Joel. Joel Malcolm. How are you feeling?"

"Better, thanks. But I'm so tired."

"That's too bad, kiddo. But I'm glad you're okay. I hate to ask you this," he continued without missing a beat, "but are you going to be able to finish the story?"

Laura knew he didn't hate to ask her at all. The sweeps story was all he really cared about. *Bastard.*

"Don't worry, Joel," she reassured him tiredly. "The piece will be finished in time. I'll be in tomorrow and the rest of the weekend if necessary to get it done."

Replacing the receiver in its cradle, Laura got out of bed and slowly walked to the bathroom. She stared at her face, pale and grayish in the unforgiving makeup lighting that Gwyneth had had installed around the large mirror.

Someone had tried to kill her.

She didn't want to die.

There was no answer at Emmett's as Laura tried for the third time to reach him. She was angry. He hadn't even bothered to call her and see how she was.

She lay quietly in the large bed, but could not fall back asleep. She had to confront her father with what she knew, had to find out what, exactly, he and Gwyneth were to one another, and what, if anything, they had to do with the death of Tommy Cruz.

There was so much to do. The piece wasn't even written, much less edited. But before she could start writing, she had to talk to Emmett. What he might tell her could solve the mystery of Tommy's disappearance.

If that was the case, the piece would be a blockbuster. A thirty-year-old mystery solved by *Hourglass*. Joel would be thrilled. The ratings would be high.

But her father would be a murderer.

130

THERE WAS NEWS on Tommy's case.

Felipe and Marta Cruz walked hand in hand into the police station a half hour after they received a call asking them to come in. A young patrolman escorted the couple into the chief's office.

"You have something new to tell us?" Felipe asked tentatively.

The chief cleared his throat uncomfortably. "Yes, Mr. and Mrs. Cruz. Someone has come forward with information about Tommy's death."

The couple waited.

"According to this source, what happened that night was an accident. A tragic, terrible accident."

Marta closed her eyes and clasped her hands in her lap as she listened to the chief's explanation.

"Apparently Tommy and his friend Ricky Potenza sneaked into the amusement park that night after it closed to collect a reward."

"A reward," interrupted Felipe in confusion. "What sort of reward? I don't understand."

The chief was patient. He had two kids of his own.

"They had been running errands all summer for the guy who ran the roller coaster. He promised them free rides when the park was closed as payment." He waited, but the Cruzes remained silent.

"Anyway, Tommy and Ricky came that night to get their rides. It seems they dared one another to stand up on the ride as it came to the roller coaster's apex and, in the force of the Cyclone's sudden descent, Tommy lost his balance and fell from the roller coaster car."

"But I don't understand," cried Marta. "What happened to Tommy? How did his body get buried?"

"The guy who ran the roller coaster and his girlfriend carried Tommy's body from the park and buried it. It was the girlfriend's cross we found near the body."

So, in the end, it was as simple as that, thought Marta, a

strange sense of peace beginning to flow over her. An accident. What fear Tommy had known was, mercifully, only momentary. No one had tortured him or sexually assaulted him. None of the terrifying scenarios with which she had tormented herself over the years had actually been inflicted on her baby.

God was good.

131

Saturday, January 29

SHE HATED TO cancel her session with Jade, but there was no way of getting around it. She had to get to the office. Matthew was meeting her there.

As she was gathering her paraphernalia into her canvas carryall, the intercom buzzed, the doorman announcing a visitor.

Startled, Laura answered, "Send him right up."

She was waiting for her father as the elevator doors opened.

"I've been trying to reach you, Pop."

"I'm sorry, Munk. I've been busy."

She gestured. "Come in. We have to talk."

Emmett's eyes swept the room, but he made no comment on the lush surroundings as he took the seat that Laura offered him.

"Are you feeling better, Munk?"

"Well enough to go to work. I have to finish my story."

"That's what I came here to talk to you about, honey."

She listened silently as he slowly unburdened himself of the story that had happened all those years ago on that late summer's night.

"And Gwyneth?" Laura asked when he was finished.

"Believe it or not, Munk, Gwyneth found your old dad quite attractive in those days. I suppose it was the excitement of dating someone her parents didn't approve of." He shrugged. "Once she went off to college, she would have forgotten all about me, if we hadn't had our secret. But later, as GiGi became more and more successful, she began to send me money. She said she wanted to help me out, since I had you and was raising you all alone and all. But when she couldn't find the cross she was wearing that night, she didn't like the idea that I'd be able to say it was her. So, you know, it was really kind of an insurance policy. So I wouldn't talk."

"And Mommy knew all this?" Laura asked, remembering the whispered conversation she had overheard between her parents as her mother lay on her deathbed.

"She didn't know about the money. That came later," answered Emmett sadly. "But she did know what happened at the park, God rest her soul. She wanted me to tell the police, but I wouldn't."

"You should have," Laura whispered with a heavy heart.

132

THE *HOURGLASS* OFFICES were quiet Saturday morning as Laura arrived, but Matthew and the editor he had called in were already screening tapes.

A handsome-looking older man was talking on the monitor while Matthew typed text of his remarks into his computer.

"Ed Alford?" asked Laura.

"Mm hmm." Matthew's fingers tapped away.

Laura watched as the retired cop gave his recollection of events and she instinctively noted the sound bite they would use in their piece. "Tommy Cruz did not fit the description of a runaway. I was positive that something had happened to that little boy, something that he had no control over. And I had a gut feeling, though I couldn't prove it, what happened to Tommy Cruz had something to do with Palisades Amusement Park."

"He was right," Laura whispered.

Matthew looked at Laura keenly and she motioned him to follow her out of the editing booth so they could speak privately. As they walked down the hallway together, Laura quietly recounted the story Emmett had told her.

"I should be glad. Our piece will be gangbusters," she concluded ironically, bitterness creeping into her voice. "We've got our ratings-guaranteed ending. We've solved our mystery."

133

IT WAS ALMOST eight o'clock when they decided to call it a day, feeling satisfied with how much they had accomplished. Laura and Matthew had finished a rough draft of their script, weaving in the various sound bites they had accumulated in their interviews over the last month, planning for the places where they would use the pictures and old film of the amusement park, picking the spots where they would bring up the sound of the various Palisades Park songs.

On Monday, they would show the script to Joel, knowing full well that the executive producer would rip their work apart critically, demanding that changes be made. That's the way the system worked and they would try not to take Joel's criticisms personally.

They speculated on how Joel would react when he learned that Gwyneth Gilpatric had helped bury Tommy Cruz, both deciding that, in the end, Malcolm would only care about the sensational result. Ratings. Ratings. Ratings.

"You look beat, honey," said Matthew as they waited for the elevator to take them down to the Broadcast Center lobby. "How about we order in some Chinese food and relax?"

Laura shook her head. "Thanks, Matthew. That's sweet of you, but you're right, I'm exhausted. I just want to go home and get some sleep. I'm sorry, but you understand, don't you?"

He kissed her forehead gently. "Of course I do."

By nine o'clock, Laura was asleep in Gwyneth's bed.

134

AFTER A MADDENING wait, the jet finally taxied across the runway at the San Juan airport.

Francheska was glad that she had been able to change her reservations and get an earlier flight out. She didn't like being away from New York.

She hated to disappoint her parents by leaving early, but she could not take one more minute of her father's reminiscences about Jaime, her mother's dragging her to Mass to pray for her dead brother.

As the plane lifted into the air, Francheska gazed out the window, thinking that there was no point in looking back.

She wanted to get home, to New York. Her life was there.

135

Sunday, January 30

LAURA'S EYES OPENED and tried to adjust to read the illuminated hands of the clock on the bedside table.

Two-fifteen.

She lay in the darkened room, her mind racing. What would happen to Emmett now? What consequences would there be for his actions thirty years ago? As much as she was heartbroken about what her father had done, she did not want to see him go to prison. How would he survive there?

She had tossed and turned, hoping for soothing sleep to return, but now she was wide awake.

Laura switched on the lights and went to the kitchen, putting a kettle of water on the stove to boil. She pulled a bag of decaffeinated tea from the canister on the counter.

With cup in hand, she wandered into the library. Perhaps something good to read would help her get her mind off everything. As she went to the wall of books, her gaze fell on the pile Francheska had left in the corner. Her new roommate's hard drive, video monitor and printer were waiting to be hooked up in its new home.

Why not? Francheska would be thrilled to find the miserable job all done when she got back. Laura knew how hard the trip to see her parents was for her friend. It would be a pleasant surprise for her to arrive and find her computer all ready to go, especially if she was, as she said, going to take some more courses to help her get a real job.

Laura lifted the parts of the computer carefully, her body still aching. She arranged the components on the small desk that they had moved from another room so that they would both be able to work in the beautiful library. She was satisfied with herself as she matched the various wires to their proper portals. Francheska's computer was now connected to its monitor, the mouse, a set of small speakers, and her own combination printer-copier-fax machine.

Now the test. Laura switched on the computer.

Beautiful, she thought, as the brief, soothing START WINDOWS music played and Francheska's DESKTOP appeared on the screen.

Laura was about to shut everything down when it occurred to her that it might be nice to create a little WELCOME HOME sign and tape it to the front of Francheska's video monitor. She took the mouse in hand and double-clicked on the MICROSOFT WORD icon and watched the program open up, presenting Laura with a blank piece of "paper." She began typing, in a large, fancy font, centering each line of text.

WELCOME HOME, FRANCHESKA!

YOU'RE ALL PLUGGED IN!

Laura brought the mouse up to the top of the screen and clicked FILE so she could print out her sign. She was just about to press PRINT when she noticed, curiously, at the bottom of the pull-down menu, the list which most word processing programs automatically prepare for their users: the last four documents that had been worked on.

GHOSTLAND GRID

FORDHAM

RECIPE

MAMA Y PAPA

Guiltily, she slid the mouse down its pad and clicked open the first document in the list.

136

FEELING GRIMY AND irritable, Francheska waited for a taxi at La Guardia Airport, along with scores of other passengers from her delayed flight.

When her turn finally came, she barked her Central Park West destination to the cab driver.

Francheska sat back into her seat and closed her eyes. In a little while she would be sleeping in Gwyneth Gilpatric's bed.

137

LAURA STARED IN disbelief at the computer screen.

Having opened GHOSTLAND GRID, Laura was now studying what looked like a financial spreadsheet. One hundred names flowed, in alphabetical order, down the left-hand column; and, next to each name, a different e-mail address for each month of the year.

As Laura scrolled down, she recognized almost of all of the names as some of the most well-known people in the print and television news media. She marveled at how much power, and money, each name represented.

About one-third of the way down the list of names, Laura's attention was drawn to GWYNETH GILPATRIC. She noted that, instead of an e-mail address, there was only one word next to Gwyneth's name: CASPER!

Laura tried to make sense of what she was looking at. She thought back to the evenings, when she and Francheska were roommates, when they had visited Emmett. She recalled Francheska's insistence that they go down to the basement to see the mini-park and the fancy her friend had taken to the Casper's Ghostland attraction with its painted cartoon characters of Casper, Wendy and Spooky.

What did all of this mean?

She decided to go back to the list of four recent documents she had discovered under the file menu. Ignoring the one entitled FORDHAM, as that was probably just a letter asking about admissions procedures, she clicked on the third document in the list.

Laura felt her pulse throbbing in her ears, her face growing hot, as she read the contents of RECIPE. It left no doubt that Francheska Lamb, Laura's trusted friend, was not the woman Laura believed her to be.

Francheska had ordered gamma hydroxybutyrate powder. It was obvious that she had downloaded, and then saved, the instructions for combining all the ingredients needed to create a substance called Liquid G.

Francheska had tried to kill her!

Laura's thoughts spun as she tried to remember the events that led up to her collapse at the fund-raiser. Francheska had left before she got sick, so Francheska didn't know that the poison hadn't killed her friend. Laura felt her stomach wretch as she realized that Francheska had left for Puerto Rico believing that Laura would be dead when she returned.

Everything was falling into place now, like a deadly row of dominoes. Laura realized that Francheska had a reason to kill Gwyneth, whom she perceived as having caused her brother's death. Francheska had a reason to kill Kitzi Malcolm, the eyewitness to her crime. Francheska could have killed Delia, too, if she thought the maid had seen her just prior to Gwyneth's death.

So engrossed was she in the horror of the betrayal that she had just discovered, Laura didn't hear the elevator doors sliding open down the hallway, as she picked up the telephone to call Matthew, three in the morning or not.

138

"LAURA, SLOW DOWN. I can't understand you, honey," urged Matthew, rubbing his eyes.

"It's Francheska! I think she was the one who spiked my drink. I think she killed Gwyneth and the others!" Laura rattled off frantically.

"Laura, you've got to calm down, sweetheart. You haven't been feeling well. It's all been too much for you," Matthew said softly.

"Don't talk to me like I'm a crazy person. I know what I'm talking about. I have proof—"

Matthew shivered as he heard a click and the line go dead.

139

THE EMERALD-RINGED FINGER depressed the button on the telephone, abruptly ending Laura's conversation.

"What kind of proof, Laura?"

Laura looked up to find Francheska standing above her, a kitchen knife gleaming in her other hand.

"Francheska, how could you?" she whispered.

"The world's a tough place, Laura. You do what you have to do. It was just a matter of time before you put things together. You'd realize that I had a reason to want to see Gwyneth dead. You'd start questioning how I had the money not to work—and I don't intend to work, Laura." She lifted her chin defiantly. "I know you too well. You're like a dog with a bone when you get hold of something. You wouldn't be able to just let things ride and I couldn't afford to let you put the pieces together."

"Murder?" asked Laura incredulously.

"It happens. Remember? Your friend Gwyneth helped clue me in on that."

Laura was silent. How was she going to get out of this?

"Get up," Francheska commanded, nudging Laura with her knee. "Your precious Matthew is probably on his way over here right now. Let's go into the living room."

Laura rose from her seat as Francheska shifted behind her. Feeling the cold blade pressed to her neck, Laura walked slowly down the hallway.

Think! Think! Laura didn't like her chances if she turned to struggle with Francheska, with that knife in her hand.

"Francheska," she pleaded, "there must be some way we can work this out."

Her friend laughed coldly. "Yeah, right! For a smart girl, you talk real stupid. *Imbécil!* Did your little Jade teach you *that* Spanish word? There's no way to work this out. I'm not going to prison for the rest of my life, or worse. I have all the money I'll ever need and I intend to enjoy it."

They were in the living room now, the Manhattan skyline still sparkling outside the terrace windows.

"But you said it yourself, Francheska, Matthew is on his way over here right now. Please, put down the knife and we'll figure out what to do."

"I've already figured out what to do, Laura. By the time Matthew gets here, you'll be gone. You were so distraught that you jumped. And I will be long gone."

"But the computer . . ." Laura's voice trailed off.

Francheska shrugged. "Matthew won't check the computer. Not tonight anyway. And by tomorrow, I'll be sure to delete the files I had so foolishly forgotten."

140

WHERE THE HELL is a taxi?

Matthew stood frantically on the corner of Third Avenue, waiting for what seemed like forever. Laura sounded so frantic. He wondered if he should call the police.

No, he decided, as he ran west toward Park Avenue, hoping for better luck getting a cab there. The police weren't necessary.

He would be able to calm Laura down.

141

LAURA STOOD IN her nightgown on the open terrace, but she did not feel the cold.

Of one thing she was sure. She was not going to go down without a fight.

But how was she going to get out of this?

"Just jump, Laura," Francheska whispered urgently, the knife pressing at Laura's jugular vein. "Make it easy on yourself."

Distract her. Laura turned to face her attacker.

"How do you think your parents would feel, Francheska, knowing about what you've done, what you are going to do? They've already buried their son, but I bet they'd rather do that a hundred times over than know that their daughter is a murderer!"

For just a moment, Francheska cast her eyes downward, giving Laura her chance.

She ran to the other side of the telescope mounted at the edge of the terrace and, with the adrenaline only the truly terrified can feel, swung the black tube smashing into Francheska's beautiful, enraged face.

February Sweeps

142

Tuesday, February 1

THE SPECIAL EDITION of *Hourglass* led with the news that police had apprehended the woman suspected to be Gwyneth Gilpatric's murderer. Francheska Lamb was lying in Mt. Olympia Hospital under police guard. Lamb was thought to be responsible, as well, for the murders of Kitzi Malcolm and Gilpatric's maid, but police would not be able to fully question her until she recovered from the head injuries sustained in a struggle with *KEY News* producer Laura Walsh, who had discovered Lamb's implication in the murders.

The last *Hourglass* segment recounted Gwyneth Gilpatric's involvement in the death of Tommy Cruz at the old Palisades Amusement Park.

As Eliza Blake signed off, Laura watched the television carefully as her first credit on *Hourglass* blazed from the screen. The moment was not at all what she had imagined it would be.

The triumph of reaching her goal and discovering what had happened to Tommy Cruz that last summer at Palisades Park was darkly clouded by the discovery of her father's role in the young boy's death. The fact that her best friend was a murderer—indeed, had tried to kill Laura herself—left her deeply shaken and uncertain of her ability to judge people.

But the ratings would be good.

143

ROSE POTENZA SWITCHED off the television set and walked over to the sofa to kiss her son.

"Are you all right, Ricky?" she asked gently, her eyes filled with the deepest concern. "Ricky?"

"I don't want to talk about it, Mom. Leave me alone."

He had just watched the most powerful hour of television he had ever seen and he wasn't sure how he felt. Just a month ago he was glad that Gwyneth Gilpatric was dead and jealous that he had not been the one to kill her—or at least confront her, as he had planned to do the night of her party.

But after watching *Hourglass* tonight, he saw things a bit differently.

It had all been an accident. Gwyneth had only been five years older than he was when Tommy had fallen to his death. She had panicked, too. The difference between them was that Gwyneth had gone on to have a hugely successful life and Ricky had just sat watching her smile week after week on television. It stuck maddeningly in his craw.

Gwyneth should have gone to the police. But then again, he could have, too. Neither of them did.

Was he really any better than she was?

Maybe now he could finally talk to the doctor at Rockland about it.

144

Wednesday, February 2

THE MORNING AFTER the first *Hourglass* broadcast of the February sweeps, Laura's co-workers tried to congratulate her on her work, but it was hard for them to find the right words.

"Great piece, but I know it must be hard for you."

"Nice work, Laura, but how did it feel to screw your own father?"

"Man, if what happened to you happened to me, I'd have a nervous breakdown. It must help, though, having come into millions and living in Gwyneth's apartment."

"I didn't figure you as a ratings hound, Laura, but I've got to hand it to you. You really know how to come up with a story."

"Hey, Laura. It's Emmy time! Figuring out who killed Gwyneth *and* solving the Palisades Park thing. You should really go for the gold when your next contract comes up for negotiation."

The soul of tact, these newspeople.

Laura hid in her office and considered handing in her resignation.

"Rough morning, huh?"

Matthew stood in the doorway.

"That's the understatement of the New Year," she said glumly.

He came in and took a seat. "I hope you don't mind, but I called a good New Jersey criminal attorney about your father."

"Mind? I'm thrilled. I've been thinking I have to do the same thing, but—"

"Don't explain," Matthew interjected. "It's all been too much. I'll never forgive myself for not calling Detective Ortiz sooner with my suspicions about Casper's Ghostland. Let me help you with *this* at least, Laura. I want to."

Laura looked at him gratefully, feeling tears welling in her eyes.

"What did the lawyer say?" she asked solemnly, holding her breath.

"Well, it's better than we thought. He says that he can't imagine any prosecutor getting involved in this case. True, Emmett shouldn't have been giving the kids rides after the park was closed, but he did not cause Tommy's death. Sad as it is, the kid did it to himself. And it seems the statute of limitations has run out for any criminal prosecution of Emmett's coverup. Prosecution had to commence within five years of Tommy's secret burial. So Emmett won't be doing any jail time for that."

Thank God! What Emmett had done was terribly, terribly wrong, and there had to be some penalty to pay. But the thought of his spending the rest of his life in state prison was more than she could bear.

"And?"

"And as far as any civil suit is concerned, even if the Cruzes decide to bring one, you can't get blood from a stone. Emmett doesn't have anything for them to get."

Laura thought of Gwyneth's money, now hers. "I have money."

"Yeah, but that's yours, not Emmett's. The Cruzes can't touch that."

She thought of the poor Cruzes. Their lives had been shattered, yet they were left to pick up the pieces without restitution or satisfaction. It wasn't fair.

"Not unless I give it to them," she answered.

145

LAURA WANDERED FROM room to room of the apartment, careful not to look out to the terrace.

This will always be Gwyneth's place. It will never feel like mine.

She knew that she was making the right decision as she

called Roberta Golubock at Sotheby's International Realty to make an appointment with her to come over and list the penthouse.

She wasn't quite sure how much the luxury apartment would bring, but she knew it would be in the millions. With that, and all the rest Gwyneth had left her, Laura knew she was a truly wealthy woman, in the enviable position of doing whatever she damned well pleased.

She could give it all to the Cruzes. Or she could keep some of the money and invest it—and have the funds to do other good things, help other people. Laughing Jade sprang to her mind and Laura was sure she would put enough aside to fund the child's college education.

And what about Ricky Potenza? He had been just a child, innocent of any wrongdoing—his life, and his family's, ruined by what had happened that long-ago night at Palisades Park. Maybe now she could help Ricky and his mother.

Laura got out a legal pad and began to write, making a list of things she could do with her money to make things better, to somehow make amends in her own way for life's inequities. As her pencil moved across the yellow page, she felt her spirits begin to lift.

There was enough there to do a lot of good.

She picked up the telephone to call Jade.

◆◆◆

PROLOGUE

◆◆◆

Thursday evening, August 18th

Deprived of sight, her other senses were intensified. She stood in the darkness, seeing nothing, but hearing the persistent roar of the Atlantic Ocean in the distance and the soft flapping of wings right above her. Her nostrils flared at the smell of must and decay. The ground was damp and cold beneath her bare feet, her toes curling in the wet, sandy dirt. She felt something brush against her ankle and prayed it was only a mouse and not a rat.

Three days in this dank chamber were enough. If she had to stay any longer, she would surely lose her mind. Still, when they found her, as she fantasized they would, the police would want to know everything. To survive this, she'd have to be able to recount every detail of what had happened.

She would tell the police how he'd leave her alone for what seemed like hours at a time. She would tell them how he'd gagged her when he left so nobody would hear her screams and how he would only lower the gag to press his mouth against hers when he returned.

The police would want to know what he'd said to her, but she would have to tell them that she had stopped asking him questions after the second day of captivity because he'd never answered. He'd expressed what he wanted by touch. She'd be sure to tell them how he'd caressed her and lifted her up, how he'd maneuvered his body against hers, how she had known she must follow his lead.

As she continued to mentally organize the information the police would surely need from her, she felt a familiar rumble from her stomach. She had eaten sparsely of the meager provisions, but that didn't really bother her. Hunger was a familiar friend. She knew the ability to survive with minimal sustenance was one of her most impressive strengths, though, of course, her parents didn't see it that way. Nor did her former friends or teachers or the health care professionals who had worked so hard to steer her away from the path she had chosen for herself. They didn't see what to her was only obvious. Not eating was the ultimate control.

As she listened to a pigeon cooing from the eaves above her, she thought more about her parents. They must be frantic with worry. She imagined her mother crying, and her father pacing and cracking his knuckles, over and over, his annoying habit whenever he was upset. Was everyone in town out looking for her? She prayed they were. She hoped that anyone who had ever wronged her, anyone who had ever snubbed her, anyone who had ever hurt her, was worried about her now.

The low rumble of the waves rolled in and out, and she began to rock to the rhythm, trying to soothe herself. It was all going to work out. It had to. She would tell the police what had happened, how he'd silently pulled her to her feet. Without words, he'd shown her what he wanted her to do by the way he moved his body next to hers. She had danced in the dark for him.

Danced again and again, trying desperately to please him. Dancing for her life.

Four hours later

The security guard raised his arm and pointed the flashlight at his wrist. Still an hour to go before his shift was over. Time for one last patrol.

Strolling along the empty paths, George Croft pulled his handkerchief from his uniform pocket, wiping his forehead and the back of his neck. Except for the excessive heat, it was a night like many others in the quiet oceanside community. An occasional throaty snore emanated from the canvas cottages he passed. The rules permitted no loud talking after ten o'clock, and most lights were off by 11:00 P.M. The combination of sun, heat, and salt air had left the summer occupants ready for a good night's sleep.

Finishing up on Mt. Carmel Way, the guard cut across the grass and stopped to check the doors of Bishop Jane's Tabernacle and the Great Auditorium one last time. The massive Victorian-style wooden structures were locked up tight as drums. The illuminated cross that shone from the top of the auditorium, serving as a naval landmark for passing ships, beamed into the night, signaling that all was well.

He was satisfied that everything was in order, but he still had another fifteen minutes before he was officially off duty. God forbid something happened before 2:00 A.M., and he wasn't on the grounds. He'd lose his job over that. And, although she didn't live in his patrol area, that young woman was still missing. If some sick nut was intent on abducting another Ocean

Grove girl, the guard wasn't going to have it happen on his watch.

Lord, it was hot. Longing for a drink of cool water, George turned his flashlight in the direction of the wooden gazebo which protected the Beersheba well. He knew the first well driven in Ocean Grove had been named for a well in the Old Testament. Beersheba's waters had been good enough for the Israelites back then, and good enough for his town's founding fathers, but he preferred the bottled stuff. Still, the gazebo was as good a place as any to wait it out until his shift was over.

With no breeze blowing in from the ocean, the night air was especially still. He trained the yellow light on the lawn in front of him and walked slowly, trying to kill time. Noticing one of his shoes was undone, he put the flashlight down in the grass and stooped to tie the lace. It was then that he heard the scratching sound.

The fine hairs tingled on the back of his clammy neck and George spun the flashlight in the direction of the noise. He squinted, trying to identify what he was seeing. A dark, motionless mound lay at the base of the gazebo.

With caution, George stepped a little closer. Just when he heard the scratching again, he detected slight movement coming from the form. Slowly, slowly, he approached until, finally, the glare of the flashlight reflected off the pale skin of a female face, blindfolded and gagged.

FRIDAY

AUGUST 19

CHAPTER ONE

Diane could feel the heat from the sidewalk seeping through the soles of her shoes as she hurried down Columbus Avenue. As beads of perspiration slipped down her sides, she wiped the dampness accumulating at her brow line with one swoop, negating the twenty minutes she had spent in front of the bathroom mirror with her hair dryer, round brush, and styling mousse. Her freshly laundered cotton blouse stuck to her back, and the starched collar was beginning to droop. The day hadn't even begun and already she was a wilted mess.

She was anxious, as usual, about being late and she wished she hadn't promised herself to walk to work. The twenty-block trek was the only dependable exercise she got these days, and she needed it. She had let her gym membership elapse since she found she wasn't using it on any routine basis. There just wasn't time anymore—not if she was going to spend the hours she felt she must with the kids right now.

Sniffing the sickening smell of garbage already baking in the morning sun as it waited to be picked up from the curb, Diane felt relief that her two-week vacation was about to begin. It would be so good to get out of the city, away from the oppressive heat, away from the noise and the hustle and the pressure. These last months had been tough on all of them, brutal really. Sometimes, it didn't feel like any of it could have happened at all. Yet, the reality was all too clear when she spotted Michelle biting her nails, or watched Anthony's shoulders slump when she caught him staring at his father's framed picture on the piano, or when she reached out in the middle of the night to the empty place in her queen-size bed.

She cut across the courtyard at Lincoln Center, stopping for just a moment at the wide fountain, hoping to catch of bit of fine spray. But there was absolutely no breeze to propel the mist her way.

Adjusting her shoulder bag, Diane continued walking. No matter. Soon she and the kids would be someplace where the air didn't stink and the water flowed cool and clear. Maybe they weren't going the way they had originally planned, maybe it wasn't the way they would have wanted it, but it was the way things were. They were going on this vacation. They deserved it. They needed it after all they had been through.

Life, even without Philip, had to go on.

Pushing through the heavy revolving door into the lobby, Diane welcomed the blast of cool air. She smiled at the uniformed security guards as she fumbled in her bag for the beaded metal necklace that threaded its way through the opening on her identification pass. Finding it, she swept the card against the electronic device that beeped to signal that she was cleared to enter the KEY News Broadcast Center. She knew that many of the other correspondents found it annoying to produce their I.D.'s. They thought that their well-known faces should be enough for entry, but Diane didn't mind. Security had an increasingly tough job, and it was easy enough for her to pull out her card. She did draw the line, however, at wearing the thing around her neck all day. That wasn't a fashion statement she cared to make.

Diane purchased a cup of tea and a banana at the coffee trolley and then walked up the long, wide ramp to the elevators, passing the large, lighted pictures of the KEY News anchors and correspondents, grouped according to their broadcasts. Eliza Blake beamed from *KEY Evening Headlines* poster. Constance Young and Harry Granger grinned beneath the *KEY to America* morning show logo. The *Hourglass* photo, taken over a year before, showed Cassie Sheridan surrounded by the news magazine's contributing reporters. Diane didn't stop to study her own face, with its blue-gray eyes and nose she wished was just a little bit straighter, smiling from the wall with her colleagues. She needed no reminder. The worry and aggravation of the past few months were showing on her face. The fine lines at the corners of her eyes had deepened, and new ones had formed around her mouth, vestiges of unconscious frowning. Lately, Diane noticed she was forced to apply concealer several times a day to camouflage the dark circles that had developed beneath her eyes.

Another good reason for a vacation, Diane thought, as she pressed the elevator button. If she could just get away and relax for a bit, her appearance would benefit. All of the female correspondents were acutely aware that the way they looked played into their success. Experience was valued, but beauty was rewarded. Those were just the facts of life for females in broadcast news. The guys paid attention to their appearances too, of course. But they could let their hair go gray, sport some wrinkles, gain a few pounds, and get away with it. The women couldn't. They groused about it with their friends, but it wasn't going to change and they knew it.

The elevator bell pinged, and the doors slid open. Walking directly across the sixth-floor hallway, Diane slipped into the ladies' room. She pulled paper towels from the wall dispenser and patted at her face, trying not to wipe off her makeup as she dabbed at the mascara that had run at the corners of her eyes. As she worked to re-create some semblance of a hairstyle, Diane heard the click of a lock opening at one of the stalls behind her.

"Hi, Susannah," Diane said as the young woman limped toward the sink next to hers and pumped out some liquid soap.

"Hey, Diane. Hot enough for you?" Facing the mirror, Susannah smiled her crooked smile, which reflected its way back to Diane.

Diane was about to start complaining about her flattened hair and her sweaty walk to work, but she stopped herself, knowing how insensitive that would be. Susannah would probably give just about anything to be able to take the brisk walk that Diane took for granted.

"Thank God for air-conditioning," Diane answered, pulling strands of ash-blond hair from her brush before putting it back into her shoulder bag. She rifled through the recesses of the satchel and pulled out a small can of hair spray. "And tomorrow I leave for a vacation with my kids. It may be hot at the Grand Canyon, but it won't be as muggy as it is here."

"That sounds fabulous," Susannah answered with enthusiasm in her voice. "Do you have all the information you need before you go? I could get a little research package together for you."

That was one of the great things about Susannah, thought Diane, shaking the can and taking the lid off. She was always so upbeat and eager to help. God knew Susannah had plenty to be down about. But she didn't play the victim. Maybe she knew that a "poor me" attitude wore thin with folks after a while.

"Oh, you're a doll, Susannah, but I don't need a thing. I'm going to just sit back and let the tour guides do their jobs. I'm looking forward to a vacation where I don't have to read any maps or make any decisions or be responsible for anything more than deciding which pair of shorts to pull on in the morning. I just want to relax with my kids for two weeks and let someone else worry about what we're going to do every day."

Diane waited until the researcher made her way to the restroom exit before pushing the button to release the hair spray. The smell of the aerosol fumes was just reaching her nostrils when Susannah called back from the doorway.

"I guess I should give you a heads-up, Diane. Joel is looking for you."

CHAPTER TWO

The detective stood at the foot of the hospital bed in the small examining room, his face impassive as he took detailed notes on Leslie Patterson's answers.

"How many times do I have to tell you?" Leslie's voice rose in frustration. "I never saw his face. I'm telling you the truth: I never saw him."

She watched the detective for a reaction. His facial expression gave nothing away. It was the way he was rephrasing the same questions over and over that tipped her off: He didn't believe her.

"Let's go over it again, Miss Patterson. You were on the boardwalk taking a stroll at midnight?" The detective stressed the last word of his question, signaling his skepticism. "Do you usually go out alone late at night like that?" he asked.

"I told you. I had a fight with my boyfriend, and I wanted to be alone to think about things. I thought a walk would clear my head and maybe tire me out so I could fall asleep."

"Your boyfriend would be Shawn Ostrander, correct?"

"Yes. I told you that, too." She picked up a spoon from the breakfast tray and threw it back down again. Some nurse had thought she was doing Leslie a favor by bringing in the tray as she waited to be released. "As if I would eat this slop." Leslie sighed as she pushed back the rolling table that held her un-touched food.

"And Shawn said he didn't want to see you anymore, is that right, Leslie?" The detective used a gentle tone as he led her on-ward.

"Yes. And that he'd met someone else." Leslie studied the raw scrape marks the handcuffs had left on her wrists and then pulled the covers up higher.

Beneath the hospital blanket, where the detective couldn't see, Leslie pinched the top of her thigh. Without a safety pin or razor blade, a manually inflicted wound would have to do. A hard, mean twist intended to make her feel better. As the sharp pain pulsed, the expression on her face never flinched.

"That must have hurt," said the detective.

Leslie blinked, for a moment thinking the man somehow knew she was pinching herself, before realizing he was referring to the hurt of knowing that Shawn had found someone else.

"Yes. It did. I love Shawn." Leslie grabbed again at her hid-den flesh and pressed the skin tight. This time, tears welled in her eyes. Not because of the physical pain, but because she couldn't stand the thought of losing Shawn. Didn't he realize that no one was ever going to love him the way she did?

"Did you want Shawn to worry about you, Leslie? Did you hope he would reconsider his decision to break up if he realized how much he missed you? Did you hope that disappearing for a couple of days would make Shawn come around?"

Leslie considered her answer. Yes, she did want Shawn to worry about her, and yes, as she'd lain in that dark, damp place for three days and nights, she was sustained by the hope that Shawn was missing her. She'd hoped that the horror she was go-ing through would all be worth it because, when faced with the thought of losing her forever, Shawn would realize that he loved her as much as she loved him.

But if she told the detective that, it might help confirm what Leslie knew he already suspected. That she had staged a three-day disappearance to get attention. She didn't want him to think that.

"Look, Detective, someone abducted me, blindfolded, gagged, and tied me up, and left me somewhere for three days. I feel like you're accusing me when you should be out there searching for a real criminal."

"We are, Leslie, believe me, we are. I'm not the only man working on this case. The better part of the Neptune police department is involved. We will get to the bottom of this. You can count on that." Something in the detective's tone made the words feel more like a threat than a reassurance.

The hospital room door opened, and the doctor who had examined her in the emergency room walked over and stood beside the bed. He looked at his clipboard before speaking. He looked at the cop, too. As part of a crime investigation, the police as well as the patient had a right to know these test results.

"The rape kit came back negative. So we have that to be grateful for, Leslie. Even though you didn't claim to be raped, it was good to have done the test anyway. You can never be too sure in a situation like this one. You could have been drugged or knocked unconscious and not even known it." The doctor smiled reassuringly and put his hand on Leslie's shoulder. "So, physically, you check out fine. Those scrapes on your wrists and legs will heal in few days. So will the cuts at the corners of your mouth. You can go home, Leslie. You're going to have to talk to someone, though, get your feelings out. Do you need a reference to a therapist? We have some excellent ones on staff."

"Thanks, but I already have a therapist." Leslie nodded, knowing that it made no sense to protest. Sure, she'd go back to therapy, and she'd fool Dr. Messinger the same way that she was fooling the emergency room doctor right now. He had no idea that she was pinching herself, over and over again, beneath the white hospital sheets.

**Read on for an excerpt from
Mary Jane Clark's exciting novel**

HIDE YOURSELF AWAY

**Coming in June 2005
from St. Martin's Paperbacks!**

PROLOGUE

He wanted to have the light on, but she was just as glad that wasn't a possibility. Any illumination coming from the playhouse windows would beckon one of the staff to come and investigate.

He also wanted to have some music and had brought along his cassette player, but she insisted on silence. They couldn't risk the noise traveling out into the soft, night air. The only undulating rhythm coming from within the cottage this night would be the slow, steady rocking of their bodies.

She lay on her back on the wrought-iron daybed, thinking of the youngsters who had napped on the mattress. She strained at every cricket's chirp and skunk's mournful whine from the field outside. She wondered if there were animals in the condemned tunnel that ran beneath the playhouse. She hoped not, since that was their predetermined escape route should they ever need it.

She was having a difficult time letting herself go. He was having no such problem. He was well into things. It was just as he was becoming frenzied that she heard the voice outside the cottage.

"Good Lord, it's Charlotte," she hissed as she pushed him away.

They scrambled to collect their clothes. He grabbed his cassette player as she slid aside the wooden panel in the floor. Into the darkness they lowered themselves, sliding the trapdoor shut just as the playhouse door above them opened.

The cold, hard dirt floor of the tunnel pressed against their bare feet.

"What are you waiting for?" he whispered. "Let's go."

"I'm getting dressed right here," she said. God only knew what was in this tunnel, and she would feel a hell of a lot better if she were clothed as they made their way to the water at the other end.

They sorted their clothes by feel and dressed in the blackness as muffled voices came from above.

"Who's that with her?" he asked.

"I can't tell."

Slowly they began to walk, arms outstretched to the tunnel walls, feeling their way out to safety. She stifled a scream as she felt something brush her leg. A raccoon? A rat? God was punishing her for her sinfulness.

Eventually, the waters of Narragansett Bay glistened from the opening at the end of the tunnel. They stepped up their pace, the moon providing scant but precious light. As they reached their goal, he stopped.

"Crap."

"What's wrong?"

"My wallet. It must have slipped out of my pants pocket."

"Oh, sweet Jesus."

He grabbed her hand. "Don't worry, let's keep going. Maybe they won't see it."

"I'm going back for it." She was adamant.

"Tomorrow. You can get it tomorrow," he urged.

She wished she could follow him out, but she knew she wouldn't sleep all night knowing that his wallet might give them away.

"You go ahead. Go home," she said.

"I'll go back with you," he offered.

"No. You have to get off the property. They can't know you were here. You have to go. Now."

"All right, but I'll see you tomorrow."

She swallowed as she watched him dart along the shoreline and disappear into the darkness. Taking a deep, resolute breath, she turned and stepped back inside, feeling gingerly against the side of the tunnel. Her fingers brushed against the hard-packed dirt and old brick, cold and clammy to the touch. She imagined what it must have been like for the slaves, running for their lives through this tunnel, inhaling deep breaths of the damp, musty smell that filled her nostrils now. Had they had lanterns to light their way? Or had they tapped blindly along in the blackness, not sure what was in front of them but willing to risk it, knowing only what horrors they had left behind?

When she estimated she must surely be close to the ladder that led up to the playhouse, her hand receded into a large indentation in the wall. Pieces of earth broke away as she pushed against it. Her pulse quickened. Was the old tunnel safe? Could it collapse and trap her inside? Would anyone ever find her?

She prayed. If she got out of this one, she vowed she would never, ever go to the playhouse again. No matter how much he wanted her to, this was the last time. She promised.

She pushed on, sniffling quietly in the darkness.

Until she tripped over something and fell to her knees. Her breath came in short, terrified pants, her heart pumped against her chest wall as her hand groped over the form. It was covered with a smooth fabric of some sort, and it was large and intractable.

A human body, still warm, but lifeless.

She had had this feeling before, but only occasionally, in dreams. The urge, the ache, the need to scream, but somehow being frozen, unable to utter a sound. She pushed back from the body and cowered against the tunnel wall, trembling in the darkness.

Later, she would realize that she had been there for only moments, but then it seemed an eternity, the terrified thoughts spinning through her mind. She should go get help. She should summon people from the big house. But she couldn't. She wasn't supposed to have been here at all, and she was mortified at the thought of having to explain her forbidden tryst.

And, even worse, what if they blamed her? What if they thought she had committed murder? She was rocking on her haunches, trying to soothe herself, when she heard the grating sound. The door was sliding open overhead.

She clamped her eyes tight, sure that this was the end. The murderer was coming to get her, too.

Instead, something fluttered from above, hitting her head, grazing her face. A piece of paper? A card?

She listened, shaking but undetected, as the door slid closed again.

Fourteen Years Later

The mining lamps that dotted the tunnel were powered by a generator, but that was one of the few nods to technology. The work was being done painstakingly, by hand. Just as the tunnel had been dug more than a century and a half before, human beings, not machines, scraped the clay and mortared the old red bricks now. Special care was being taken, inch by inch, foot by foot, to make sure that the walls were sturdy and firm. When the job was completed, thousands of tourists and historians and students would have the opportunity for the first time to walk the path American slaves had trod on their desperate flight to freedom. This tunnel had to be safe.

"We've got a soft spot here," called an expert mason, his words echoing against the walls of the underground passage.

The trowel tapped against the soft, red clay. Clumps of earth fell to the tunnel floor. The indentation in the wall grew larger.

The burrowing continued, revealing folds of material embedded in the clay, discolored and shredded by dirt and time. Still, some metallic threads managed to glitter in the light of the mining lamps. Gently, the mason brushed away the clay, following the trail of golden fabric.

The other workers in the tunnel gathered to watch the digging, and when they saw it they were grateful that they were all together. No one would have wanted to find such a thing alone.

A human skull and bones, swaddled in yards of gold lamé.